*Hell, Josh thought, it was wrong to feel—he didn't even know what— about Candace.*

*Unsettled* was as good a word as any, he decided as he sat in his truck, engine idling, pondering which way to turn.

He wasn't used to a beautiful woman being off-limits for any reason other than marriage. And Candace Thompson was definitely beautiful. If not for her history with his family, he would already have done things with her that would make a grown man blush.

Instead, he wasn't supposed to see her, talk to her…even *think* about wanting her.

He damn sure wasn't supposed to help her change a flat tyre, then go home with her, bandage her scrapes and touch her in a way that brought those soft, erotic whimpers from her, as he had tonight.

Clutching the steering wheel tightly, he turned away from Candace, towards Tulsa. A night on the town, too much to drink—and, if he did it right, come tomorrow morning, he wouldn't remember a thing about tonight.

Right?

# Available in January 2004 from Silhouette Special Edition

*Sean's Reckoning*
by Sherryl Woods
*(The Devaneys)*

*Completely Smitten*
by Susan Mallery
*(Hometown Heartbreakers)*

*The Family Plan*
by Gina Wilkins
*(The McClouds of Missippi)*

*The Trouble With Josh*
by Marilyn Pappano

*Just a Small Town Girl*
by Patricia Kay

*There Goes the Bride*
by Crystal Green
*(Kane's Crossing)*

# The Trouble
# with Josh

# MARILYN PAPPANO

SILHOUETTE®
SPECIAL EDITION™

*First published in Great Britain 2004
Silhouette Books, Eton House, 18-24 Paradise Road,
Richmond, Surrey TW9 1SR*

© Marilyn Pappano 2003

*ISBN 0 373 24533 5*

*23-0104*

*Printed and bound in Spain
by Litografía Rosés S.A., Barcelona*

## MARILYN PAPPANO

brings impeccable credentials to her writing career—a lifelong habit of gazing out windows, not paying attention in class, daydreaming and spinning tales for her own entertainment. The sale of her first book brought great relief to her family, proving that she wasn't crazy but was, instead, creative. Since then she's sold more than forty books to various publishers and even a film production company.

She writes in an office nestled among the oaks that surround her country home. In winter she stays inside with her husband and their four dogs, and in summer she spends her free time mowing the garden that never stops growing and daydreams about grass that never gets taller than two inches.

You can write to her at PO Box 643, Sapulpa, OK 74067-0643, USA.

## Chapter One

Visit all fifty states:
√Mississippi
√Arkansas
√Oklahoma

In the months since she'd almost died, Candace Thompson had made a list of all the things she wanted to do while she still had a chance. It filled six pages on a dog-eared legal pad and wasn't in any particular order, except in her mind. She had crossed off plenty of them—things like *Spend a week on the beach* and *Apologize to Craig,* whom she'd dumped her senior year in high school, for the manner in which she'd done it.

There were still plenty to be crossed off—another thirty or forty years' worth, by her reckoning—but the time had come to take care of the number-one priority on the list: *Make amends with Natalie.*

Nothing like setting her goals too high. It would be easier, she suspected, to sprout wings and fly to the moon, but she had to try. She'd made promises—to God, to the doctors, to herself. She had to do her best to keep them.

It had taken some effort, but she'd finally located her former best friend, living on a ranch outside Hickory Bluff, Oklahoma. She'd had the address and phone number for five months now and had done nothing with them. Forgiveness of this magnitude wasn't something that could be asked for over the phone, and doing it by mail struck her as cowardly—too easy, too impersonal.

Hey, no one had said all the things on the list would be pleasant or fun. Some were supposed to hurt, to require guts and courage and looking people in the eye.

This was definitely one of those.

She'd arrived in Hickory Bluff nearly twenty-four hours earlier, after taking the scenic route from Atlanta, and had spent the time getting settled. In planning the trip, she'd discovered there wasn't a motel in town, but there was an RV park at a lake two miles north. Since she'd recently come into possession of a fairly comfortable motor home, she'd reserved a space, much to the amusement of the campground owner—obviously October wasn't a busy period for them. Once she'd settled in at the park, she sweet-talked a friendly guy named Rick at the nearest car rental agency into delivering a car to her.

And she'd found out exactly where this ranch of Natalie's was. She was all set.

Except that she'd been sitting at this intersection of two dirt roads for more than ten minutes and couldn't bring herself to go on.

Natalie wasn't going to be happy to see her, and Candace couldn't blame her. If the situation were reversed, she would wish Natalie off the face of the earth. It would be a cold day in hell before she would give even scant consideration to forgiving her. Since Natalie was sure to feel the same way, and Candace had come all the way here, maybe she could give herself credit for trying, scratch it off her list and go on to the next goal.

But that would be cheating. No surprise there. She'd been a cheat and a user and a manipulator all her life. No one who truly knew her expected honesty from her.

It was a pathetic excuse for a human being who couldn't be honest with herself.

Drawing a deep breath, she checked the crossroad in both directions, even though not one car had passed in the minutes she'd been sitting there. It took a major effort to press the accelerator down, another major effort to not turn right or left to avoid the destination straight ahead.

She kept her speed down—because she didn't want gravel flying up to damage the rental car, and because Rick the friendly rental agent had gone to some trouble to get her a convertible and she didn't want to show up at Natalie's all dusty. Not because she was trying to delay her arrival at the ranch.

The road ran straight and true with little to see on either side—open grassland and woods, an occasional cluster of buildings. She couldn't imagine Natalie voluntarily settling down someplace like this…but a lot of her choices had been taken away from her. Her career, her reputation, her relationship with her father—none of it had survived Candace.

Up ahead something appeared in the road. She squinted behind her sunglasses to bring it into focus. Large, shaggy, brown and white—cows. A whole herd of them. Just sort of milling around on the road.

She slowed to a snail's pace, then stopped about ten feet from the nearest bovine. Most of them appeared taller than her low-slung little sports car, and they seemed to have zero interest in her. The ones that were munching grass at the sides of the road continued to munch, and the ones that were just standing around blocking her way continued to stand and block.

She was reaching to tap the horn when a voice from someplace much too close behind her said, "I wouldn't advise honking the horn. They tend to associate that with feed and come running."

As she twisted in the seat to see who'd spoken, a cowboy reined in his very large horse next to the driver's door. He wore jeans, a T-shirt and scruffy boots, along with a cowboy hat that shaded his face. He was dusty and sweaty...and cute. Very definitely cute. His hair was brown, his eyes the same color and crinkled at the corners. His smile was crooked and so was his nose, and the hands that held the reins were big and powerful.

She had a thing about hands...and power.

"Sorry about the delay," he went on. "Neighbor's buffalo took down a section of fence, and the dumb animals decided they'd rather eat the grass over here."

She managed what she hoped was a friendly smile. "Well, you know what they say. The grass is always greener on the other side."

"Not that it matters much to the cows." He shifted in the saddle with a creak of leather. "You're not from around here."

"Aw, what gave me away?" The fact that she was lacking that luscious, slow-lazy-day accent of his? Or maybe that she was wearing sandals instead of Justins, a ball cap instead of a Stetson, and linen pants instead of Wranglers?

"Let's start with the fact that I've lived my entire life here and never run into you," he said with a grin. "You wander off the highway and get lost?"

"No. I'm just taking a drive." No doubt, knowing everybody's business was the small-town, country-folk way, but she kept hers to herself. She looked at the cows. "Do you leave them here until they've eaten their fill and wander back to the right side of the fence?"

"No," he drawled, then lifted one hand in a gesture too lazy to be considered a wave.

She turned just as another very cute cowboy on another great big horse came through the trees. He tipped his head in greeting, then began herding the cows over the downed wire and into the pasture, with the help of one of the biggest dogs she'd ever seen. Damn, all the creatures around here were big enough to intimidate her—especially the men.

Understandable, since she hadn't gotten close to one who wasn't wearing a stethoscope around his neck in...oh, eleven months.

"Don't you need to help?" she asked.

"Nah. The dog does most of the work."

It looked to her as if the cowboy and the dog were sharing the job equally, but she wasn't going to argue. "I guess a dog provides cheap labor on a ranch. He can't ask for a raise, doesn't get drunk and fail to show up for work, can't talk back...."

"Give 'im a little chow, and he's happy," he said with a grin. "Ol' Red there is extra cheap—he belongs to our neighbor, so we don't even have to feed him. He just likes working cattle."

"Red?" she echoed. "He's black as night."

"You noticed." He didn't offer an explanation as the last couple of cows crossed the road. "Well, I guess you can go on your way now."

She glanced ahead and smiled weakly. "I guess I can."

"Enjoy your drive."

"I will." She pulled forward a few feet, then stopped. "Would you happen to know if there's anyplace around here where I could get a cold beer and a greasy burger for supper tonight?"

"You can have one or the other, but not at the same time. For a greasy burger, try the Dairy Delight in town. For a cold beer..." He removed his hat with one hand, shoved the other through his hair, then reseated the hat. Damned cute, indeed. "I tend to do my drinking at Frenchy's. It's about a mile north of town. You can't miss it." He made a clicking sound with his tongue, and the horse started around the car and toward the broken fence. About halfway there, he looked back at her with a grin and a wink. "Maybe I'll see you there."

"Maybe you will." Candace was smiling as she drove away. A handsome cowboy who was either single or didn't care that he wasn't…what more could a woman on a quest ask for?

But her smile faded. Although there actually was a mention of a cowboy on her list—*Pick up a handsome cowboy/ soldier/cop/jock*—that wasn't her priority right now.

Natalie was.

According to her calculations, the ranch should be just a short distance ahead…and sure enough, long before she was ready to reach it, there it was—a large house, a barn and some other stuff out back, Natalie's classic old Mustang parked in the drive.

Candace stopped at the end of the driveway and tried to take a deep breath, but couldn't. Her chest hurt. Her stomach hurt. Even her fingers hurt from clenching the steering wheel so tightly.

She couldn't do this. *Couldn't.* She didn't care if she'd driven all this way, didn't care if she was letting herself down. The only thing that mattered was that she *could not* face Natalie. Not now.

Maybe not ever.

"Have you ever met a pretty woman you didn't flirt with?"

Josh Rawlins glanced up as his half brother, Tate, swung to the ground beside him. They would do a temporary fix on the fence for now, then come back out later to do it right. He would rather do damn near anything than fix barbed wire. It was his least favorite job on the ranch.

No, that wasn't quite true. The job he hated most was digging post holes for barbed-wire fences. It was a general rule in Oklahoma that wherever you dug, you were bound to hit rock. Sometimes it seemed as if the entire ranch was nothing but a foot of dirt on top of one huge slab of sandstone.

"I didn't flirt with your wife," he pointed out at last, then grinned. "I like women, and they like me."

"She didn't look like your type."

Josh scoffed. Pretty, blond, blue eyes and a nice body. What could possibly be not his type? "*All* women are my type, Pop."

"Don't call me that."

"J.T. does."

"He calls me Papa, and he's allowed. You're not."

As they got to work, Josh laughed at the scowl accompanying the last words. "What're you going to do? Give me a whippin'?"

"I've done it before. I've also saved you from more than a few of them. Don't antagonize me or I won't do it again."

"Well, hell, big brother, you haven't been to a bar with me since you got married. If somebody decides to kick my ass, you're not gonna be there to stop 'em anyway."

Tate shook his head. "You know, Mom and I keep hoping that at some point, you'll outgrow this habit of fighting in bars and getting thrown in jail."

"Hey, I haven't been arrested in a year, and that last time wasn't my fault. She told me she didn't want to leave with that guy."

Tate gave him a dry look as he spliced two strands of wire together. "She was underage, and that 'guy' was her father. You're lucky all they did was lock you up until you were sober."

"She *looked* a lot older. Even the sheriff thought so."

Josh faked a sorrowful look. "It's a sad day when a man has to ask a woman in a bar for ID to find out how old she is."

"Then again, a man could try meeting a woman someplace other than a bar."

Josh cheerfully shook his head. "Sorry, but we're fresh out of pesky reporters wanting to write about the old man." That was how Tate had met his wife. Retired senator Boyd Chaney had hired Natalie to write his biography, and had required that she gain the cooperation of his six ex-wives and nine children, including the illegitimate son he'd never recognized—Josh himself. There had been a little passing around of identities, a quick trip out of town for Josh and his mother, plenty of lies and deception and, ultimately, a happy ending. Tate and Natalie had been married four years now and had a little boy, J.T.

But how many times was something like that likely to happen? Maybe once in a blue moon? Which meant Josh was out of luck. He had to settle for meeting women the old-fashioned way…not that he was looking to settle down just yet. He figured one of these days the carousing would stop being fun, and then he would know it was time to give it up. To pick one woman, get married and start acting respectable, like Tate.

Of course, Tate had been acting respectable ever since he was eighteen, when his girlfriend had handed their newborn son, Jordan, to him, then walked out of their lives.

And Josh hadn't behaved respectably in…well, ever. He liked being the disreputable Rawlins, the one with plenty of wild oats to sow, the impulsive one, the fun one. He wasn't in any rush to give that up.

"You have any plans for this evening?" Tate asked.

Other than dates when he was seeing someone in particular, Josh had a tendency to not make plans. He was single, his own boss—at least, when Tate wasn't giving him orders—and he had no responsibilities outside his family. He was free to go where he wanted when he wanted. Why mess it up with plans?

But when he opened his mouth to say no as he snugged the last broken strands together to splice, the wrong words came out. "I thought I might drop by Frenchy's—have a beer and play a game or two of pool."

"Gee, what made me think that's where you'd be?" Tate teased. "Must have been you telling the pretty woman it was a good place for a cold beer. Maybe a good place to have a dance or two, pick up someone like…hmm, maybe her. At least this one's definitely past the age of consent."

Josh scowled at him as he swung into the saddle. It would serve Tate right if Josh proved him wrong and showed up for supper tonight just like he did most other nights, then went home—alone. Though he wasn't quite sure how his sleeping alone tonight while Tate snuggled up with his wife would prove anything.

"Why don't you go on and start checking the fence?" Tate suggested. "I'll take care of this, then meet you back at the house for lunch."

Josh didn't argue. He just nodded in agreement, then turned his gelding north. He'd lived all but the first few years of his life on this ranch, and he couldn't imagine living anywhere else. It hadn't been an easy life to start. Lucinda had had her hands full trying to run the ranch and raise two boys without much help from their fathers. By the time Tate had turned fifteen, he'd put in a full day at school, plus another on the ranch, and he'd still managed to find time to play football and baseball and get his girlfriend pregnant.

Josh had skipped the sports, other than a little rodeoing, and the pregnant girlfriend, thank God, but other than that, his life had been pretty much the same. It wasn't so bad now. The days were still long, the work still hard, but their mom helped out, and when Tate's son, Jordan, came home from college on weekends, he did more than his share.

Even Natalie—the best example of a city girl Josh had ever known—was more than willing to saddle up or mend a fence when necessary.

They didn't have the biggest spread around, but it was about as big as they could handle, and big enough to provide them with a comfortable living. They would never get rich, but, hell, that had never been a priority in their lives. Tate had wanted to be a good father to Jordan, hang on to the land, stay close to his mother and brother, and someday expand his own family, and he'd done that. Josh just wanted to maintain the status quo—live on and work the ranch, see his family every day and have a good time. He'd enjoyed the first thirty-three years of his life, and he intended to enjoy the rest of it just as much.

Though the sun was shining brightly overhead, occasionally there was a chill in the breeze as it shifted directions. October in Oklahoma couldn't be beat anytime, anywhere, in his opinion. The hundred-degree-plus temperatures of August and often September were gone, the leaves were turning red and gold, and even the air smelled sweeter. The sky was a clear blue this morning, with only a few thin clouds that one good wind would blow into nothing but fluff, and the fragrant scent of wood smoke from the north indicated that their neighbors were burning the timber they'd bulldozed last spring.

That was a job he had to do soon—after putting it off for eight years, he'd finally cleared out some trees around his house—but he was waiting for the nights to get colder. He planned to pick some weekend when Jordan and Michaela Scott, his nephew's best friend and their neighbor, were home from college, and the two families could get together for a wiener roast. There wasn't much better than a cold night, a blazing fire, hot dogs, roasted marshmallows and a pretty woman.

The horse maneuvered through timber and over sandstone without much guidance from Josh, who checked the five strands of barbed wire that ran from post to post. This was a mindless job—one that he liked, of course. He was good at mindless tasks because his thoughts certainly liked to wander. For a moment he let them wander to the stranger.

Where was she from? What had brought her here? And why had she chosen their little dirt road for a drive? He was pretty sure she wasn't visiting anyone locally—in a town like Hickory Bluff, news like that got around—and that meant she wasn't staying locally since the nearest motel was twenty miles away in Dixon. Well, there was that old campground up at the lake—though not much of a campground and not much of a lake. Besides, she sure didn't look the camping type. Or the small-town type. Definitely not the country type.

That left the here-for-a-day-or-two-then-gone type. Most definitely *his* type.

The sun was straight up in the sky when he got back to the barn. Natalie was standing at the corral fence, her arm around J.T.'s middle as he balanced on the top rail. She looked over her shoulder and smiled in greeting. Long-legged, red-haired and blue-eyed, she was exactly the sort of woman Tate had always been a sucker for. Looks aside, she was also sweet, generous, kind, and loved Jordan as if he were her own. If Josh knew his brother, he'd started falling in love with her the moment they'd met—and hell, if Tate hadn't, maybe Josh would have.

"Hey, Uncle Josh!" With Natalie's help, J.T. scrambled to the ground, then ran over, arms extended. Josh swung him onto his hip. "Look at me! I'm a nastronaut!"

"That's pretty cool, J.T. Are you going off in a space-ship?"

The boy bobbed his head as he said, "Nooo, silly. This is for 'alloween. I'm jus' pretendin'."

"Well, good, because I'd miss you if you went off into space."

J.T. wriggled out of his plastic spaceman's helmet, leaving his hair standing on end. Except for the reddish tint to his hair, courtesy of his mother, he looked remarkably like Jordan had at his age—who, according to the family album, had looked remarkably like Tate. Occasionally Josh wondered if he would see the same resemblance in *his* kids someday…but only occasionally. Once every few years.

"What're you gonna be for 'alloween?" J.T. asked.

Josh pretended to think about it as he walked over to the fence where Tate had joined Natalie. "How about if I go as a cowboy?"

"Uncle Josh, you *are* a cowboy. You gotta go as somethin' you ain't."

"There's a whole world of possibilities," Josh murmured as J.T. made a leap into his father's arms. "Hey, Natalie, Tate."

"Hey, Josh," his sister-in-law replied. "We were wondering if you'd be joining us for lunch. It'd be a shame if you missed it, considering I've fixed ribs, baked beans and the last of the Silver Queen corn from your mom's freezer, along with a chocolate cake for dessert."

As they started toward the house, J.T. hitching a ride on Tate's shoulders, Josh slid his arm around Natalie. "You know I love your ribs—and the rest of you ain't too bad," he teased. "There's not much that could drag me away from my favorite food fixed by my favorite sister-in-law."

"How about a pretty blonde in a silver convertible?"

Josh gave both her and Tate a pitying look. "Your lives must be disgustingly boring if you find my being sociable with a stranger passing through worthy of discussion. Yes, she was blond, she was pretty, and she was driving a convertible. And she has about as much significance in my day as that hawk flying up there." He shook his head sorrowfully. "Poor old married folk."

Natalie elbowed him for that last remark. "One of these

days, Josh, you're going to fall in love and get married, and then you'll see what you've been missing.''

''Maybe…when I've done all there is to do, seen all there is to see, and life no longer has meaning.'' Opening the screen door, he held it for them while they went inside, then followed them into a kitchen filled with incredible aromas. His mother was a decent cook, though she didn't really like the fuss, and Jordan excelled at breakfasts and desserts, but Natalie's every effort was outstanding, and she enjoyed it, too. The Rawlins family had never eaten so well until she came into their lives.

He washed up in the laundry room sink while Tate took J.T. to the bathroom to clean up and change out of his astronaut costume. Just as Josh reached for a towel, the doorbell rang, followed by Natalie's call. ''Can you get that, Josh?''

Cutting through the dining room, he dried his hands, then tossed the towel over one shoulder as he reached the door. The bell rang again an instant before he pulled it open. ''Well, well.''

Standing there was the pretty blonde, looking uneasy and edgy. Out of the car, he could see that she was a half foot shorter than him, slender, with hints of curves in the right places. The ball cap was gone, revealing her very short hair, shorter even than his own. She wore linen trousers that were pressed and creased, a long-sleeved white shirt, open at the neck and sleeves rolled halfway to her elbows, and shoes that gave her a few inches of extra height—probably a casual look where she came from, but not in Hickory Bluff.

When she didn't speak but continued to give him a look that was at the same time blank and startled, he leaned one shoulder against the doorjamb. ''Let me guess. You were so dazzled by my charm and boyish good looks that you came back for more.''

"I…I— You—" She drew a deep breath. "I'm looking for Natalie Rawlins. Is she here?"

"Yes, she is, but trust me, darlin', I'm more your type." With a grin, he leaned back and called over his shoulder, "Yo, Nat, it's for you."

"Who is it?" Natalie called back, and he looked questioningly at the blonde.

Her mouth worked a time or two without producing a sound, then she took another of those deep breaths. "Tell her.…" Pitching her voice loud enough to carry, she said, "It's me, Natalie…Candace."

The sound of shattering glass echoed through the house, making Candace flinch inside and out. That was not a good sign. In fact, that was a get-in-the-car-and-get-the-hell-out-of-town sign, or the next breakable might be aimed at her. She wanted nothing more than to run away, wanted it with an intensity that surprised her, but her feet wouldn't move. She couldn't do anything but stand there and indulge in a mild panic.

Was the flirtatious cowboy the Rawlins from whom Natalie had gotten her new name? Had Candace been thinking mildly lustful thoughts about her former friend's *husband*, for heaven's sake? And what kind of idiot was she, to think that Natalie might ever offer the remotest hint of forgiveness?

The cowboy was looking from her to the back of the house, and the grin was gone. No doubt she'd heard her last friendly word from him. Once he realized who she was, she'd be lucky if he didn't run her out of town on a rail, or tar and feather her, or whatever they did to unwelcome varmints in these parts.

As footsteps slowly approached the door, she caught her breath. This was it. The moment she'd been anticipating, dreading, visualizing. She'd imagined it a thousand times, with every outcome possible. Nine hundred ninety-nine of them had ended badly.

Finally her feet obeyed, took a step away from the door and toward the driveway, but it was too late. The woman she'd adored, loved, envied, idolized and destroyed appeared in the doorway next to the cowboy, and she was looking at Candace with quiet loathing.

She hadn't changed much in the five-plus years since Candace had last seen her. Her hair was still long, curling wildly, still the color of new copper, and her skin was still pale and creamy smooth. The clothes were different—faded jeans, scuffed cowboy boots, a chambray shirt—but she was still elegant. Still beautiful. And she still hated Candace.

"What do you want?"

Candace had imagined the question a hundred times and formulated as many answers. She'd been ready. But the instant Natalie had spoken, all the eloquent answers flew right out of Candace's head. All she could do was stammer and sputter. "I…I want— I'd like—" She breathed, then exhaled the words in a rush. "Can we talk?"

"No." Reaching past the cowboy, Natalie gripped the door and started to swing it shut.

"Please, Natalie—"

"You couldn't possibly say anything that would interest me. Get the hell off our property and don't—"

"Mama said a bad word!"

Candace's gaze slid past Natalie. The other cowboy, the one who'd worked alongside the dog while the flirt flirted, came to join them, carrying a small child. Though the boy's hair was auburn, there was no denying the resemblance between him and the man, which suggested *he* was Natalie's cowboy, which meant the other wasn't. It was a selfish thing to consider at the moment, but Candace couldn't help it. She was relieved.

The second man slid his free arm around Natalie's waist and hugged her close. "What's going on, babe?"

Pale and steely-eyed, Natalie replied, "Nothing. She was just leaving."

Candace cleared her throat. "Natalie, please... I don't blame you for not wanting to talk to me, but please, just listen to what I came to say."

"Listen to you lie, twist the facts and manipulate the details? I don't think so."

She started to close the door again, and Candace blurted out, "I just wanted to tell you how sorry I am—"

The door closed with a quiet click.

Candace stood there a long time, staring at the door. She wanted to ring the bell again and apologize for disturbing them. She wanted to climb in her car and drive as far away and as fast as she could. She wanted to beg for just a moment of Natalie's time.

When her lungs began to burn, she finally remembered to breathe, a quick soft gasp that sounded unnervingly close to a sob. Of course it wasn't. Candace Thompson was tough, ambitious, self-centered. She didn't cry. She made other people do it. She had cried only twice that she could recall in the past thirty years, the first when she'd thought she was going to die the way she'd lived—alone and unloved—the second, soon after. She hadn't been able to name a single soul who would mourn her passing, and that had sent *her* into mourning.

Once she forced her feet to move, she hurried down the steps, then covered the ground to the car in a dozen long strides. She didn't glance at the house as she backed around an ancient oak, then headed down the driveway. She didn't wonder if they watched through the blinds with relief that she was leaving.

By the time she'd reached the intersection with the first paved highway, her breathing was relatively normal. She forced her jaw to relax, then eased her two-fisted grip on the steering wheel. She'd tried and failed. End of story, right? So she could mark that goal off her list and go on to the dozens of goals that remained. Right?

Right.

With an overwhelming relief rushing over her, she checked for traffic, then pulled onto the highway. She didn't intend to waste any time. She would contact the accommodating rental car guy and make arrangements to turn in the car this afternoon, get the RV ready and hit the road first thing in the morning. She had places to go and things to do. She had a life to live. She'd wasted most of the thirty-eight years she'd been given, but she intended to make the next thirty-eight—or however many she had left—worthwhile.

The two-lane highway led her east into Hickory Bluff. The smallest place she'd ever lived had more than 175,000 residents. She wasn't sure if Hickory Bluff appealed to her in spite of that, or because of it. According to the sign on the edge of town, it was home to 990 two-legged residents, and probably twenty times that of the big, shaggy four-legged variety.

Nothing about the place was fancy. The buildings downtown were built mostly of native stone, and the houses on the blocks extending out from downtown were plain and functional. Most had porches, even the trailers, which weren't gathered in a mobile home park as she'd come to expect, but were mixed in with the more permanent structures.

High school athletics seemed to be an important part of the community. The water tower was painted green and gold, with the legend Go, Wildcats! Store windows bore hand-painted cheers, pennants or bumper stickers, and a disproportionate number of the people she'd seen wore green ball caps with the Hickory Bluff High School initials embroidered in gold.

It was a rather shabby, worn, homey town, and if she

were staying, she would probably be tempted to write an article about just how homey. *If* she were still writing.

Once she turned onto the main street, she intended to drive straight through town and to the campground. Instead, she found herself pulling into a parking space in front of Merrill's, a store that could provide you with a driver's license to drive to the lake, a fishing license to use while you were there, beer and sandwiches for a late lunch and ice to keep them cold. Through the window she could also see a selection of fussily hand-painted T-shirts, a display of plastic Halloween lawn ornaments and stacked-up cases of motor oil, supporting videotapes for rent. At first glance, it seemed an odd combination of goods and services, but she could remember a time when it would have met every one of her father's needs, especially the beer.

It was hunger that had made her stop—she'd been too nervous to eat breakfast that morning—along with the desire to avoid one more solitary meal. She'd had enough of those in the past eleven months to last a lifetime.

Norma Sue's Café was in the middle of the block and was one of only three places to eat in town. The others were the Dairy Delight, great for burgers, according to the obviously some-sort-of-relative-to-Natalie's-husband charmer, and Pepe Chen's Mexican and Chinese Buffet, an experience she thought she might be better off skipping.

A cowbell jangled over the café door when she went inside. A few people glanced up, and the waitress behind the counter called, "Have a seat wherever," but that was the extent of attention. She'd expected a few more curious glances but was grateful to be wrong. She wanted to be with other people, but she didn't necessarily want their attention. Just seeing other faces, hearing other voices, would be enough.

She'd barely settled in an empty booth when the waitress brought her iced water and a menu. She ordered a chicken salad sandwich and pop, then eyed the mile-high meringues on the pies that filled a display cabinet on the counter. She could turn down candy, ice cream and cake, but a good pie would undermine her best intentions every time. Natalie had once suggested that it was because she associated pies with easier, more innocent times—growing up, holidays, family closeness.

Candace hadn't told her there'd been nothing easy or innocent about her childhood. There had certainly been no family closeness.

Thinking of Natalie stirred an ache in her chest. She'd known all along what the outcome of this trip would be— had known the odds against her succeeding were over-whelming. Still, someplace deep inside, she'd hoped....

If she left Hickory Bluff tomorrow, there could be no more hope.

Listlessly she pulled the legal pad from her bag. It was wrinkled, torn and stained, but the writing was still legible. To be on the safe side, she'd copied its contents into her journal, but there was something satisfying about this original with its stains, tears and doodles. That neatly written list on heavyweight pristine journal paper could well be nothing more than a someday dream, while this one was being made real, slowly but surely.

But not by giving up after one lousy failure.

She was staring at that failure—*Make amends with Natalie*—when a shadow fell across the paper. Expecting the waitress, she looked up with a faint smile. Seeing the handsome cowboy, she let it fade.

Without waiting for an invitation, he sat down across from her and leaned forward. "I don't know what the hell you think you're doing, but you're not welcome here," he said in a low, cold voice. It was an amazing change—from the appreciative looks, the lazy drawl and the easy charm to this cold, hard hostility. And he didn't even know her. Just think how much he could hate her if he did.

"What I'm doing is none of your business," she said,

making an enormous effort to keep her voice as well as her hands steady as she turned the legal pad facedown.

"The hell it isn't! No one comes around here making trouble for my family without making it my business."

"I'm not making trouble."

"Natalie says you are. She says you're a liar, that you'd backstab your own mother to get ahead. She says you're dishonest, unethical and untrustworthy and that she wishes she'd never met you."

Candace stared hard at the tabletop to stop the moisture trying to well in her eyes. No surprises there. She'd known of all the challenges and goals she'd set for herself, this would be the most impossible. Natalie wasn't inclined to feel an ounce of forgiveness, and understandably so. If Candace were in her place, she wouldn't feel very forgiving, either. But if she could just find it in her heart to listen—not forgive, not forget, just listen....

"Do us all a favor and get the hell out of town. If you set foot on the ranch again, we'll have you arrested, and if you go near Natalie again, I swear to God, I'll make you *damn* sorry." He delivered his warning in a voice so fierce, with such force behind it, that she had little doubt he meant every word of it. Then he slid to his feet, almost bumping into the waitress.

"Hey, Josh, can I get you—" The waitress broke off, perplexed, to watch him walk away, then slowly shifted her suspicious gaze to Candace. Making no effort to be friendly, the woman set the dishes down with a thud, sloshing pop onto the cardboard back of the legal pad, then walked away.

So was that the kind of influence the Rawlins family held in Hickory Bluff? Candace wondered wearily as she stared at a chicken salad sandwich big enough for three. Their enemies were the town's enemies? Was the waitress's loyalty to Josh in particular, or was the entire town likely to turn against Candace if she stayed?

She was feeling perverse enough to find out.

## Chapter Two

Supper at the Rawlinses' house that evening was an unusually somber affair. Natalie was withdrawn, Tate concerned about her, and Josh.... Truth was, Josh was pretty much in the dark. He didn't know exactly who Candace Thompson was—someone Natalie had once been friends with, whom she now despised, whose name couldn't even be mentioned at the table without stony silences or, worse, an awful hurt look sliding over Natalie's features.

But, bottom line, Josh didn't need to know any details. Rawlinses stuck together. It was how they got through the bad times, and it made the good times that much better. He didn't need to know what Candace had done. Natalie was family, and her enemy was the family's enemy.

Too bad her enemy was so damn pretty.

He finished the supper dishes he'd volunteered to wash and dried his hands, then went into the living room. Tate was sitting on the couch, J.T. snoozing on his lap and Natalie curled up against him. She looked as if she were a thousand miles away, in a place too melancholy to bear.

"I…I guess I'll head on home," he said.

"See you in the morning," Tate responded.

Moving closer, Josh gently ruffled J.T.'s hair, then squeezed Natalie's hand. She didn't lift her head from Tate's shoulder but gave him a sad smile.

The night was chilly, making him glad he'd brought a jacket. The sky was dark and clear, the stars so bright that it seemed he could reach up and touch them. He whistled tunelessly as he crossed to his pickup, then headed home. He lived on the south end of the property, a half mile west of the road in a stand of timber. He and Tate had built the house themselves eight years ago, working in their free time. They'd had precious little of it, so the place was plain and purely functional, which suited him just fine. He didn't spend much time there, and if he ever married and had kids, he would have to build on. Any prettying-up could be done then.

The road that ran between the two houses was little more than two ruts in the grass. Just before it entered the trees, another narrow lane angled off to the left, giving him quick access to the county road through a rickety gate. The main road went straight, then zigzagged through the trees before finally reaching the clearing where the house stood. It was a simple frame house, painted a dark rusty red. The front porch stood only a foot off the ground, so he hadn't bothered with railings, and he generally ignored the steps centered in front. He parked at the side, stepped directly up onto the porch, then went in.

The place always seemed so quiet compared to Tate's house—though this evening next door had been an exception. Of course, having a three-year-old in residence made a hell of a difference. It was nice to walk into Tate's and hear laughter, chattering and singing, to smell scents like food cooking, perfume and other feminine things, to see childish and womanly touches all over.

Just as it was nice to come in here and find the quiet and privacy he expected.

As he settled on the couch, he listened to the messages on the answering machine. Two were from Theresa, the steadiest of the recent women in his life, one just asking for a call, the other inviting him over later in the week. The third was from the wife of one of his buddies. They were going to a concert in Tulsa on Saturday and would he be interested in going along with her cousin, Stacey.

He grimaced. He'd met Stacey before, and while she was gorgeous, her biological clock was ticking loudly, making her eager to get married. Every time he spent even a few minutes with her, he felt lucky to have escaped unharmed—or unhitched.

It was barely eight o'clock. Too early for bed. He turned on the television and flipped through the channels but found nothing that caught his interest. He considered returning Theresa's call, but figured she'd be busy grading her fifth-graders' papers. He ate an apple and tried to finish the thriller that had been sitting on the end table since the last time he'd put it down over two weeks ago. Obviously, it wasn't thrilling enough.

What he needed was a distraction, and where he usually found his distractions was Frenchy's, the same place he'd recommended to Candace Thompson for a cold beer. What were the odds she would show up after their conversation at Norma Sue's? What were the odds she was even still in the county?

And so what if she was and she did go to Frenchy's? That didn't mean he had to speak to her or anything. For damn sure he didn't have to stay home and avoid one of his regular hangouts just because *she* might be there.

He wasted another ten minutes, trying to talk himself out of it, but when he was done, he grabbed his jacket and

Stetson and returned to his truck. When he drove through the gate and onto the county road, he turned left, the shortest route to the bar. He looked for the blonde's car in the parking lot and was satisfied when he didn't see it. As tension he hadn't even been aware of drained from his shoulders, he parked and headed for the door.

Frenchy's wasn't much—but then, nothing in Hickory Bluff was. The building was long and squat, built of concrete blocks that had been painted red once upon a time, then white and most recently, gray. Of course, *most recently* was about ten years ago, so patches of all three colors, as well as bare concrete, showed through.

The floor inside was cement, and the interior surface of the blocks was painted black, as if the windowless building hadn't already been dark enough inside. Booths lined three walls, and the floor space was shared by tables and chairs, pool tables and a dance floor. A bar ran the length of the back wall, and a bandstand took up one end of the building. Frenchy's offered live music every other weekend, some of it pretty good. The rest of the time they made do with a juke box, and it was pretty good, too.

Josh knew everyone in the place, and said hello a half dozen times on his way to the bar, where the owner was wiping the counter. He wasn't French, and his name was Otis. Rumor had it that back in his younger days, he'd met a singer in Paris by the name of Genevieve. They'd fallen in love, and he'd come back here to build this place, where he would tend bar and she would provide the entertainment, but she'd never come to join him and he'd never found out why.

One night, when Otis had been drinking away his profits, he'd confided in Josh that the only Paris he'd ever been to was in Texas and that Genevieve was his shrew of an ex-wife who'd given him good reason to leave that great state.

By the time Josh reached the bar, an icy long-neck was waiting for him. "How's it going, Otis?"

"Can't complain. It's a sad commentary on life in Hickory Bluff that you guys keep me busy. 'Course, what can you expect in a town where the only place to go is away?"

"Aw, it's not as bad as that. You know, most of us—yourself included—live here because we like it."

"Because we don't know no better," Otis retorted as he moved to wait on a customer at the opposite end of the bar.

Josh turned for a look around the room. Some of his buddies were occupied at the two pool tables at the far end, and a half dozen more sat at the big round table they'd claimed for their own. While he was debating which group to join, his gaze settled on Calvin Bridger, alone in a distant booth. He didn't ask permission to join Cal, since he'd probably say no and Josh would do it, anyway. He just slid onto the bench across from him.

"I didn't know you were back in town," Josh remarked.

Cal took a deep drink from his beer, then scowled at him. "I didn't ask you to sit down."

"Good thing I've known you all of our worthless lives, or I might think you were being rude. When did you get home?"

"A couple days ago."

"Where's Darcy?"

Cal mumbled something and shrugged, then took another long swallow.

The three of them—Josh, Cal and Darcy Hawkins—had gone to school together from kindergarten on. When just about everyone else went out for football, basketball or baseball, Josh and Cal had started rodeoing. Cal had been a lot better at it—had turned it into a career and made a living at it for fifteen years and counting. He'd also married Darcy a few years back, and seemed to be pretty good at that, too.

"You guys staying at your folks' or hers?" Josh asked.

"Uh-huh."

"Which one?" It made a difference if a person wanted to go visiting, since the Bridger ranch was a few miles west of the Rawlinses' and the Hawkins place—called the Mansion with a derisive sniff—was on the east side of Hickory Bluff, high atop a hill and looking down on the town just as the Hawkinses had always looked down on its people.

Cal drained his beer and signaled Otis for another, then fixed a hostile stare on Josh. "I'm staying at the ranch. I don't have a clue in hell where Darcy is. She didn't want to go to this last rodeo with me. She didn't want to come home with me. Here lately she doesn't want to do much of anything with me. Now will you go the hell away and let me have one beer in peace?"

Josh didn't argue or press for more details. Taking his beer, he stood up, then turned back. "Let me know before you leave."

Though it wasn't a question, Cal nodded. "Yeah, sure."

Josh never gave a lot of thought to the state of people's marriages. Some of his buddies changed wives the way other people traded cars. A few had been married a long time and seemed satisfied with their wives, three kids and a dog. Some swore they'd never get married, and he believed them. Some swore the same, and he didn't. But Cal and Darcy...damn. They'd been together a long time. If asked, Josh would have said they had the second-best chance at staying together forever. First, of course, went to Tate and Natalie.

Looked like he would have been wrong.

He crossed to the round table, into which some joker had carved The Knights, and pulled up a chair, swinging it around backward to straddle. The conversation was football—the college games played the weekend before and the Wildcat game coming up on Friday. Both Tate and Jordan had been Wildcat stars, both scouted by college teams, and Jordan was attending Oklahoma State University on a football scholarship. For those reasons, people seemed to think that made Josh an authority of some sort. Truthfully, he didn't know any more about the game than anyone else—and didn't care as much as most of them. Tossing a football around and risking life and limb against guys twice his size didn't appeal to him at all.

He'd by far preferred risking his life and limb against bulls *ten* times his size, he thought with a grin.

He'd finished his first beer and was nursing his second and thinking about asking the pretty brunette at the bar to dance when Dudley Barnes hollered his name from the vicinity of the pool tables. "Rawlins, get your scrawny carcass over here and give me a chance to win back that forty bucks you stole from me last week."

Shooting pool with Dudley was about the easiest money Josh had ever come by. He could beat him blindfolded and with one hand tied behind his back. There was no challenge to it, but it was something to do. Besides, that pretty brunette taught at Theresa's school, and Theresa might not take kindly to him paying her any attention.

Crossing to the table, he laid a twenty-dollar bill next to the one already on the edge, then circled to take a cue stick from the rack on the wall. He chalked the tip while Dudley racked the balls, then bent over the table to break.

"How 'bout you lose twenty to me and twenty to my friend?" Dudley suggested.

"Aw, you don't have any friends," Josh replied. The cue ball hit with a clean *cra-ack* and the balls rolled in every direction. He moved to the end of the table and bent over, bracing his hand on the felt.

"I've got one, and she's the prettiest girl in the place. Talks real pretty, too, 'cause she's from…where was it, honey?"

"Atlanta." The voice was feminine…and familiar, even though he'd never heard it before that morning and had confidently thought he would never hear it again.

He made his shot, then slowly looked up. It was easy enough to overlook anyone standing beside Dudley. At six foot six and three hundred pounds, he was a big boy. But once Josh's gaze connected with Candace Thompson, Dudley faded into the background.

She'd changed clothes for slumming at the local honky-tonk, into jeans that clung the way they were meant to and a red button-front shirt. Her boots were brown, thick-soled work boots that hadn't seen much, if any, work, and she wore a black cowboy hat that was way too big for her head. Seeing that it belonged to Dudley, it was probably too big for everybody's head.

"Buddy, this is Can—"

Josh interrupted Dudley's introductions. "We've met," he said rudely, then turned his back on them to make the next two shots.

She waited until he'd straightened again to speak. "Technically, we haven't. I know your name is Josh because the waitress called you that, but—"

He hit the next ball with more force than he'd intended, but it rolled into the intended pocket, anyway. Then he faced her impassively. "I'm Josh Rawlins. Tate Rawlins's brother. Natalie Rawlins's brother-in-law. And you're Candace Thompson. And that's all that needs to be said, isn't it?"

*And you're Candace Thompson.* Candace hadn't known it was possible for someone to put so much pure loathing in the four syllables of her name. No doubt he'd picked that up from Natalie, a fact that sent an ache through her, but she hid it. Instead she coolly watched as he methodically sank ball after ball.

She'd talked herself out of coming here more than once through the afternoon and early evening, but somehow she'd found herself walking through the door, anyway. She'd figured Josh wouldn't be there, on the chance that she would, but he was the first one she'd seen when she'd come in. Then Dudley had stepped between them, blocking Josh from sight, and she had gratefully accepted his invitation to join him for a drink—something she wouldn't have done if she'd known he would soon invite Josh over, too.

But she was here, and so was Josh, and what did it matter? Clearly he didn't intend to talk to her, and she had nothing to say to him. Enlisting his help in gaining access to Natalie was out of the question. Not only would she not ask, but he would surely refuse if she did. And with Natalie between them, that pretty much ruled out anything else.

He finished the game without Dudley even getting close to the table, scooped up the forty dollars and shoved them into his pocket and started away.

"Hey, what about the next game?" Dudley said. "You afraid to play the lady?"

Josh slowly turned and let his brown gaze slide over Candace as if he were taking inventory and coming up short. "What lady?"

Dudley pushed away from the table with surprising speed for a man his size. "That was uncalled for," he said flatly, his voice empty of good humor. "You owe her an apology."

"Like hell I do."

"You sure as hell do. You can give it on your own, or I can help you with it. It's your choice."

Josh's gaze narrowed and turned even colder. "You remember the last time you tried to make me do something I didn't want to do?"

"You broke my nose." Dudley jutted out his jaw. "But that ain't gonna happen this time."

Tired of the blustering, Candace stepped in front of Dudley and laid her hand on his arm. "You promised me a beer."

"Right after he gives you an apology."

"I don't want an apology. Come on, a drink and a dance,

then I have to go home.'' She maneuvered him around until he broke eye contact with Josh and finally looked at her. Sweeping off his cowboy hat, she gave him a coaxing smile. ''Come on. I haven't danced in ages.''

After a tense moment he let her pull him around tables to the dance floor, then grudgingly took her in his arms. With one last glare in Josh's direction, he looked down at her and smiled.

The music was country and slow, and she stumbled over her own feet and Dudley's only a time or two. There had been a time when she'd danced as naturally as breathing— a time when a lot of things had come naturally to her. She'd taken a great deal for granted...but not anymore.

She wasn't counting on Dudley to remain silent, and sure enough, around the middle of the song, he asked, ''What's between you and Josh?''

''Nothing.''

''Oh, come on. He's not usually like that.''

''What's he usually like?'' she asked, though she'd seen a good example that morning, before he'd known who she was.

Dudley was quiet for a moment, then he grinned. ''His mother says the trouble with Josh is he likes women...a lot. Trouble for her, because he's never gonna settle down and give her some more grandchildren. No trouble at all for the women around here. He's been involved with every pretty woman in a hundred-mile radius. I should have expected that he'd already met you, too.''

''And how many grandchildren does his mother have that she needs more?''

''Two. Jordan's twenty and the little one's 'bout three.''

Natalie mothering the three-year-old was an easy enough image to conjure, but a twenty-year-old? When she was only thirty-six herself? Of course, how much mothering did a twenty-year-old need? Candace had been on her own for two years before her twentieth birthday, and she'd done all right.

She'd just been lonely. Alone. Ambitious. Driven. Afraid.

"Have you settled down and given your mother grandchildren?" she asked to keep him from returning to Josh.

His grin was remarkably boyish. "A time or two."

"For the settling-down or the grandkids?" she asked dryly.

"Two marriages, two divorces, two grandkids. What about you?"

"No marriages, no divorces, no kids." And no mother around to nag her for babies to spoil.

"You've never been married? The men in Atlanta must be blind."

To the contrary, she thought as the song ended. They just had so many better women to choose from than her.

When the music stopped, she stepped out of his arms. "Thank you for a nice evening."

"What about that drink?"

She regretfully shook her head. "I'd better skip it and get on home."

"How long are you going to be around here?"

If the Rawlins family had their way, no longer than it would take to cross the state line. In a weak moment that would be her choice, too—had been her choice that afternoon after seeing Natalie.

But she couldn't allow herself to be weak. A weak woman couldn't survive everything she'd been through in the past year. Though she'd often been weak in body, her spirit had been strong, and she had to keep it that way. Living another thirty-eight years depended on it.

"I don't know," she answered honestly. "Maybe a few days. Maybe a few weeks."

"Then I'll see you back here again sometime."

How long had it been since anyone besides a doctor had wanted to see her again? Too unbearably long.

She smiled at Dudley with real pleasure. "Yeah. You'll see me again."

With that she got her suede jacket from the stool where she'd left it, pretended not to notice Josh or the icy stare centered on her back and walked out into the chilly night. As she unlocked the car, she gazed up at the sky, midnight dark and filled with more stars than it was possible to see in Atlanta. She picked out the brightest one, focused hard on it and tried to make a wish, but only one word would form. *Please.*

It wasn't particularly articulate for someone who'd earned her living with words, but it pretty much covered everything. Please let Natalie give me a chance. Please let me live a long, healthy life. Please don't let Josh look at me like that again. Please help me be strong. Please let me have just one friend…and please let Natalie be that friend.

Yep, that one word said it all.

Smiling with a satisfaction she hadn't felt in far too long, she climbed into the car and headed off through the dark night.

√Dance.
√Have some fun.
√Wish upon a star.

For a brief time the day before, Candace had thought she would be crossing the Arkansas state line around ten this Wednesday morning. Instead, she was enjoying a beautiful fall day in downtown Hickory Bluff. She'd had a late breakfast at Norma Sue's and had spent more than an hour examining an appealing mix of junk and antiques. She had a shopping list tucked in her purse—mostly groceries, plus an inexpensive lawn chair for enjoying the weather. Patsy

Conway, who ran the campground with her husband, Dub, had filled her ear that morning with memories of Octobers as warm as any summer day and as bitter cold as the dead of winter.

Right now the temperature was in the midseventies, the sun was shining brightly, and there was a pleasant breeze blowing out of the northwest. It was so nice that Candace had done her morning meditation outside, sitting cross-legged on an old quilt spread over straw-like grass. She'd finished secure in the knowledge that she'd made the right decision in not running away this morning. One attempt to talk to Natalie didn't constitute *making amends*. Hell, it hardly even qualified as trying. She was a journalist, which meant she possessed many qualities. Among the better ones was tenacity.

Natalie, also having been a journalist, probably didn't even expect her to give up after one refusal. She'd taught Candace better than that—though she'd lived to regret it.

The owner of the antique store had directed her down the street to find a lawn chair. Just a few yards short of her destination was a pay phone. Though she tried to ignore it as she walked, her gaze kept drifting back to it. Even though it was the last thing she wanted on such a beautiful morning, she was going to stop and make a call before finishing her shopping. She was going to pick up the receiver, drop in the correct change and dial the number she'd committed to memory.

Rejection number two, coming up, she thought as she listened to the phone ring. It was answered after the third ring, making her catch her breath until she realized it was an answering machine. So Natalie wasn't home, or she was screening her calls. It would make a lot of difference if she knew which.

It was the husband's voice on the machine, his message simple and to the point. ''You've reached the Rawlins residence. Leave a message and we'll get back to you.'' Just before the beep came a childish, ''Yee-haw!''

Candace took a few shallow breaths, then hung up. She didn't like pleading on tape where strangers could hear. Not that she was above doing it if she had no other choice, but only then.

Feeling as if the day were somehow less bright, less perfect, she crossed the final few feet to the store. Its name, U-Want-It, was emblazoned across one plate-glass window, and a life-size wildcat, its mouth open in a snarl, was painted on the other. The place appeared to have a little of everything—clothing, books, tools, toys, sports equipment, auto parts and even an old-fashioned soda fountain. The electronic bell on the door played the first few notes of a catchy tune, but the voices that greeted her were none too friendly.

They came from the checkout and belonged to two women—one with jet-black hair, probably in her forties, and the other a sullen blonde, maybe half that age. Candace gave them a vague smile, then wandered down the main aisle. That wasn't enough distance, though, to block out their conversation.

''You can't tell me what to do!'' the blonde snapped in a tone that suggested this wasn't the first time she'd said it. ''My daddy—''

''Your daddy may run everything else around here, but this store is *mine.* I'm your *boss,* Shelley, and you know what that means? I *do* get to tell you what to do. Dusting shelves is a part of your job, as is being here on time and not making personal calls on store time.''

Shelley sniffed haughtily. ''Dusting is a dirty job, and it's hard on my nails, and I'm not going to do it. And I was *only* twenty minutes late.''

''For the third time in a week.''

''What—are you keeping track?''

"Yes, I am. It's called a time card," the woman said impatiently. "That's how I know how much to pay you."

"Hey, you can't hold it out of my check just because I was a minute late! That's not fair!"

"What's not fair is you spending an hour a day on the phone, chatting with your—" As if on cue, the telephone rang. As Candace peeked up from the Christmas decorations that filled the center aisle, both women grabbed for it, but the older one was closer and quicker. "U-Want-It, we got it," she said brusquely. "This is Martha.... No, Shelley can't come to the phone now."

"Hey!" Shelley shrieked, trying to get the phone before Martha hung up but failing. "You can't treat me like this, or I'll quit, and then you'll be in trouble. You'll never find anyone to replace me."

"Oh, honey, my arthritic grandma over in the nursing home can work circles around you, and without whining, too."

"That's it!" Shelley jerked off the red vest that passed for a uniform, tossed it on the counter, then stomped toward the door. There she did an abrupt U-turn and swept back to grab the purse Martha rather loudly plunked on the counter. Back at the door, Shelley faced her once more. "Don't even think about asking me to come back. You'd have to triple my salary, and even then I'd still rather eat dirt."

"I'd be happy to serve it up for you," Martha called after her as she left the store.

The quiet that immediately followed echoed in Candace's ears. She hesitated a moment, then slowly approached the counter, where Martha was rubbing her temples. When Candace cleared her throat, she looked up, then smiled apologetically.

"Great service, huh? You come in for a simple purchase and instead get to watch the owner and clerk fight. I'm so sorry about that."

"Don't worry about it. Though, honestly, I don't know how you expect to find good help if you expect them to show up and actually work. That's a bit unreasonable, isn't it?"

Martha laughed. "It certainly is to Shelley. Oh, well…I only hired her because my husband works for her daddy. I'm sure he'll hear about this, but…" She shrugged. "That's life. Is there anything I can help you with?"

"Do you have any lawn chairs?"

"Only the cheap aluminum kind that you usually have to throw away at the end of the summer. All the way at the back on the left."

Candace headed toward the back, marveling at the variety of merchandise. Besides the Christmas display, inexpensive Halloween costumes and decorations were packed into one section of the main aisle, along with paper Thanksgiving turkeys, tablecloths and such. Women's clothing was on the right in the front half of the shop, men's at the rear and kids' in between. Exactly where Martha had said, she found the last of the lawn chairs and picked up one, then optimistically added another. Who knew? Maybe Patsy Conway would join her for coffee some morning.

Back at the checkout, Martha rang up her total, and Candace handed over a twenty. After returning her change to her wallet, she hesitated. "Will you be hiring someone to replace Shelley—at least, temporarily?"

"I have to. I can't be here most afternoons right now. My mother just got home from the hospital after having hip surgery, and I'm the only one who lives close enough to stay with her." Martha's shrewd gaze swept over her. "You interested?"

"For a while."

"You have any experience?"

"A little." She'd worked as a cashier on the three-to-eleven shift at a convenience store back when she was in school—the scariest job she'd ever had. At least here, she wouldn't have to worry about someone coming in with a shotgun and blowing her away.

"You mind getting your hands dirty?"

Candace laughed. "I'd much rather clean dirt than eat it."

"When can you start?"

"Today."

It was that easy. No references, no application. Four questions, and Martha was handing her the red vest Shelley had discarded. "Welcome to U-Want-It. I'm Martha Andrews."

"Candace Thompson."

Martha showed her the cash register and gave her a quick tour of the store, including the stock room and bathroom. Then, dust mitts in hand, Candace set to work.

A year ago she'd thought dusting and cleaning so far beneath her that she'd paid someone else quite a lot to do it for her. She hadn't worked so hard to get through school and then to advance her career just to spend her spare time chasing dust bunnies and scrubbing toilets.

Now the career was on hiatus, possibly gone for good since there wasn't much demand for a writer who'd stopped writing. Now she supported herself working temporary jobs, and although she still wasn't fond of scrubbing toilets, she'd found a measure of satisfaction in other jobs she'd once considered too menial.

She began dusting at the back of the store and worked her way up one aisle and down the next. The bell on the door sounded fairly often, but the customers paid little attention to her, and she stayed focused on her work.

When she reached the front, she started on the tall glass jars that lined a display next to the cash register. They were filled with candy—fat, multicolored peppermint sticks, candy necklaces, wax lips, straws that poured flavored sugar, tiny candy-covered chocolates. She remembered many of them from childhood trips to the store with her father, when he loaded her up with so many sweets that she'd often been sick by the time they returned home.

She was on her knees, dusting the jar that held the candy necklaces, when a young child crouched beside her. Prepared to smile, she glanced at him, but the smile wouldn't form. She'd seen him for mere seconds the morning before, but she would have recognized him anywhere. If she were a better person, she would have been there when he was born, would have been named his godmother and been called Aunt Candace as soon as he'd learned to talk.

Now Natalie would be furious if she so much as spoke to him.

"Hi," he greeted, his voice soft.

She looked around guiltily but saw no Rawlinses close enough to hear. "Hi."

"I'm gonna buy some candy for me and Petey. Petey's my horse. I named him myself."

"Th-that's nice." She started to stand up, to retreat someplace safe until the boy and whoever had brought him were gone, but he spoke again.

"What kind of candy do ya think Petey would like?"

"I don't know. What kind do you usually get him?"

"He likes plain ol' sugar. And apples and pears and peaches and watermelon." He rubbed his nose with the back of his hand. "But *I* like candy."

"Well, maybe you should—"

"*J.T.*" Seemingly coming from nowhere, Josh Rawlins tossed some items on the counter, then swung the boy into his arms and held him away from Candace as she, too, stood up. "Remember what your mama and daddy tell you about talking to strangers?"

"Not to."

"And she's a stranger, isn't she?"

The boy shook his head. "She's the one that made Mama say a bad word. She was at our house."

"But she's still a stranger, and you're not supposed to talk to her. Do you understand?"

"Yes, but—" J.T. took one look at his uncle's frown, then sighed. "Okay."

"Good." Josh set him down. "Why don't you go sit on one of the stools over there, okay?" He watched as J.T. ran to the soda fountain, then clambered onto a stool. Slowly he turned back to Candace, but before he could speak, Martha, who had apparently witnessed the exchange from the far end of the counter, joined them.

"Teaching a kid to be careful of strangers is a good idea, Josh, but don't you think he needs to know the difference between your garden-variety stranger and the clerk who's trying to wait on him?"

Though Candace's gaze had settled somewhere around his feet, she knew the instant *his* gaze touched her. It made her face grow hot and her nerves tingle—made her wish she were only three inches tall so she could duck behind the register or crawl into a drawer to hide from his stare.

"You've got to be kidding. You *hired* her?"

"Yes, I did. You want to make something of it?"

His gaze didn't shift. "Get J.T. an ice cream cone while I pay for this, will you?"

Martha hesitated, then crossed the room to the fountain counter.

His voice low but no less dangerous, Josh accused, "You said you were leaving."

Candace aimed for mild inoffensiveness. "No. You suggested it. I chose not to follow your advice."

"No one wants you here."

Clenching her jaw, she moved behind the cash register and began ringing up his purchases—an air filter for a truck, a pair of boot laces, a spool of white thread and a can of paint thinner. Before she totaled it, she stiffly asked, "What about J.T. and Petey's candy?"

"He'll get his candy at the grocery store."

Candace hit Total, then sacked everything while he pulled his wallet from his pocket. She made change, which he accepted as if touching her might soil him. He didn't grab the bag and the kid, though, and put some distance between them. Instead, he leaned closer, so close she could smell the faint tang of sweat and the…well, horsey scent of a horse. So close she could hear the short, even rhythm of his breathing and see the muscles tightening in his jaw.

So close she could wonder, just for an instant, if he ever put all that passion into a kiss.

"You're not welcome here."

Her presence had been unwelcome to people far more important to her than some Oklahoma cowboy, no matter how cute he was. That fact gave her the strength to keep her gaze level and her mouth shut.

"Natalie's not going to talk to you, not now, not ever."

She didn't have to talk, Candace thought. All she had to do was listen. If she would simply agree to that, then Candace would say what she needed to say, then leave.

But that was between her and Natalie, and no matter how adamantly he might insist otherwise, it was none of his business.

Then he repeated his words from the day before. "Do us all a favor and get the hell out of here."

She let him turn away, let him take three or four steps, before she softly spoke, drawing him back around to face her. "I'm not interested in doing favors, Josh, and frankly I'm not interested in your advice, your opinions or your threats. I came here for a purpose, and I don't intend to leave until…" Until she succeeded? Or, more likely, until she admitted failure? "Until I'm satisfied with what I've done."

He gave her a long, scathing look, then scooped up J.T. "How much for the ice cream?"

"It's on the house," Martha replied.

With a curt nod he left without looking Candace's way again.

"Well..." Martha gazed at her from the opposite counter. "*You* have some talking to do, my friend. Pull up a stool and tell Auntie Martha all."

Not on her life, Candace thought grimly. She had enough enemies in Hickory Bluff in the Rawlins family. She couldn't afford one more.

# Chapter Three

When it came to precipitation in Oklahoma, it seemed there was no such thing as a balance. Months of drought were often followed by so much rain that the lowlands flooded, the dirt roads turned to mud and a smart cowboy stayed inside.

But no one had ever accused Josh of being smart.

After a day and a half of constant downpours, he'd decided he might as well be antsy someplace else. He'd knocked off work early Friday, cleaned up and packed a bag and was heading for Tulsa. He intended to visit some old friends, maybe catch a movie or two and eat in a restaurant other than Norma Sue's. Hell, he might even call Jerry Lee and see if they still needed a date for the concert for cousin Stacey.

Or maybe not. He had enough frustration right now without adding a beautiful woman desperately seeking a husband and father for her children.

He hadn't told Tate and Natalie anything about running

into Candace Thompson at Norma Sue's...or Frenchy's...or U-Want-It. If one of them had mentioned her, he would have said something, but he hadn't seen any reason to bring it up out of the blue.

Unfortunately, J.T. wasn't as big on discretion as Josh was. He'd wanted to know whether the nice lady really was a stranger. Natalie hadn't been happy that Candace had gotten so close to her son, and Tate had called Josh irresponsible, and things had gone downhill from there.

Josh *was* irresponsible at times—he knew that, and if he ever forgot, there were plenty of people who were more than happy to remind him. But it had pissed him off, coming from perfect Tate, who'd never made a mistake or failed to live up to a responsibility in his life. Even getting his high school girlfriend pregnant hadn't been his fault—the condom had failed.

So perfect Tate was staying home with his perfect wife and son, and Josh was going off to spend a few days someplace where no one expected him to be anything but a screw-up. And when he came back Sunday, it would be as if no harsh words had ever been spoken.

Though it was usually quicker to cut across the back roads and catch the highway about eight miles north of Hickory Bluff, because of the rain, Josh headed for the nearest paved road. It took him into town, where the streetlights were already shining and the only people out were the ones who didn't know better. The Wildcats' game would start in two hours, and they would play to a full stadium in spite of the weather, but he was grateful he didn't have to be there. He'd never missed any of Jordan's or Tate's games, but his obligation was over until J.T. was old enough to play.

Maybe he'd get him to rodeo instead.

With the radio tuned to a country station and the windshield wipers keeping time, he drove through town, then passed Frenchy's. About a half mile past the bar, his headlights glinted off a car on the side of the road—a sleek little silver convertible, with a sleek little blonde crouched beside the right rear tire.

It was a hell of a time for a flat, though he couldn't think of anyone who deserved it more than Ms. Thompson. He didn't take his foot off the gas as he drove by. She didn't need help from him. A deputy would be by sooner or later, or some Good Samaritan on his way to the game—or, hell, he'd seen the cell phone on the seat beside her Tuesday. She could call the garage in town. Ol' Chief Ebersole would be happy to change the tire for her, and he probably wouldn't charge even half his usual rate, what with her being so pretty. She would make out fine.

And telling himself that didn't stop him from swearing as he swung onto the dirt road that led to the campground, turned in a tight circle, then headed back toward town.

Pulling onto the shoulder so his truck was nose to nose with her car, he sat there a moment. With the headlights in her eyes, he doubted she could see who he was, but she didn't look the least bit concerned...until he got out and she recognized him. Then wariness crept into her eyes, her body language, her manner.

Had any woman *ever* looked at him like a deer caught in headlights? None that he could recall, and it pissed him off that she did. Granted, he'd been unfriendly, but it wasn't like he would actually hurt her.

"Need any help?" He tried not to sound as if he'd rather be anywhere else in the world, but he didn't pull it off. He sounded rude, hostile and exactly as if he'd rather be any-place else.

"No, thanks."

Though her clothes were soaked and water dripped from her hair, she was holding an umbrella now to protect the car manual from the rain. He moved close enough to see that she'd looked up how to change a tire. She'd gotten as far as opening the manual and removing the jack from the trunk.

Ignoring her refusal, he went to the trunk, found it open but pushed down to keep the rain out, and removed the lug wrench and the spare. The wrench wasn't good for anything besides acting as a lever on the jack, and the spare was an undersize doughnut—one of the worst ideas the auto industry had ever come up with, in his none-too-humble opinion. He tossed both on the waterlogged ground, then stalked back to his truck to remove his own lug wrench.

"I'd really rather do this myself," Candace said when he returned.

He glared at her in the gloomy dusk. "Why?" If she said one word about him or his behavior, he would get back in his truck and—

"Because I think changing a tire is a good thing to know, and I need to learn."

He stared at her a moment, all too aware of the cold rain dripping from his hair and down his back. Finally he stepped back and offered her the lug wrench.

She tossed the manual into the passenger seat, then folded the umbrella and left it on the roof. Crouching in front of the tire, she tried the various ends of the X-shaped wrench in search of one that fitted.

Her hair was plastered to her skull, and he would bet whatever makeup she'd had on was gone. Her clothes were plastered, too, her pants clinging to her thighs and calves, her cotton shirt hugging curves and revealing the lines of what appeared to be a pink lace bra. Her breasts weren't very big, but he wasn't a breast man himself. There was so much to appreciate about the female body. Why limit himself to one—er, two parts?

She found the right end of the lug wrench, fitted it over a nut and pulled. Really pulled. Put her whole body into it.

Nothing happened.

She tried the next nut, and the next, with the same result.

On the fourth one, she pushed on one side of the wrench and pulled on the other with so much force that when it slipped, she tumbled to the ground.

"Well, hell." She maneuvered back onto her knees, brushed grit from her left arm, then gazed up at him. "If there's a secret to this, now would be a really good time to share it."

He held out his hand, and after a moment she gave him the wrench. "No secret," he said, kneeling and manhandling the nuts loose. "You're just not strong enough."

He didn't miss the face she made at him but ignored it. "You just want to loosen the nuts, but don't remove them yet. If you do, the tire could come off when you jack the car up."

After laying the wrench aside, he moved the jack into place, then reached for her hand. Her fingers were slender and cold, and the contact startled her—he could feel it in how stiff she'd become. It wasn't a good idea—he could feel that in how stiff *he* was becoming.

He moved her hand along the undercarriage of the car. "Feel that? That's where you want this part of the jack to go."

He wasn't sure if she pulled away or he let go, but suddenly they weren't touching anymore and she seemed to concentrate unusually hard on positioning the jack. He moved back, then stood up and backed off a few more steps just to be safe.

Safe from what? he wondered cynically as he watched her. She was six inches shorter than him, slender and delicate, like a fragile little china doll that belonged on someone's shelf. She was beautiful, sure, but that didn't count for much, considering that she'd betrayed Natalie's trust and broken her heart.

That was a lot to forgive, and Rawlinses didn't forgive so easily.

Following his directions, she removed the flat tire, put

on the doughnut, then let the jack down. After she tightened the lug nuts, he tightened them another half turn, then lifted the flat tire into the trunk while she got the jack.

When she closed the trunk lid, she was wearing a self-satisfied grin, as if she'd succeeded at something really important. "I know you wish it had been anyone but me, but thank you."

"Yeah." He picked up his lug wrench and took a few backward steps toward his truck. "Get that fixed first thing in the morning. That doughnut's not safe."

"Okay."

He was halfway to the pickup when she spoke again. "Hey…I'm staying right up the road, at the campground, if you'd…if you'd like to dry off a bit or…or have a warm drink or…" She shrugged as if she'd run out of words…or courage.

The answer was an easy one. *No,* he didn't want to dry off, and *no,* he didn't want to share a drink with her. Easy, easy answer…so why didn't he just say it? Why did he have this feeling that if he opened his mouth, the wrong words would come out?

After a long moment in which he said nothing, she shrugged again. "It's okay. Thanks. I, uh, appreciate…" She grabbed the umbrella from the roof of the car, then slid behind the wheel and started the engine. By the time he climbed into his truck, she'd already backed up a dozen feet and was easing onto the pavement.

Turning around, he headed for Tulsa once again. Then, for reasons he couldn't even begin to understand, when the convertible turned off the highway onto the campground road, so did he.

A quarter of a mile in, the road branched, the right fork going to the old Conway house, the left curving another half mile to the lake and a dozen RV sites. Only one was occupied, by a small motor home bearing Georgia tags. Candace parked beside it, in the pool of light cast by a nearby streetlamp, got out and waited for him in the rain as if it were a warm, sunny afternoon.

Obviously, she wasn't as delicate as she looked, he thought as he followed her to the RV. This was hardly his idea of a good safe place for a woman alone to stay. With no neighbors for more than a half mile and only two street-lights burning, it felt isolated, lonely and spooky. All kinds of things could happen out here, with no one ever the wiser.

She unlocked the door, then stepped inside. When she closed the door behind him, she noticed his duffel bag. "You have some dry clothes?"

He nodded.

"I'll get some towels and you can change out here." She headed toward the back of the motor home, turning on lights on the way. A moment later she was back with two beach towels, then she disappeared again.

Josh stripped down, dried off and dressed in clean clothes from his bag. Leaving his shoes near the door, he used one of the towels to dry his hair while he looked around the place.

It was small, cramped, comfortably cluttered. Books were scattered over the dining table—mostly fiction, women's stuff—and on the built-in sofa across the narrow aisle was a quilt tied with pink ribbons. There were pillows, too, and a small tape player, along with a stack of tapes. He picked up the top one, *Becoming the Best You Possible,* then laid it down again.

He was standing in the aisle, listening to the rain drum on the roof and thinking he'd be better off going home and giving Tulsa a try the next day, when she returned. She didn't make any noise that he recalled hearing. He just knew she was there. And when he turned, sure enough…

She wore plaid flannel pajama bottoms and a tank top. The bra strap that edged out from beneath the fabric was pale green and made him wonder why she bothered. Her hair stood on end, as if she'd just crawled out of a bed where she'd done everything but sleep, and her feet were bare and somehow sexy.

She stopped in front of the compact refrigerator and pulled open the door. "I have bottled water, caffeine-free pop, and I can do hot chocolate."

What kind of woman invited a man over for a drink, then offered him hot chocolate? he wondered, then answered his own question. The kind who didn't have anything else on her mind. And that was good, because he damn sure didn't need to have anything else on his mind, either. Not with this woman.

"Hot chocolate's fine." He sat down on the couch and watched as she fixed the chocolate. Her toenails were painted red, he noticed, and she wore a ring with a silver heart on the middle one. It was silly and something of a turn-on, and he was starting to think he really should have invited Theresa along this weekend.

Grateful that her hands weren't shaking, though she could pass it off as a chill if they were, Candace carried the two mugs to the couch. She handed one to Josh, then sat on the bench across the aisle. After one awkward moment, then another, she grasped the first topic to come to mind, gesturing toward the bag next to his shoes. "Were you going somewhere?"

"Yeah."

"I'm sorry. If you need to call someone—"

"No." After a moment he shrugged. "No one's expecting me. It wasn't a sure thing."

Well, that was the extent of her small talk. It amazed her that a reporter who'd asked a lot of tough questions and written a lot of powerful pieces could find herself so completely at a loss for words. But what did she expect? Except for her friendship with Natalie, she'd had no personal life to speak of. If she were interviewing Josh for a story, she would have more questions than he wanted to answer.

But she wasn't interviewing him. She was quietly admiring him, and maybe even lusting after him, just a little bit, and those weren't easy for her, particularly when she knew what he thought of her.

At least that gave her something to say. "Why did you come back to help me?"

He glanced at her, then away, sipped his chocolate and plucked at a ribbon on her quilt. After a time he shrugged as if his actions were unimportant. "Around here that's what we do."

"So if it hadn't been you, some other properly raised Oklahoma cowboy would have stopped."

He nodded.

"So…why did you come back? You didn't need to, if you knew someone else would help."

His brow drew together in a frown. "Lucinda Rawlins has certain expectations of her sons and grandsons. Leaving a woman stranded alongside the highway isn't one of them…no matter who she is."

She would have been happier if he'd kept those last five words to himself. But none of this was about her happiness—at least, not directly.

Holding in a sigh, she cradled her mug and let the heat seep through her chilled skin. Her fingers had been cold ever since she'd left work…except for those few minutes alongside the road when Josh had taken her hand. She knew it sounded sappy and romancey, but she would swear she'd felt some kind of charge pass between them. For a few moments she'd forgotten that she looked and felt like a drowned rat. For those few moments she'd felt warm and tingly, and she'd wondered how much warmer and tinglier she might feel if he *really* touched her. If he brushed her hair back from her face or slid his arm around her waist and pulled her close….

How appalled would he be if he knew she'd had such thoughts? Enough to drop the chocolate, leave his shoes behind and run screaming into the night.

"Your arm's bleeding."

Though she continued to gaze at him, it took a moment for his words to register. She lifted her left arm from the table and saw blood smeared across the surface, then twisted the arm to one side, then the other, searching for the source. "I must have scraped my elbow when I lost my balance. Excuse me."

With a tight smile she went to the tiny bathroom that separated the kitchen from the bedroom. It was easier to see the cut in the mirror there. It wasn't bad, but it continued to ooze blood. After cleaning it with a damp cloth, she located the largest adhesive bandage she had, squirted a dollop of antibiotic ointment on the gauze pad, then tried to gauge the proper alignment in the mirror.

"Let me." Josh stepped into the cramped space, turned her for a better look, then smoothed the bandage in place. His fingertips were rough when they slid from the bandage to her skin—callused from years of hard work, but gentle, bringing back memories of other times, other hands....

Candace couldn't breathe. Couldn't speak. Couldn't escape. Worse, she didn't *want* to escape. She knew it was wrong. Reckless. He was the last person in the world she should want to get involved with, and there were a hundred reasons why. Natalie was between them. Her life was nothing but uncertainties. She was afraid. Afraid, afraid, ninety-five times afraid.

But his fingers were still touching her, lightly stroking from bandage to skin, and she was amazingly warm and aware, and even if it was reckless, she couldn't recall ever feeling so secure.

A soft sound drifted on the air between them, not really a moan or a whimper so much as a wordless plea. It was heavy with pleasure and need, and she realized when his dark eyes hardened and turned cold that it had come from her.

Embarrassed, she took a step back and felt the commode

against her legs. Forcing a smile that felt every bit as phony as it was, she lowered her arm to her side. "Th-thanks for the help. Our, um, chocolate is getting cold."

Taking a deep breath, she squeezed between him and the door frame and beat a hasty retreat to the living area. She grabbed the quilt from the couch, then slid all the way back on the bench flanking the dining table. With her legs stretched out in front of her, the table on one side and cabinets on the other and the quilt tucked over her, she felt relatively protected.

But from whom? Josh? Or herself?

She half expected him to grab his shoes and clothes and go. The way he looked at them when he passed suggested the thought had crossed his mind. But instead, he settled on the sofa with his hot chocolate. When he spoke, his tone was conversational, his voice steady. "I had a quilt like that when I was five. I was being forced to go to school against my will, so my grandmother made it to cheer me up. It was made from my old worn-out jeans and tied with yarn."

She plucked at one of the ribbons until she recalled the image of his long, tanned fingers doing the same. Resolutely she folded her arms over her chest. "I have no talent for sewing. A friend made this for me."

The friend's name was Betty, and Candace had known her only online. They'd met in a chat room and had built the only real friendship she'd had since Natalie. That was a sad commentary on her life. "It's my security blanket," she added with an awkward shrug.

She half wished he would ask her something personal— what friend? Security from what? Of course, he didn't, so after a time she asked him, "Does your grandmother live in Hickory Bluff?"

His gaze narrowed, and she knew exactly what he was thinking—that she was asking because of Natalie, digging for information on Natalie. Though, really, what possible good would it do her to know where Natalie's husband's grandmother lived? Would it persuade Natalie to meet with her, or make her view Candace with any less disdain? Of course not.

Presumably, he reached the same conclusion, because at last he answered the question. Barely. "No."

It wasn't much encouragement to go on, but hey, she'd once been a damn pushy reporter, and she had the awards to show for it. "I only ask because I find families interesting. You've heard the joke about putting the fun back in dysfunctional?" She waited for his faint nod. "That's my family. We weren't fun, but we damn sure were dysfunctional."

"So that's your excuse? You can't be held responsible for what you did to Natalie because your family was dysfunctional? Your father was a drunk and your mother didn't love you, so you're entitled to behave however you want without suffering the consequences?"

Now it was her turn to simply look at him. Was he guessing? After all, that was about as stereotypical as a rotten family could get.

Or had Natalie repeated all of Candace's confidences to her new family?

"I'm not blaming anyone but myself," she said evenly. She'd been self-absorbed, ambitious and greedy. She'd wanted everything Natalie had had—hell, she'd wanted to *be* Natalie. And for a few years she had more or less succeeded. While her former friend had disappeared with her career in ruins, Candace had moved on and up. *She'd* become the hotshot female reporter making a name for herself. Even Natalie's father, a legend in the field who'd always found his daughter lacking, had accepted and welcomed her. Though he'd never lifted a finger to help Natalie follow in his footsteps, he'd extended a very generous helping hand to Candace, giving her the support and encouragement that should have gone to Natalie instead.

For a while. Until Candace had disappointed the great man by letting illness come between her and her career. In Thaddeus Grant's mind, *nothing* interfered with the job. His wife's death thirty years ago hadn't distracted him, and neither had the young daughter he was supposed to raise in her mother's stead. The career, journalism, the news, was all-important.

Until she'd gotten sick, she'd agreed with him. Now she knew better. The job was nothing if you didn't have a life—friends, family, anyone who cared.

Feeling the faint flutters of depression settling in her chest, she laid the quilt aside and slid to her feet. She pulled a plastic shopping bag from a kitchen drawer, stuffed Josh's wet clothing in it, then held it out. "You should probably go on to wherever you're going." It wasn't the most polite invitation to leave, but it was the best she could come up with, considering her limited experience in dealing with visitors. And she *wanted* him gone, before she got anymore blue.

He got to his feet slowly, trading his mug for his shoes. They were work boots, and looked none the worse for the time they'd spent in the rain. He shoved his feet inside and laced them quickly, shrugged into a dry jacket from the duffel—fleece-lined denim—then picked up the two bags. "Thanks for the chocolate." His tone was civil, nothing more.

"You're welcome. And thanks again for your help." She watched as he opened the door and gazed for a moment at the rain, falling even harder than before. The cold air seeping in made her shiver and hug herself tightly. "For the record—"

He glanced back at her.

"My father was the sweetest, most good-natured drunk I ever knew, and while my mother never wanted a child, she tried to make the best of having one. It's not her fault her best wasn't much."

The look in his eyes shifted, edging into embarrassment or perhaps chagrin. Maybe Natalie hadn't spilled her secrets, Candace thought with a hint of relief. Maybe he'd gone for the stereotype, never dreaming it was true.

Without saying anything, he stepped out into the rain, then closed the door behind him.

Candace stood there a long time, until her chills were gone, until the cold fresh scent of the rain gave way to the RV's usual citrus-and-vanilla potpourri. She rinsed the two mugs, then turned on the tape deck, sending the relaxing sounds of the ocean through the motor home. Grabbing her legal pad and an ink pen, as well as her quilt, she stretched out on the couch, plumped pillows behind her back and breathed deeply of potpourri and the faint hint of Josh.

She settled in for another Friday night alone.

√Learn a useful skill.
√Indulge in a lustful fantasy.

Josh followed the dirt road back to the highway, then sat there, engine idling for a moment. If he turned right, he could still make it to Tulsa in plenty of time to hook up with his buddies and do some much-needed relaxing. If he turned left, he could be home in ten or fifteen minutes and…and what? Spend the night alone watching TV? That was pathetic. Invite Theresa over? Maybe even sweet-talk her into cooking dinner for them, and then…

Something that felt a lot like guilt made him move uncomfortably on the seat. Theresa liked cooking, and she especially liked cooking for him. But, hell, there was just something wrong about calling her when he felt so damn…he-didn't-even-know-what about Candace. Not *interested*. Not *turned on*.

Unsettled. That was as good a word as any. He wasn't used to a beautiful woman being off-limits for any reason other than marriage—and Candace Thompson was definitely beautiful. If not for her history with Natalie, he would have already done things with her that would make a grown man blush. Instead, he wasn't supposed to see her...talk to her...even think about wanting her.

He damn sure wasn't supposed to go home with her or bandage her scrapes or touch her in a way that brought that soft, erotic whimper from her.

Clutching the steering wheel tighter, he turned right onto the highway, toward Tulsa, away from Candace. A night on the town, too much fun, too much to drink—all sounded pretty good at the moment.

And if he did it right, come tomorrow morning, he wouldn't remember a damn thing about tonight.

"Your mother needs a book of stamps from the post office, and your brother wants this stuff." Natalie slid a list bearing Tate's writing across the kitchen table. "And here's the grocery list. And can you drop off Jordan's sports coat at the cleaners? He wants to take it back to school with him this weekend. Let's see, is there anything else?"

It was a sunny, cool Monday morning, and given a choice, Josh would spend it on horseback. Not that his sister-in-law had given him a choice. Bossing him around came as naturally to her as it did to Tate and their mother. It was a good thing for the family that being bossed around came naturally to him.

"I can't think of anything," she said as the phone rang. Being closest, she rose to answer, said hello, then frowned and hung up.

"Nobody there?"

"No," she said flatly. "Oh, can you tell Martha to go ahead with the ice cream cake we talked about? I'll need it Saturday morning."

Couldn't that be done by phone? he wanted to ask. Better yet, couldn't they skip the ice cream cake altogether and order a regular cake at the grocery store bakery? Of course, if he asked, Natalie would want to know why, and then he'd have to tell her that Candace was working at U-Want-It. Somehow that hadn't been made quite clear in their shouting match—er, conversation—last week, and no doubt that would somehow be his fault.

"Anything else?" he asked as he stood up.

"I don't think so."

"Then I'll be back in a couple hours." He folded the lists and slid them into his hip pocket, grabbed his nephew's coat from the back of a chair and picked up his own jacket. He was passing the wall-mounted phone when it rang again, and though Natalie moved as if to answer, he picked it up. "Hello."

There wasn't silence on the line—he could hear voices in the background, the sound of a bell—but whoever had called apparently didn't want to talk. After a few seconds the line went dead. "Nobody again," he said as he hung up, then headed for the door. "See you, Nat."

He'd made the drive into town so many thousands of time that he swore he could do it blindfolded. He didn't have to think about traffic, his speed or where to turn—it was as if his truck was on autopilot—which meant he had all that time to let his mind wander.

He'd gotten back from Tulsa last night to find three more messages from Theresa on his machine. She hadn't sounded nearly as friendly on the last one as the first, so he figured he'd better ask her to dinner some night this week. It didn't have to be anything fancy—she would be happy with burgers at the drive-in and a few turns around the dance floor at Frenchy's.

And he'd make up to her for his inattentiveness by taking her to The White House in Burning Bow over the weekend. That was about as fine as dining got in this part of the state, and it was one of her favorite restaurants. Saturday was J.T.'s third birthday, which meant a family dinner at home, so that was out. Natalie wouldn't mind at all if he brought a date, but he was no fool. He knew better than to invite any woman to a private family celebration unless he intended to marry her, and while Theresa was sweet, he had no such intentions at the moment.

So he would have to convince her to miss the Wildcats' home game Friday night and go then. She felt, as a teacher, she should attend all the extracurricular events, but she could be persuaded otherwise.

Satisfied with his decision, he parked in front of the post office, went inside to pick up his mother's stamps, then returned to the truck. The smart thing would be to climb in and make his stops at the feed store and the grocery store, then call Martha. There was nothing so complicated about "Natalie will take the cake and will need it Saturday morning" that it couldn't be said over the phone as well as in person.

It was a good plan, a *smart* plan. But when he opened the pickup door, he didn't climb in but merely left the stamps on the console. Then he slammed the door and crossed the street.

The annoying sounds of "Boomer Sooner," the University of Oklahoma fight song, made him grimace as he walked through the door. With his nephew playing football up in Stillwater, the Rawlins family were all Oklahoma State Cowboy fans, and they didn't much cotton to Sooner fans.

"Hey, Josh," Martha greeted him. "How're you doing?"

"Better before I heard that poor excuse for a song." He tried hard, damn it, to keep his gaze on her, to not let it wander even a few feet away. If he was lucky Candace wasn't working, and if she was he'd get out without seeing her.

Though he was having a hard time convincing himself that not seeing her could in any way be considered lucky.

"Hey, don't make fun of my Sooners," Martha said, tugging at the red-and-white college sweatshirt under her vest. "As the song goes, 'I'm Sooner born and Sooner bred.'"

"Or, as they say in Stillwater, 'I'd sooner be dead than red.'"

She shook her finger at him in a mock threat, then rested both hands on the counter. "I know you didn't come in here to debate which team is better—the many-times-national-champion Sooners or the fumbling Cowboys. What can I do for you?"

"My brother's bossy redhead sent me. She wants a cake for Saturday."

"We can take care of that for her. Come on over here."

He followed her to the soda fountain, taking advantage of her inattentiveness to do a quick visual sweep of the store. There was no sign of Candace anywhere. That was good.

So why didn't he feel more relieved than let down?

Martha went behind the counter, and he took a seat on one of the stools. Grabbing a binder and an order form, she leaned on the cool marble countertop in front of him. "Okay, she wants the spaceman cake?"

"Sounds about right. She just said the one you'd talked about."

Martha flipped through the binder until she found a photo of the cake. It was shaped like an astronaut drifting in space, with the dark visor of his helmet reflecting yellow stars and one impressive purple-ringed planet.

"You make these yourself?"

She laughed as if he'd told a knee-slapping joke. "Oh, good Lord, no! Any cake I might bake would be likely to break your pearly whites. No, my cousin's niece over in Fort Gibson does them." She filled out the order form while she talked. "It's hard to believe the little stinker's turning three. It seems like just last week that his mama and daddy were getting married.''

Sometimes it seemed to Josh that Tate and Natalie had always been a part of each other's lives. Other times, when they looked at each other a certain way, it was like it was all brand-new. Those looks had a way of making Josh feel lonely…and he wasn't a man who *ever* felt lonely.

"Okay. The cake will be ready anytime after nine o'clock on Saturday." Martha handed him a copy of the order form. "What are you getting him?"

"Getting him?"

"For a gift." At his blank look, she swatted his shoulder. "You're the boy's only uncle. You've got to get him a gift."

"I know that." He just hadn't thought about it. Truthfully, Natalie or his mom usually picked out his gifts for J.T., wrapped them, then traded the gifts for his cash. He'd just assumed they would do so again, though neither of them had mentioned it, and he hadn't thought to ask.

"Why don't you go on back and see if you find anything you like? Our stock is limited but quality."

"Yeah, sure." He slid to the floor and headed deeper into the store, only to humor her. He would look, then tell her he had no clue what to get his nephew and that he'd better leave it to the women in the family, as usual.

Rounding a corner, he came to an abrupt stop. Kneeling there on the floor, right in the middle of the toy section, was Candace. She wore denim overalls with a white T-shirt, and headphones that pushed back her hair like a headband. She was stocking a shelf with books while listening intently to a tape in the small tape deck hooked to the hammer loop on the overalls. As slender and small as she was, with the clothes, headphones and her feathery short hair, she looked about fifteen years old.

And all he could think was that he wished he'd kissed her in her bathroom Friday night.

After a time his brain finally gave a command that his feet obeyed. He covered the distance between them, not stopping until he was right beside her.

She noticed his feet first, then his legs. Her gaze kept climbing until her head was tilted back and her eyes were locked on his face.

Slowly, gracefully, she stood up, then pushed the headphones down to dangle around her neck. Before she pressed Stop on the tape player, he heard flutes, a harp and the sort of quiet, monotonous voice that could put an insomniac to sleep.

She ran her fingers through her hair, then laced her hands together. "I...I got my tire fixed Saturday. Thanks again for...for helping me."

He nodded once.

"I'm going now, Candace," Martha called from the front. "If you need anything, you can get me on the cell phone. Josh, next time you're in, we'll discuss what it'll cost to make me forget to tell Natalie about the bossy-redhead remark. In the meantime, you're in good hands. Make the most of it." With a grin and a wink, she slung a huge purse over her shoulder, waved and walked out the door, setting "Boomer Sooner" playing again.

Josh glanced at Candace again, his gaze going to her hands. Good hands, Martha had said. Small, delicate hands. Her nails were painted a few shades lighter than the rusty color of barbed wire past its prime, and she wore rings on six fingers. They weren't hands accustomed to heavy work—capable of it, maybe, but never forced to prove it. Hands capable of giving a great deal of pleasure.

Abruptly she moved, setting an empty box aside, picking up another and using a utility knife to slice the tape that sealed it. "How was your weekend?"

Even though she was deliberately not looking at him, he shrugged. "I danced with every beautiful woman the city of Tulsa has to offer."

She had nothing to say to that as she lifted a stack of action figures from the fall's most popular kids' show from the box. After fixing a price sticker to each package, she hung it on a metal rod extending from the pegboard display, then reached for another.

He wanted her to say something. He didn't know what, damn it. Just…something. "What did you do this weekend?"

"I meditated. Did some reading."

"What kind of reading?"

Balancing an armful of Kasdor, Evil Warlord, figures, she moved a few feet down the aisle, picked a book from the top shelf and returned to hand it to him. It was the paperback version of one of last year's runaway bestsellers—he knew that because it was emblazoned across the front cover in red type—and was written by a fluffy female self-help guru who fed people a line via an afternoon talk show. He'd rather castrate their own prize bull than watch five minutes of the woman's way-too-perky touchy-feely manure, but his mother liked it.

"I see by the smirk that you're not a fan."

He looked from the book to Candace. "I'm not smirking."

"No, now you're frowning. I wonder what Dr. DeeDee would say about that."

"I don't think I care what a grown woman who calls herself Dr. DeeDee thinks about anything." Sliding past without touching her—too bad—he returned the book to its slot.

"So you're not a believer in the self-improvement movement."

"What's to improve?"

She eyed him up and down with a look so dry it left his throat parched before she returned her attention to stocking the toys. "Well, not all of us are blessed with perfection, so we have to do the best we can with what we've got."

"You want to know the secrets to being a good person? Be nice to everyone. Share your toys. Go to church. Laugh at least once a day. Watch the way a person treats an animal or a child—it'll tell you a lot about him. Respect the law. Respect your elders. Respect yourself."

She almost smiled. "And that's the gospel according to…?"

"My mother. She's never wrong."

"That's quite a compliment."

"She's quite a woman."

"And your father must be quite a man."

He scowled before he could stop himself. "Quite a bastard."

"I'm sorry."

"Why?" As she hung the last warlord on the display, he scooped up half a box of Kashmiri, Warrior Princess, figures and handed one to her. "I'm not. He's never mattered in our lives and he never will."

When she fumbled with the price stickers, then dropped a figure twice before managing to hang it, he realized he'd made her uncomfortable. Too late he remembered the mother who hadn't wanted her and the alcoholic father. Maybe her dysfunctional family was too sensitive a subject for her to appreciate his screw-him-who-gives-a-damn attitude about his father.

But then, she didn't know his father. She must be one of the handful of Americans who hadn't forked over thirty bucks for the bastard's biography a few years earlier.

He handed her the last doll, then glanced around the empty store. "You know how to make a cherry limeade?"

She shook her head.

"Come on and I'll show you."

"I really should—"

"You'll get this done. Come on."

He didn't know why he'd offered, or why he'd even

called her attention to him in the first place. It was something he would think about later.

And as for why, when she remained reluctant, he took her hand and pulled her toward the soda fountain, he wasn't going to think about that at all.

He didn't think he'd like the reason.

## Chapter Four

As Josh circled the counter, Candace climbed onto the middle bar stool, rested her palms on the counter and swiveled from side to side. There was no question he was more familiar with the work area than she. He knew exactly where to find the fresh limes, the maraschino cherries and the cherry syrup, and in what proportions to mix them. She watched him for a moment before asking, "Did you work here when you were a kid?"

"Ranchers don't work as soda jerks."

"But kids aren't ranchers."

"Tate and I were. We had way too much to do at home to ever work elsewhere. Not that I wouldn't have gladly traded baling hay or castrating bulls or fixing fence for whipping up cherry limeades, at least for a while."

"Sounds like hard work."

"Damn hard work, and you'll never get rich at it."

"But you no longer want to trade it for anything else."

"What would I do with an easier job? How would I stay

out of trouble then?'' He set a tall foam cup filled with ice and fizzy pink liquid in front of her, tossed a straw on the counter, then slid a straw into his own cup and took a deep drink.

She did the same. "Umm. Sour."

"As it should be."

"So how did you learn to make a cherry limeade?"

"My girlfriend in the eighth grade worked here after school. So did my girlfriend in the ninth grade." His forehead wrinkled in a frown. "Come to think of it, so did my girlfriend at the beginning of tenth grade, before she got a job at Dairy Delight. And my girlfriend in the winter of tenth grade—"

With a laugh, Candace held up one hand. "Okay, I get the picture. Hickory Bluff had few places for a teenager to work, and you had lots of girlfriends."

He leaned against the counter behind him, the pop machine on one side and a jar of giant dill pickles on the other. "Oh, like you didn't have a lot of boyfriends in school."

Fishing out a cherry, she bit into it and savored its overly sweet flavor before swallowing. "No, not a one."

"Come on…"

"I'm flattered that you think so, but—" she shook her head "—no guys ever looked twice at me in school. I was brainy, shy, short. I had long hair that was as straight and limp as spaghetti, and I wasn't the least bit interested in sports, dances or clubs. I just wanted out."

"Why did you cut it?"

It took her a moment to realize which part of her tale of woe he'd focused in on. To celebrate graduating from college, she'd had her waist-length hair cut so it brushed her shoulders, and she'd worn it that length for the next fifteen years. Now she raised her hand self-consciously to her shoulder, then remembered she had to aim higher if she wanted to touch her hair. It was silky, and she knew from studying it in the mirror that it gleamed beautifully.

But it was *short.*

"I got tired of it," she lied. "It took forever to wash, dry and fix. This—" she gestured with an open hand "—takes about two minutes, and I'm done."

"Yeah, but long hair is sexy."

A shiver of cold and a blast of heat collided in the pit of her stomach. She wanted to tell him that she wasn't the least bit interested in sex or being sexy, but it would be another lie. Though it was on her list of goals in various forms—*Pick up a handsome cowboy/soldier/cop/jock. Share a romantic interlude. Indulge in a toe-curling kiss. Be wicked. Have incredible sex*—she'd known when she'd written them that every one would likely go unfulfilled. She was such a coward.

"You said you just wanted out," he went on. "Out of where?"

"The neighborhood. The projects. The poverty."

"Actually, I meant what city."

Her reflection in the mirror behind the soda fountain showed the pink that tinged her cheeks. "Oh. Atlanta."

"Have you always lived there?"

"I spent a few years in South Carolina and Alabama." She sneaked a peek at him. "That's where I met Natalie."

Her words made a muscle in his jaw twitch, then tighten, but when he spoke, he ignored the remark. "So you grew up poor in the big city and that made you determined to make a better life for yourself, no matter what the cost."

"Sounds like something out of a movie, doesn't it?" Affecting a melodramatic Southern accent, she declared, "'As God is my witness, I shall never go hungry again!'"

"Did you?"

"Go hungry?" She thought of all the paydays when her father hadn't come home at his usual time, when her mother had grown angrier by the hour, when he'd finally staggered in in the wee hours, after having traded a week's wages for too much booze and a few unlucky hands of poker. "No, we didn't go hungry." They may have eaten rice or beans for days on end, but at least they'd eaten.

"We were never hungry or homeless. We just never had enough. Little luxuries like going to the doctor or buying brand-new clothes or having Christmas weren't within our means."

There was a look akin to pity in his eyes, and it made her wish she'd shut up sooner. She didn't want anyone's pity. She'd stopped being that needy little girl years ago. She'd studied hard, gotten scholarships and loans and committed everything in her to erasing all but the memories of the past. She'd sacrificed her personal life for her career. She'd wanted to be not just good, but *the best*.

And then she'd found out that being *the best* meant nothing when you were utterly alone.

After a moment's silence Josh pushed himself away from the counter. It was a simple movement, but he did it so well—lazily, fluidly. Just watching made her want to sigh in feminine appreciation. Instead she gulped a mouthful of her sweet-tart drink and curled every taste bud on her tongue.

"I'd better finish my errands and get back home." Removing a battered wallet from his hip pocket, he pulled out three ones, then dug in his front pocket for a quarter. "The limeades are a buck-fifty each, plus tax. That'll cover it."

"I can pay for my—" Candace broke off when she saw his scowl. With a faint smile, she picked up the money from the counter. "Thank you."

He was halfway to the door before she thought of anything else to say. "Were you looking for something—" *like me?* "—when you came in, or did you just want a limeade?"

"I ordered a cake for—" Abruptly he stopped, and a guilty look crossed his features. He'd been about to say, *for Natalie*—she knew it as sure as the autumn air smelled sweetly of change. Did he not want to give her a chance to talk about Natalie? More likely, he felt guilty for talking to her at all. He knew his sister-in-law hated her, and it stood to reason that his brother felt no more kindly toward her. He probably felt disloyal to his family for not hating her, too.

After a stiff moment he shrugged. "Anyway, Martha sent me back to the toys to look for something for my nephew's birthday."

"You didn't get a chance to really look."

"Nah. I'll let his mom pick out something for him." He curled his fingers over the door handle, pushing the door open far enough to activate the electronic tune, then turned back. "Unless…"

The look he gave her was speculative, measuring. It made butterflies swoop in her stomach and her chest grow too tight to allow a deep breath. Sliding to the floor so her knees wouldn't shake, she cocked one eyebrow and oh, so carelessly asked, "Unless what?"

"I won't have any trouble finding something for him in Tulsa."

So much for butterflies and anticipation. She'd never been to Tulsa before, but she knew it was a fair-size city and the shopping destination of choice for most people in this part of the state. She also knew it was filled with beautiful women susceptible to a handsome cowboy's charm.

And she knew she'd made a huge leap in thinking, from nothing more than his look, that his "unless…" might have anything to do with her.

Crossing to the checkout, she rang up the limeades, deposited his cash, then offered the change. When he shook his head, she dropped the coin in the need-a-penny cup.

"Well?" he prompted.

"Well what?"

"Do you want to go?"

The butterflies started their dance anew but for no reason, she warned herself. He wasn't asking her *out,* like on a date. He was looking for advice on what to buy his nephew, and he had no objection to taking hers. As if she knew anything about little boys and birthdays.

Before she could give an answer—before she'd even figured out for herself what the answer would be—a customer arrived. Josh opened the door for the woman, murmured a greeting, then waited until she'd disappeared down an aisle before repeating his question. "Do you want to go?"

She shouldn't. It wasn't a good idea. Natalie wouldn't like it. She was too susceptible to his charm. She wasn't sure she had the right to a relationship of any sort. Clearly, her answer was no.

And just as clearly, when she opened her mouth, she said, "Yes, I would."

"I'll pick you up at the campground around 5:15." He waited long enough for her to nod, then left.

Candace gazed after him with what felt like a truly goofy smile on her face. There couldn't be anything between them, so it wasn't a date, and she would make sure she remembered it. But shopping—and, presumably, dinner—with a gorgeous guy was so opposite from the ways she'd spent the past 330-plus nights that it couldn't help being fun.

"You're not Martha."

Candace drew her gaze from outside, where Josh had long disappeared, to find the customer standing at the checkout. The woman looked about eighty, wasn't a centimeter over five feet tall, and had flaming orange hair as unruly as any Candace had ever seen.

"No, ma'am," she said with a polite smile. "My name's Candace."

"Hmph. My name's Eunice, only most folks around here call me Miz Harjo."

"It's a pleasure to meet you, Miz Harjo." Candace picked up the old lady's purchases—two boxed sets of handkerchiefs, thin squares of cotton edged with ribbons and lace—and rang them up.

"How long you been in town?" Miz Harjo asked as she handed over a crisp twenty-dollar bill.

"Since last week."

"How long you staying?"

"I don't know." How long constituted a fair-enough effort? When was it acceptable to admit defeat? Should she be counting days, or the number of times Natalie rebuffed her?

"Well, I'm not surprised you already met that Rawlins boy. He fancies himself something of a ladies' man. Of course—" a wicked smile brightened the woman's creased face and competed with her orange hair for attention "—what man wouldn't, when women are always throwing themselves at him?"

Candace had no trouble believing that as she made change. Marriage had never come high on her list of priorities, but she'd worked with enough single women to know how rare it was to find a handsome, intelligent, hardworking eligible man.

The woman continued without encouragement. "He dallies with one, then another, but he don't ever stick around too long. I hear right now he's goin' out with that Martin girl who teaches over at the grade school, but after seein' him just now, I'd lay odds that that's about done with."

"You certainly read a lot into what you just saw." Candace tempered her words with a smile. "Josh came in to order a cake for his sister-in-law, not to see me." Though he'd been there a whole lot longer than the few minutes needed to order the cake. Which meant *nothing*.

"Hmph. I may be old, but I can see what's in front of me." Miz Harjo tucked her change into an old-fashioned coin purse that opened with a squeeze, then patted Candace's hand. "You mark my words—it won't be no time at all before that boy sweeps you right off your feet."

"Now, Miz Harjo, I've never been swept off my feet in my life, and I'm thirty-eight years old. I don't think it's going to happen now."

"Oh, every woman should experience it at least once. Why, I'm eighty-two, and I've been swept off my feet a dozen times or more, and I'm fully expectin' it to happen again. You should give it a try. As long as you remember that it's all in fun, that Rawlins boy can make it well worth your time." Stuffing the shopping bag Candace offered into her large purse, the woman gave her a wink and a lascivious smile, then left the store.

The butterfly dance that had tickled Candace's rib cage turned to warm discomfort and…was that disappointment? What did she have to be disappointed about? Her heart was uninvolved, remember, and intended to stay that way. She was here for herself, and for Natalie. Josh was merely a distraction. A side benefit. Currently involved with a grade school teacher by the last name of Martin. They could be friends, if he was willing, but under the circumstances— his, hers, Natalie's—that was all. And that would be enough.

It had to be.

Josh was half in his truck when Tate came out of the barn. "You headin' home?"

Slowly he eased back out and faced his brother over the hood. "Yeah."

"Coming back for dinner?"

"Uh, no. I'm…going out."

"With Theresa?"

Instead of deliberately lying, Josh shrugged, then changed the subject. "If the day's calm, I thought I'd burn off that timber out in the southeast section tomorrow. And Floyd said he should have that part for the tractor in tomorrow. Oh, and if you talk to Jordan, tell him Shelley wants him to call."

"Do I have to?" Tate asked with a scowl.

Josh grinned. Around the ranch, they called Jordan's old girlfriend "Cheerleader Barbie," because she was so blond, perky, tiny and about as genuine as the doll. She'd cornered Josh at the grocery store that afternoon—literally, between two freezer cases, a center-aisle display and her own shopping cart. She'd moved in too close, laid her hand on his arm and batted her lashes while asking about Jordan. In the process she'd given him a few none-too-subtle reminders that she was no longer a kid, including stating flat-out that she would be turning twenty-one in another month.

She'd made him feel his age and then some. In spite of his run-in with the sheriff a year ago regarding the underage girl he'd met at Frenchy's, he did *not* have a taste for very young women—especially one who knew his nephew intimately.

"Hey, I passed on the message," Josh said. "What you do with it is up to you. I'll see you in the morning."

With a nod Tate started to walk away, then he turned back. Already in the truck, Josh had to roll down the passenger window to hear his question.

"Why don't you invite Theresa to dinner Saturday night?"

"Uh…I don't think so. She's not that kind of girl."

"She's not the kind you invite to dinner?"

"Not with family. Not for a special occasion. If I do that, she'll get the wrong idea. She'll start thinking—"

"That she actually means something to you?"

"Hey, I like Theresa just fine," Josh protested. "But in a short-term, not-too-serious sort of way. I sure can't see myself spending the rest of my life with her."

"Is there any one woman you can see yourself spending the rest of your life with?"

Catching Josh off guard, an image formed in his mind—delicate features, wispy blond hair, blue eyes. It was so completely the wrong answer that his face grew warm.

"Jeez, I'm not even thirty-five. It's not like there's any hurry. Besides, there are so many beautiful women I haven't met yet."

"You're just like J.T. when he picks out a new toy. It's hard for him to choose this one when the one he hasn't seen yet might be even better."

"Unlike you, who fell for the first two females who ever caught your eye."

"And it was the right choice both times. Stephani gave me Jordan, and Natalie's given me everything else I ever wanted."

Which made his brother a damned lucky man. Tate knew it, too, and was thankful every day.

"Yeah, well, why don't you go see Natalie, and I'm gonna get cleaned up and gone." Josh returned his brother's wave, then headed for his house. He showered and shaved in record time, dressed in faded jeans and a clean shirt, then left again. At exactly 5:14 he parked next to the convertible in front of Candace's RV.

He could have offered to pick her up at work—she got off at five—but truth was, he hadn't wanted anyone seeing them leave together. It was one thing for customers to see him talking to her in the store, since it was the only place in town to buy most of the stuff they sold. It would be another thing entirely for them to see her climb into his truck, not to return for several hours.

He'd shut off the engine and was halfway around the truck when she came out, locked the door behind her, then started down the stairs. She wore wheat jeans, along with a blue sweater that fell past her hips. It hid any hint of the curve of her breasts or the narrowness of her waist, and gave no clue that her hips flared nicely underneath its bulk. But *he* knew. For some reason that knowledge made him too warm for the leather jacket he was wearing.

"You didn't have to get out," she remarked as she got nearer.

"I told you, my mother has certain expectations of Tate and me. Staying in the truck instead of going to the door would probably earn me a slap on the back of the head." He opened the passenger door and she climbed in, then he closed it and circled around to slide in behind the wheel.

"That's nice," she said as she fastened her seat belt.

"That my mom would smack me?"

She gave him a chastising smile. "No. That she has expectations. The only thing my parents ever expected of me was to stay out of their way. Sometimes I wonder...."

He wanted to prod her to go on, but when she didn't, he merely backed out and started toward the highway. "Your folks still in Atlanta?"

"I doubt it." Again she smiled, but this time it was a tight little grimace. "It's hard to imagine misplacing your own parents, isn't it? I got a full scholarship to the University of Georgia at Athens, which is about seventy miles away. I didn't have the money or the means to go home very often. The last time I managed...they were gone. I was able to track them to Savannah, then I found my mother again a few years later in Orlando. The last she'd heard, my dad was living in Macon, or maybe it was Mobile or Memphis, and she was getting ready to move to Chicago. She wasn't interested in keeping in touch with me, and I guess he wasn't, either. I have no idea where they've been the past fifteen years."

Odd family. Josh knew, and always had known, within a few miles where his mother was at any hour of the day. As far as that went, he'd also found it fairly easy to keep track of his father, what with the old man being on the nightly news throughout his lifelong career as a senator. Even retired, he still popped up on a regular basis.

"Do you miss them?"

She considered her answer awhile before sighing. "I miss my father some. My mother...we never managed to make a real emotional connection. She was a reasonably nice woman who found herself in the position of having to take care of a child she didn't want. She didn't like it, but it was her duty and she did it, and as soon as she could stop doing it, she did. I guess, more than actually missing my parents, I miss the overall concept of parents. The idea of having two people who love each other and love you, who always have and always will…. It's a powerful thing."

Josh glanced at her before shifting his gaze back to the road ahead. He'd never had the two-loving-parents deal, either, but his mother and her parents—well, at least her mother—had more than made up for the missing father. What would it be like to have no one? To know all your life that neither of them wanted or loved you? To know that they thought so little of you, they could move away, never see you again and not care?

After a few miles passed in silence, he felt her gaze brush across him. "I'm sorry. I'm not used to answering personal questions. Sometimes I don't realize when I've said too much."

"Don't apologize. I asked, you answered."

After another, shorter silence, she asked, "Have you always lived in Oklahoma?"

"Yeah."

"Has your family always been in ranching?"

"Yeah."

She turned as far in the seat as the belt allowed. "Oh, gee, I forgot. The first rule of conducting an interview is to ask questions that can't be answered with a simple yes or no."

"But you're not interviewing me."

"Isn't that more or less what most conversations are? Asking questions to gather information about someone?"

"You sound like—"

For a moment the air in the pickup seemed thicker, heavier. Then Candace softly said, "Natalie. You can say her name. And I'll take that as a compliment, because she taught me a lot.''

''And look how you repaid her.'' He regretted the words the instant they were out, but didn't bother with the futility of wishing them unsaid.

Looking even more fragile than usual, she faced forward again. ''What do you know about it?''

''Enough.'' Enough to put all the blame on her, even if it wasn't exactly fair. But Natalie was family, and when it concerned family, he didn't have to be fair. In fact, that was one of the reasons he hadn't asked for details—because he didn't need them to know that his place was on the family's side. Blind loyalty, *My family, right or wrong* and all that.

''Would you like to hear the details?''

''No.'' Gripping the steering wheel tighter, he took another glance at her. ''The only way this is gonna work is if we keep Natalie out of it. Okay?''

Candace's first impulse was to assure him that she would be fair in her recitation of events. She wouldn't spare herself one bit of the guilt and shame she'd earned. Her second impulse was to ask him to define *this*. Was he talking acquaintanceship? Friendship? More? But she reined in both impulses. He wouldn't believe the first, and she might very well be disappointed by his answer to the second. Better to wonder if he could ever want more from her than to ask and know for sure that he couldn't.

''All right,'' she said at last. ''We won't talk about Natalie. But before that rule takes effect, can I ask one question?''

His only response was a grudging shrug.

''Is she happy?''

A muscle in his jaw flexed, and he looked as if he'd rather talk about anything else than this. But after a beat or two, he stiffly said, ''She could never find a family that loves her more.''

Wearing a faint smile, Candace directed her attention out the side window, where forests interspersed with pasture rolled past. Being part of a family was all Natalie had ever wanted. God knows, her father wasn't the paternal sort and he lacked any real capacity for caring. Worse, even though he'd had no love or affection to give his daughter, he'd deliberately kept her from the extended family who would have adored her.

But now she had the Rawlins family with their fiercely protective nature. She was lucky.

No one had ever wanted to protect Candace. Most people who'd had the misfortune to cross paths with her had thought *they* needed protection, not her. And most of them, she was ashamed to admit, had been right.

If she got nothing more from this quest than the knowledge that Natalie was happy, she would find a way to be satisfied. It wasn't as good as her goal of making amends. It certainly wasn't as good as her closely held, secret goal of salvaging their friendship. But at least she would know she hadn't ruined Natalie's life forever.

"Can I ask you one more question?"

In the ever-dimmer light inside the truck, Josh glanced at her.

"Can I buy you dinner while we're in Tulsa?"

"Nope. But *I'll* buy *you* dinner while we're there. What do you like?"

"Everything. Anything."

"Watch it. There's a sushi bar just down the street from where we're going. You might find yourself facing a plate-ful of octopus or squid."

She thought of the crumpled list inside her bag and an entry on the third page: *Try sushi.* She couldn't resist a smile. "Do you eat octopus?"

"Yeah, but I like eel better. Have you ever had it?" When she shook her head, he grinned. "Want to give it a try?"

"Sure. I know this is going to sound snobbish, but I don't think of a small-town Oklahoma cowboy as the sushi type."

"I do wash off the manure and make it into the city with civilized folk from time to time," he said dryly, then relented. "I used to date a woman who'd grown up in Japan. She introduced me to it."

The trouble with Josh, Dudley had told her last week in the bar, was that he liked women—a lot. He'd had more relationships than any ten people she'd known, while all she'd ever had were liaisons. One-night, two-night or occasionally even two-month stands—all for the sole purpose of satisfying those sexual urges that occasionally grew too strong. She gave nothing but physical pleasure and took nothing but the same, and when they ended, she forgot and was forgotten.

Just once she wanted not to be forgotten.

"What was her name?" she asked as countryside gave way to city.

"Keiko."

"So she wouldn't be the Miss Martin you're seeing now who teaches school."

He gave her a long look, his eyes narrowed, before traffic required his attention again. "What do you know about—Miz Harjo. That crazy old woman's the biggest gossip you ever saw."

"Just because it's gossip doesn't mean it's not true. You *are* seeing someone named Martin, aren't you?"

"Sort of. Sometimes. Yeah." He combed his fingers through his hair before resettling them on the steering wheel. "But it's got nothing to do with my being here with you."

Of course it didn't. Because this wasn't a date, or even a man spending an evening with a woman he found attractive. This was just two people who could carry on a conversation with relative ease going on a shopping expedition for kiddie birthday presents. A man with something to do and a woman with nothing to do but sit home alone.

And lonely.

For a time she focused on highway signs, but after he'd switched from a state road to a toll road to an expressway, she gave up. Why tax her brain? It wasn't likely she would come back to Tulsa on her own, but if she did, she would manage to find her way without help. She'd been doing it on her own for twenty years, and probably always would.

He exited the expressway into a heavily commercialized area, with stores and restaurants as far as she could see in both directions, and bumper-to-bumper traffic thrown in for good measure. "Is this normal traffic for a Monday night in October?" she asked as they waited through a second red light without moving forward even one car length.

"This is nothing compared to the weeks between Thanksgiving and Christmas. It seems most of Tulsa's growth in the past few years has been out this way."

"Did you ever want to live in the city?"

"Nope."

"Never? Not even as a teenager?"

"That was Tate's dream, not mine."

"What stopped him?"

"Jordan. Tate had just turned eighteen when Jordan was born. His mother signed away her rights, left town and never came back, and Tate forgot about leaving the ranch and raised his son instead."

"He must be a quite a man."

"That's Tate, all right. He's as honest, responsible and respectable as the day is long."

"And what are you?"

He flashed a grin her way that could brighten a dark night or warm a frozen heart. She felt the heat seeping deep inside her—felt the tingle from it swirling in her stomach. "I'm the *ir*responsible one. The disreputable one. The one most likely to do anything but succeed."

Though she suspected there was some truth to his statements, she was sure much of it was just talk. For the moment, though, she liked the footloose-and-fancy-free image his self-description conjured, so she didn't argue the point with him.

Their first stop was a brightly lit store filled with a breathtaking array of toys. If she had ever set foot in such a place when she was a kid, she would have thought she'd died and gone to heaven. She would have been thrilled to get just one brand-new toy for Christmas or her birthday.

Instead both days had been just another day in the Thompson home—nothing special, no reason to celebrate. Her first Christmas on her own, she'd bought a tree and ornaments, and had cooked the whole traditional dinner, and discovered that Christmas for one was even more depressing than no Christmas at all.

Ditto on the birthdays. There was no point to celebrating if there wasn't someone to celebrate with. But she had a new birthday coming up before long—the first anniversary of her clean bill of health—and she intended to throw herself a party, regardless of whether she was alone. In fact, *especially* if she was alone.

After Josh had chosen and paid for a couple of space toys, they drove the few blocks to the sushi bar. The L-shaped bar filled one-half of the restaurant, while tables and booths occupied the other half. The hostess showed them to seats side by side at one end of the bar. It was close quarters, Candace thought. Too close. But she immediately amended that to not close enough. Close enough to smell his cologne, but not enough to touch. Enough to see the subtle shadings in his brown eyes, but not enough to feel the steady beat of his heart.

She waited until they'd wiped their hands with the steaming cloths the waitress brought, until he'd ordered miso soup and iced tea, along with a host of exotic foods—*ika, tako, ebi, unagi* and *maguro*—to turn sideways in her seat and face him. "Do I want to ask what those things are?"

"I'll tell you when they come."

"So I'm supposed to be a trusting sort."

"Hey, you saw all the restaurants we passed. You had other choices. Besides, if I was asking you to trust me, I wouldn't tell you what they are until *after* you've eaten them."

Ask me to trust you, she silently urged. She would.

But, to keep herself from accidentally saying so, she asked, "What happened between you and Keiko? Did you break her heart?"

"Nah. It was never really serious."

"You ate raw fish for her, but it wasn't serious?" She shook her head with exaggerated disbelief. "I wonder what you'd do for someone you *were* serious about."

"Something important, I imagine. Like…going against my family."

Candace looked away, her face suddenly hot. Having anything at all to do with her constituted going against his family. Natalie and Tate hated her, so he was supposed to. But that didn't mean he felt anything for her. It certainly didn't mean he might get serious about her.

And it for damn sure didn't mean she would feel anything.

Hearing a rustling beneath her hand, she looked down and focused on the paper sleeve that held a pair of chopsticks. Wonderful. Not only was she going to eat new, strange foods, but she was expected to do it with two thin sticks. She slid them out, broke them apart at the end, then held them experimentally.

"Like this." Josh reached for her hand, repositioned her fingers on the sticks, then showed her how to move just the tips. The first time she tried on her own, she managed to pick up the thin paper wrapper the chopsticks had come in. The second time, she dropped one stick and the third time she dropped both. That earned her another hands-on lesson from Josh that made her grow warm inside and out, and left her hand shaking badly enough that even if she could pick up anything with the chopsticks, she wouldn't be able to hold on to it.

Luckily the waitress brought their soup, and there was no more time for lessons. The dish was…interesting, Candace decided—broth made from fermented beans, with bits of seaweed and tofu floating in it. Then the food came, and, true to his word, Josh identified each item before she ate it. The squid wasn't to her taste, the octopus was chewy but delicately flavored, and the eel was warm, a little crispy and served with a wonderful sauce. She liked the shrimp—hey, it was cooked and peeled; what wasn't to like?—and the tuna was tasty, though the texture reminded her with every bite that it was raw.

The best part, though she kept it to herself, was the little mound of sticky rice that came with each piece of seafood. And the pickled ginger…oh, and she could easily develop a taste for the eel…and she would like to try one of those rolls another customer had ordered, with rice, seaweed, avocado and crabmeat.

And the really best part was that she didn't make too big a mess. She managed the chopsticks *almost* as well as the six-year-old girl seated a few chairs away.

"Okay," Josh said as they were walking out. "That was an introduction. Next time we'll try some of the specialties. They do a tuna platter here that's incredible, and a salmon roll and a squid salad…"

Candace knew he was still talking, but she couldn't get beyond those two words—*next time*. He wanted to come back *with her.* The thought was so intriguing that she hardly noticed the night chill as they crossed the parking lot.

Their next stop was a bookstore a few blocks away. Candace followed Josh to the kids' section, where a clerk directed them to a series of books. Each title began the same—*When I Grow Up, I Want to Be…*—before getting specific. *A Cowboy, a Doctor, a Veterinarian* and *a Teacher* were just a few of the titles. As Josh picked up the astronaut version, she asked, "When J.T. outgrows his astronaut fantasy—"

"If he does."

"—will he follow in his dad's footsteps and be a rancher?"

"I'd say it's about twenty years too early to guess."

"What about your older nephew? What are his plans?"

"Jordan's going to teach high school math and coach football—and, yeah, he plans to continue helping out on the ranch."

"That's nice," she remarked, picking up, then putting down, *I Want to Be a Reporter* without opening it. "How many generations back does ranching go in your family?"

"My grandfather has a small place in southern Oklahoma, and there's Tate and me and someday Jordan."

"What about your father?"

He gave her a sidelong look. "Probably the closest he's ever gotten to a ranch is the filet mignon he chows down at his fancy dinners."

"What kind of fancy dinners? What does he do?"

After pinning her for another moment with that steady gaze, he started down the aisle. When he found the section he was looking for, he handed the astronaut book to her, pulled a thick volume off the shelf and held it out for her to see.

The book had been a major bestseller, the face smiling up from the dust cover familiar to every American with a working television set. Former senator Boyd Chaney of Alabama had been one of the most powerful and influential politicians the country had ever seen for the better part of his life. He'd hobnobbed with presidents, kings and dictators, and it wasn't exaggerating to say that in one way or another he'd affected the lives of every single American—

and didn't intend to let anyone forget it. As a retired senator, he was as much in the news as ever, due in part to the facts that he was wealthy, much-married and oft-divorced and patriarch of a large brood of spoiled, lazy ne'er-do-wells.

She looked from Chaney's face to Josh's. His gaze was on her, his expression impassive. "Boyd Chaney...is your...?"

He flipped the book open, scanning the pages upside down, before offering it for her perusal again. It was the last page in a section of photographs, with only two photos on the page. The first was a high school yearbook photo, fifteen, maybe twenty years old. The face was younger, the hair longer, the shirt more cowboyish, with its pearl snaps and stitched yoke, but there was no denying it was Josh somewhere around seventeen or eighteen years old.

The second photo had been taken at a rodeo. As pictures went, it was a good one. It was a side shot that easily could have been turned into a poster titled *Sexy Rodeo Cowboy*. His jeans were snug, and the chaps that covered most of his legs made them seem even snugger and...er, impressive. His cowboy shirt was a bold stripe, dark blue on white, his gloves were heavy, and his cowboy hat was pulled low, casting most of his face in shadow. Only the stubborn line of his jaw was clearly visible, but that was enough to identify him. Of course, the big number attached to his back would have helped, too.

The caption offered little information: Senator Chaney's illegitimate son, Joshua T. Rawlins, in high school (above) and at a Texas rodeo (below).

Candace studied the pictures, unsure what kind of reaction he expected from her. After a time she looked up. "How'd you do that night?"

If not the right response, it must have been close, because he blinked, then the tension seeped from his jaw and his shoulders. "I ended up in the dirt. No win, no glory." He returned the book to the shelf, then took her hand as if it were perfectly natural. She hated reaching the checkout counter, because it meant he had to let go to pay for his nephew's book.

From the bookstore they headed back to Hickory Bluff. The return trip seemed to take mere minutes, though she knew that was just her mind playing tricks. She didn't want the evening to end. She wanted to ask him a million more questions—wanted to stave off her usual solitude just a while longer.

Long before she was ready, he turned off the highway, then followed the dirt road to her RV, where he parked in his usual spot—not that three times really qualified for a "usual" designation. By the time she'd unfastened her seat belt and opened the door, he'd come around, and he walked to the motor home with her. He stopped a few feet away. "Thanks for going with me."

"I enjoyed it." She unlocked the door and set her purse inside, then turned back. "Would…would you like to come in?"

He shook his head but didn't offer a reason. Did he need to get home, was he tired, was he going to Frenchy's? Or had he had enough of her company for one day?

She moved a few steps closer, then hugged her arms to her chest. He'd shoved his hands inside his jacket pockets, but he looked as chilled as she felt. "Well…" Her breath formed a wispy fog that disappeared almost immediately. "Thanks for dinner. Next time it'll be my treat. And thanks—"

He touched her—brushed his fingers across her hair— and she forgot every coherent word in her head. Then he did it again, only this time it was his mouth touching hers so lightly—a sweet, innocent kiss. Then he drew back. "Good night," he murmured as he spun around and re- turned to his truck.

He started the engine, then waited for her to go inside.

She did so, closing and locking the door before leaning against it. Her chill was gone, her lips were tingling, and those blasted butterflies were back with reinforcements.

It was a sad comment on her love life that a simple kiss could affect her so.

But she didn't feel the least bit sad. Later she would have all kinds of regrets, but tonight, for the next few moments, she was going to pretend she was entitled. That nothing was stopping her from forming a normal, healthy relationship with a man. That Natalie wouldn't stop her from forming that relationship with Josh. That just this once, she could be the lucky one.

Tomorrow was soon enough for facing the truth.

√Eat sushi.
√(With chopsticks.)
√Indulge in a sweet tender kiss.

## Chapter Five

Two minutes before his alarm clock was set to go off, Josh reached over in the predawn darkness and shut it off, then resumed staring at the ceiling. His lousy night's rest made him grateful his job was so physical. Even though he'd been lying there wide awake and gritty-eyed for a couple of hours, he knew from experience that if he stopped moving during the day, he would be liable to fall asleep.

With a grunt of protest, he got out of bed and headed for the bathroom. He'd told Tate he would burn the downed timber if the day was calm, but if the creak of tree limbs rubbing against the roof peak was anything to judge by, they had a pretty good wind blowing. That meant he'd be taking supplemental feed out to the herd instead and helping Tate round up the cattle they'd sold to a man in the next county. Then there'd be two bulls to doctor, the part for the tractor to pick up, the tractor to fix....

He'd really rather just go back to bed.

Within twenty minutes of getting up, he was ready to

walk out the door, but the ring of the telephone stopped him at the threshold. Nobody called this early in the morning besides Tate, who knew he'd be up, and Jordan, who knew he wasn't likely to find him at home any other time of day. Closing the door and tossing his hat on the table next to it, he crossed to the phone in a couple of long strides. He was reaching for it when the answering machine clicked on.

"Hi, Josh, it's Theresa," a sleepy voice said. "I was hoping to catch you before you left for work, but I guess I'm too late. I'm not even going to ask you to give me a call, since you haven't returned my last half dozen calls. You know, I'd heard you were better at brush-offs than this, but it doesn't really matter, does it? The message is the same whether it comes in person with sincere regret or is delivered through silence. Hey, it was fun while it lasted, wasn't it? But we both knew it would end sooner or later. We all know you just don't have what it takes to make a commitment."

There was a soft sigh, a yawn maybe, then rustling. It was the sound of bedcovers against bare skin, he realized.

"Well…like I said, it was fun. Unless you plan on avoiding me forever, I'll see you around."

The line went dead, then the tape stopped. An instant too late—or maybe it was exactly the right time—he grabbed the receiver. "Theresa?"

All he got was a dial tone.

Feeling lower than a snake, he left his house and headed for Tate's. He hadn't meant for Theresa to take his lack of attention for a lack of interest. Hadn't he planned to take her to dinner this weekend? He just hadn't found time to call her about it.

Though he'd found time to help Candace change a tire, then go to her RV for hot chocolate.

And he'd found time to spend the weekend in Tulsa.

And to hang out at the store talking to Candace yesterday. And to go shopping and to dinner with her last night.

In fact, if Theresa were Candace, she wouldn't have had much time at all to feel ignored.

And *that* was the problem: Theresa *wasn't* Candace.

His jaw was clenched so tightly it hurt by the time he reached the main ranch house. He parked near the barn, then crossed frosted grass to the back door, listening to it crunch under his boots. It was cold this morning—high thirties, he estimated, with a wind chill in the twenties. By midafternoon, the temperature was supposed to make it into the high sixties—another perfect fall day if the winds died down.

Natalie's kitchen was warm and full of mouthwatering smells. He hung his coat in the utility room, then hugged his mother, who was frying eggs at the stove, and his sister-in-law, transferring biscuits from a baking sheet to a towel-lined basket. After fixing himself a cup of coffee, he nudged Tate on the shoulder on his way to a chair across the table from him.

His brother wasn't much of a morning person. He glanced up, eyes bleary, and nodded a greeting, then went back to staring at nothing.

"We're a cheerful bunch this morning," Lucinda remarked as she carried a platter of bacon and another of scrambled eggs to the table.

"It's too early to be civil, much less cheerful," Tate muttered.

Natalie added the basket of biscuits and a large dish of gravy to the table, then hugged Tate from behind. "Some of us get cranky when our sleep is disturbed, don't we, darlin'?"

"Depends on what it's disturbed by," Josh teased.

His mother swatted his arm, then waited for everyone to bow their heads. After she said the blessing, she began passing food in opposite directions around the small table.

There was relative silence until everyone had been served and had taken the edge off their morning hunger, then Natalie spoke.

"We missed you at dinner last night, Josh."

He spread a spoonful of his mother's home-canned plum jelly over a biscuit before almost meeting Natalie's gaze. "I went out."

"Big surprise. With Theresa?"

"No."

"Then with whom?"

He faked a scowl at her. "Hey, nosy, you're my sister-in-law. Not my mother and certainly not my social director."

"But I *am* your mother," Lucinda said. "Who were you with? Are you two-timing that little Martin girl?"

"Would I do that?"

Lucinda and Natalie exchanged looks, then answered together, "Yes."

He gave an exasperated shake of his head and changed the subject. "When is Jordan coming home?"

"He'll be here Friday afternoon," Tate replied.

"Is Mike coming, too?"

"Michaela," Natalie corrected him automatically. "Yes, she is."

"Good. Maybe she'll help me with the tractor."

Michaela Scott, known as Mike before Natalie came into their lives, was their neighbor's only kid and Jordan's best friend. She was taller, smarter and a better ranch hand and mechanic than most of the boys around, which meant none of them had ever seemed to realize she was a girl. The last time she'd come home from college, Josh himself had realized it fully for the first time. Mike had been…well, like a nephew to him all her life, but Michaela was nobody's nephew. Somewhere along the way she'd gotten pretty and had acquired breasts, hips and amazing legs. Like Shelley

Hawkins she'd made him feel his age—and a little twisted as well.

With an exasperated shake of her head, Natalie changed the subject back. "Seriously, Josh, are you not seeing Theresa anymore? Because I know several women who have just been waiting for their chance at you."

"Now don't go— Who?" He knew without seeing his mother and Natalie roll their eyes that it was a crass question, but they couldn't blame a guy for being curious, right? Besides, it wasn't as if this thing with Candace was going to go anywhere. Before long she would saddle up her RV and head on back to Atlanta, and he would need someone to take her place.

If that was possible.

Of course it was. There was always the promise of another woman in his future. Hadn't Theresa said it just this morning—everyone knew he couldn't make a commitment. Though that wasn't entirely accurate. He could, and would, once he met the right woman, but it wasn't his fault he hadn't met her yet.

And he *hadn't*. Even if a lot about Candace felt right, his first loyalty was to the family, and they wouldn't accept her. Though last night he'd told her he might defy them for the right woman, he didn't think he'd really meant it. Tate and their mother had always been there for him. They'd sacrificed, loved and forgiven him an awful lot. They'd taught him, supported him and given him a place where he belonged so completely that he wasn't sure he could ever leave.

Could he really turn his back on them for a mere woman?

Abruptly he became aware that three gazes were fixed on him. His face growing warm, he shrugged defensively. "Is it a crime to want to know my options? Who do you know who's been waiting for me?"

Rising from the table, Tate gave him a poke on his way to the coffeepot. "She already told you, little brother, but your mind was elsewhere. You handle doctoring those bulls alone, and I'll tell you who it was.''

Josh looked from his mother to Natalie to Tate, then shook his head. "If those bulls can do that much damage to each other, they could rip me a new one. Besides, all I have to do is wait for word to get around that Theresa and I aren't together, and my phone will start ringing off the hook.''

Though it sounded like boasting, it was true. It was just as true that at the moment he couldn't stir up interest in a single woman in the county…but one. The one who'd kept him awake most of the night. The one he'd been going out of his way to see even when he knew it was the worst idea he'd ever had.

The one he'd kissed last night.

Hell, it was hardly even fair to call it a kiss. He'd been kissing girls since he was thirteen, and using his tongue since he was fourteen. That kiss had been a handshake sort of kiss. There'd been nothing personal about it, nothing intimate.

But it had made the muscles in his gut clench. All the way to his truck he'd been tempted to go back and *really* kiss her. All the way home he'd regretted that he'd resisted the temptation. And all through the night he'd lain awake, wondering what in hell he was doing.

He still didn't know.

Losing his appetite, he laid his fork across an empty plate, then stared at it, more than a little dim-witted. He'd eaten a heaping helping of eggs scrambled with peppers and onions, a half dozen slices of bacon and countless biscuits with gravy or jam, and he couldn't remember taking more than a bite or two.

He had to get a grip on himself.

He carried his dishes to the sink, swallowed the last gulp of his coffee, then said his goodbyes and went to the laundry room. He was halfway to the barn when the kitchen door closed and someone—Tate, he figured—crunched across the ground behind him. He turned to speak, then bit back a grimace when he saw his mother.

Leaning against the corral fence, he waited for her to catch up. When she did, she copied his position—arms on the top fence rail—and gazed at the horses while he gazed at her. Her life hadn't been the easiest a woman could wish for, but it didn't show. At the age of fifty-eight, she was just about as pretty as she'd been forty years ago. Okay, so there were a few lines around her eyes and mouth that weren't present in the old photos, and her blond hair came out of a bottle these days, but it was still easy to see why married men had forgotten their wives, their vows and their good sense around her.

When she realized he was studying her, she swatted his arm, then gestured toward the horses. "Don't they look good?"

"Yeah," he agreed. Truth was, with their winter coats coming in, they looked shabbier than their usual sleek lines, but sturdier, too. Even Petey, J.T.'s pony, looked less the runt for the time being.

"I told Tate to keep you away from those bulls until this distraction passes," Lucinda said at last. "I didn't put all those years into raising you just to lose you now that you've become interesting to talk to."

"Aw, Mom, I've always been interesting," he said with his best grin. Then he shrugged. "I'll be all right. I've just got a few things on my mind this morning."

"A woman?"

He settled for another shrug that, technically, neither admitted nor denied her guess.

"But not Theresa."

"It wasn't serious with her."

"No, Josh, it wasn't serious with *you*. It never is."

Petey wandered leisurely to the fence, then pressed his nose between two boards to sniff first Josh's, then Lucinda's, pockets. He struck out with Josh, but struck gold with Lucinda, who pulled out a small apple and fed it to him.

"You and J.T. need to quit feeding that animal all the time," Josh remarked. "Petey thinks everyone who comes around is supposed to bring him a treat."

"He's just a little greedy," Lucinda said, affectionately rubbing the pony's neck. "So…this woman you don't want to tell us about—do you think it might be serious?"

Josh could swear his mother to secrecy, then confide in her, and she would never repeat a word to anyone. But she would offer her opinion—negative, of course; how could it be otherwise?—and she would be disappointed in him for choosing a stranger over his own brother and sister-in-law, even though it would be a short-term choice. Especially because it would be a short-term choice. At the moment he wasn't up to her disapproval or disappointment.

"There's no woman, Mom," he lied, and guilt stabbed through him. Not because he was lying to his mother— he'd done that plenty of times in the past, though only when it was for her, or his, own good—but because he was denying Candace's existence. It seemed disloyal. Wrong. But how could it be disloyal? They hardly knew each other.

And he wanted to know her a whole lot better.

Though he'd probably go to hell for it, along with all his other sins, he let the lie stand. "Like I said, I've just got a few things on my mind."

Lucinda studied him in the thin light, and for a moment he would have sworn that she *knew* he was lying. But she didn't call him on it. Instead she clasped his hand in both of hers. "If you decide you want to talk about them, you know where to find me."

"Yeah, out with Mr. Scott most of the time," he said with a grin. "When are you gonna let him make an honest woman of you?"

Even the dawn light couldn't hide the blush that turned

her cheeks pink. "You handle your love life, sonny, and I'll handle mine."

"You're a mother and a grandmother. You're not supposed to *have* a love life," he teased.

She fixed a haughty gaze on him. "Some things get better with age, you know."

"No, I didn't, but I'm glad to hear it. So, Lucinda Mae—" he narrowed his gaze and rubbed his jaw the way his grandfather always did "—do I need to pay Mr. Scott a visit and find out what his intentions are?"

She smacked him lightly on the arm. "You're *so* good at changing the subject, young man, but you know what? Unlike you, I'm not easily distracted. Teasing me about Arthur isn't going to make me forget your problems."

He wrapped his arms around her and hugged her tightly. "How could I have any problems? I have a beautiful mother, a family I love, a job that keeps me out of trouble—"

"Mostly."

"—and this land that keeps me happy. What else could I want?"

"What else, indeed?" Lucinda murmured, then quietly added, "Besides a woman and a family of your own."

It was less than an hour until closing time, and Candace was ready to go home. She'd had a busy afternoon at U-Want-It. It was only in the last half hour that things had settled down, and she was pooped. But when the door opened and that blasted fight song started to play, she fixed a smile on her face, swept the dust into the corner and leaned the broom there. "Afternoon," she greeted the newcomer. "Can I help you with anything?"

The woman gave her a look totally lacking in curiosity, which was curious in itself. Candace swore a fair number of customers came in just to see the new clerk and try to ferret out a little information. "You can dish my ice cream, or I can do it myself," the woman said. "Though I warn you, I may not come up for air until I've cleaned out the freezer."

Candace circled behind the soda fountain. She washed her hands, then dried them as the woman slid onto a stool. "Sounds like you've had a tough day."

"I broke up with my boyfriend this morning…or he broke up with me. I don't know. I thought things were going so well. Not that we'd been dating very long, but…" She smiled ruefully. "Oh, well, easy come, easy go, right? And what does it matter if the big three-oh is only two weeks and four days away and I'm not only still single, but now single and without a prospect of ever changing that?"

"Hey, there *is* life beyond thirty for us single folks. I passed that milestone eight years ago, and it was hardly even a blip on my radar screen."

The woman's gaze was equal parts astonishment and interest. "You're thirty-eight and you've never been married? And you don't feel like the oldest old maid to ever live?"

"I didn't until you started talking," Candace teased. "Okay, what'll make you feel better?"

"Well…I don't suppose you could make Ben Affleck walk through that door with eyes only for me."

"Sorry, I'm fresh out of rich, young, handsome actors."

"Then I'll settle for a banana split with chocolate-chunk ice cream and all the usual toppings, heavy on the whipped cream. By the way, I'm Theresa."

"Candace. Nice to meet you." Though she'd never made a banana split in her life, Candace had eaten enough of them to know the steps. The banana practically slipped from her hands while she was cutting it, and it took her a while to dig out three scoops of rock-hard ice cream, but the final product looked almost as good as the picture on the menu.

"What brings you to Hicktown?" Theresa asked as she spooned up a mouthful of whipped cream.

"A motor home."

"And where it will take you when you leave?"

"Atlanta."

"Hmm. I'd love to live in Atlanta…or Tulsa…or, hell, even Muskogee. *Anyplace* has to be better than here."

"So why don't you move?"

Theresa concentrated on eating for a moment or two before shrugging. "I don't know. I'm a coward. I grew up here. My family's here. I'm stuck in a rut that's not quite uncomfortable enough to make me do something."

Candace understood that feeling. Even when the familiar was boring or filled with unhappy memories, it was still familiar, and that counted for a lot. That was part of the reason she'd returned to Atlanta when she'd left Montgomery, and it was a large part of the reason she stayed there.

"Thirty-eight," Theresa said with a shake of her head. "Wow. Thanks for making thirty look not so bad."

Thanks for making thirty-eight sound decrepit, Candace thought as she began cleaning up after herself. Maybe she should find a rocker, give up this job and start living off her old-age pension.

After another silence, Theresa spooned up an overflowing dollop of hot fudge sauce, then stabbed it in midair toward Candace. "Men stink. They come on to you, give you those charming little-boy grins and sweet-talk you right off your feet. Then, when you get used to having them around, they stop coming around. They *really* stink."

Unlike virtually every other woman who'd played the dating game, Candace couldn't chime in. She'd never stayed with a man long enough to get used to having him around, and had never gotten involved enough emotionally to miss him when he was gone. At an age where most single women had nursed at least a heartache or three, she was heart whole.

Was that something to be proud of? Or regret?

"You know, if God wanted us to marry men and spend

the rest of our lives with them, He could have given us a fair chance. He could have at least made them more reasonable, more rational—less manly.'' Theresa smiled. ''He could have made them more like us.''

Candace sneaked a look at the clock. Thirty-four minutes to close, and no other customers to see to. As long as she was standing behind a bar—er, counter—she might as well play the part and lend a sympathetic ear. ''But if they were less manly, would we still want them?''

''Probably not,'' Theresa answered with a sigh. After a few more bites, she asked, ''Don't you *want* to get married?''

The muscles in Candace's stomach tightened. Getting married wasn't on her list of goals—with the exception of *Make amends with Natalie,* they were attainable wishes. But if she was honest—and being unflinchingly honest with herself *was* on the list—deep down inside, *did* she want to get married?

''Why do you ask?'' Okay, so she was still working on the honesty bit.

''Well…'' Theresa licked marshmallow creme from the spoon, then stuck it in the remaining mound of ice cream. ''You're pretty. Smart. Nice. Surely you've been asked.''

*Nice.* It was as benign as a compliment could get—a throwaway comment that really didn't mean much. But it just might be the most flattering thing anyone had ever said about her.

Instead of acknowledging that no, no guy had ever asked her to marry him, she pulled two cups from the dispenser and filled them with ice. ''You want something to drink?''

''Water, please.'' While waiting, Theresa spun the stool around 360 degrees, then rested her chin on her hands. She was a pretty woman, with gorgeous pale skin, hazel eyes and freckles dusted across her nose. And hair…hers was long, thick and gleamed a rich coppery hue under the fluorescent lights. It reminded Candace of Josh's remark that long hair was sexy and made her miss her own longer hair all over again.

Candace set the cup of water in front of Theresa, then took a sip from her diet pop before redirecting her thoughts. "So you want to get married."

"Well, I don't want to be single forever. Besides, my mother's grandbaby craving has kicked into high gear and since I'm an only child... Doesn't your mother nag you?"

"No." Wouldn't it be something if she did? If she could love any children Candace might have, even though she'd never truly loved Candace?

"Lucky you. My mother nags, my grandmother nags. Even my father nags me to get married and pregnant—in that order—just to make them happy."

Candace was trying to think of an appropriate response, other than repeating Theresa's words *lucky you* when "Boomer Sooner" signaled the arrival of another customer. She automatically smiled when she saw it was Josh. Her smile faded, though, when he stopped abruptly and a trapped-in-the-headlights look crossed his face.

Theresa glanced over her shoulder, then slowly swiveled around to face him as the pleasantness faded from her expression. "Josh."

"Uh...Theresa."

Candace glanced from one to the other, then carefully set her pop on the counter so the sudden tremble in her hand wouldn't slosh it over the cup's rim. So Theresa was Miss Martin, the schoolteacher, and Josh was the boyfriend who'd done her wrong. And for some reason *she* felt guilty about it, though she knew that was silly. There was nothing between her and Josh. Not even after that kiss last night.

"What a coincidence," Theresa said, her tone friendly on the surface but clearly angry underneath. "For two weeks you act as if I don't even exist, and the day I finally call it quits, you show up. Why?"

His gaze flickered past her to Candace, then instantly

back again. In addition to the trapped look, now there was also embarrassment, along with more than a hint of shame. For the way he'd treated Theresa? Candace wondered. Or because of *her?* Logic voted for the first. Emotion—hot, taut, churning—suggested the second.

He didn't say hello to her. Didn't catch her eye and nod. Certainly didn't smile. He pretended she was a total stranger and focused entirely on Theresa.

And it hurt.

Without a word Candace walked around the counter and toward the back of the store to give them privacy. There was nothing for her to do back there but dawdle, try not to sneak peeks at them and wait…wonder. Restless and edgy, she went into the storeroom, closed the door and sat down on a tall stool in front of a work counter.

Maybe they were making up out there. Despite her talk about men stinking, Theresa would probably take him back with no more incentive than a charming grin. He should give it to her—the grin, an apology and his best kiss. Really, Candace hoped he would. They looked good together, and they would have good-looking kids, and both their mothers would stop nagging. Obviously, his family had no problem with Theresa and would welcome her into their midst, and they could all live happily ever after on their ranch.

While Candace went back to Atlanta alone.

Though she strained to hear, not a sound reached her. Because of the closed door and the distance between soda fountain and storeroom? Or because they were finished talking and working their way past cuddling to kissing?

"Boomer Sooner" sounded abruptly, giving her a start, but she didn't rise from the stool. If they'd left, she would know soon enough when she went out to lock up. If it was a customer arriving, one of them could damn well yell for her.

When moments passed and no yell came, she sighed, slid

to her feet and headed up front. She was only a few yards from the checkout when she realized she wasn't alone. Though there was no sign of Theresa, Josh was leaning against the cabinet behind the cash register. Her steps slowed, almost stopped, then she resumed her usual pace.

"You didn't get things patched up with Theresa?" she asked as she picked up the broom and started sweeping once again.

"I didn't come here to patch up things with her."

Don't ask, she counseled herself, and yet the words slipped out, anyway. "Then why did you come?"

Pushing away from the cabinet, he reached her in a couple of strides and took the broom. "Damned if I know."

Candace stepped aside and watched him sweep for a moment, then went to the cash register. She didn't make daily deposits, since Martha preferred to do that herself every morning. All she had to do was balance the drawer, then leave the money in the safe in the back room. Then she would flip the Closed sign over, shut off most of the lights and…go home? Maybe get some dinner?

She stole a look at Josh, wondering if he had any suggestions. If she were more like Theresa, she could ask, but what if he hadn't even considered the possibility of spending the evening with her? She would feel like an idiot.

By the time he finished sweeping up, she was on her third count of the ones from the drawer. He set the broom in the corner, then leaned on the counter. "What's taking so long?"

"I'm two dollars short."

"That's easy enough to fix." He pulled his wallet from his hip pocket, withdrew two bills and added them to the pile. "There. Go put it up so we can get out of here."

Candace wavered. She'd rather figure out where the two bucks had gone than let him make it up. That seemed wrong, and was taking the easy way out, which heaven knew, she rarely did. Even when things didn't have to be hard, she sometimes made them so.

"If you're in such a hurry to go, then go," she said politely as she began neatly stacking and clipping the bundles of bills. "You don't have to wait around on my account."

"What are you doing tonight?"

Her stomach dipped the way she imagined it would on a roller coaster, but she tried to play it cool. "I'll probably have a sandwich at home, then watch TV or read."

"Jeez, if that's how you spend your evenings now, what are you going to look forward to when you get old?"

"According to your girlfriend, I've already got one foot in the grave."

"She's not my girlfriend," he said promptly, then asked, "How old are you?"

"Thirty-eight, and sincerely hoping to see forty-eight, fifty-eight and maybe even eighty-eight." She watched him closely for a reaction, but he didn't even blink. "How old are you?"

"Old enough."

"You've got it backwards, Josh. I'm supposed to be the one who's coy about my age, not you. How old are you?"

"Thirty-three." He scowled at her. "I'm not a kid."

As she zipped the money and balance sheet into the bank bag, she laughed. "I'm afraid you are. Thirty-three in man years is, like, twenty-two in woman years."

He gave her a mocking smile as she went to lock up the cash. Five years wasn't such a big difference, she told herself, especially when they were at least in the same decade. It made her feel strange, though. She'd never even gone out with a man her own age, much less one who was a year or two younger. But five years…

…was nothing between acquaintances, or even friends. Age only mattered when it came to the long-term, like marriage, and that likely wasn't in her future.

When she returned with her jacket and purse, he was waiting at the door. He'd already changed the sign from Open to Closed and was gazing outside. He didn't turn but was aware of her approach, anyway. ''Invite me over and I'll slice the tomatoes and onions for the sandwiches.''

She stopped, jacket half-on. She couldn't think of anything else she would rather do than just that, which worried her. But since she couldn't bring herself to turn him down, she offered him an easy way out. ''I don't usually get that fancy with my sandwiches. I'm talking bread, meat and mayonnaise.''

''All right. So invite me over, and I'll stop at the grocery store on the way and pick up the good stuff to go with it.''

''Okay.''

He held the door for her, waited while she locked up, then followed her to her car. His truck was parked next to it. ''I'll see you,'' he said.

She nodded as she climbed into the car, then backed into the street. He followed her for a block before turning into the grocery store parking lot. Listening with half a mind to one of her self-actualization tapes, she let the rest of her brain anticipate the evening ahead. Would he stay long or just have supper, then leave? When he left, would he want to kiss her again—really kiss her? And if he wanted to, would she let him?

She wanted, for her own sake, to believe the answer to that last question was no, but the tautness that spread through her suggested otherwise. All she could do was her best. Be friendly, but not too friendly. Keep things impersonal. Tamp down all the lovely, terrifying romantic images he inspired.

The floodlights were coming on with an annoying buzz when she parked beside the motor home and got out. She started to hurry inside, so she could change clothes, touch up her makeup and straighten the RV. Instead, she took a moment to stand in the barren yard, to breathe deeply of the clean air and listen to the sounds—water lapping against the lakeshore, crickets chirping, the faintest of breezes rustling the browned leaves in the blackjack oaks. It was a quiet evening, peaceful, a good time for relaxing and smelling the proverbial roses—or, she thought as she sniffed again, the distant wood smoke.

Finally she went inside and gave the living space a critical look as she shrugged out of her jacket. Everything was pretty much where it belonged, except for the note paper on the dining table, along with a few old photographs. The top sheet of the stationery was dated that morning, and she'd managed a few lines. *Dear Natalie, I know my showing up here has been something of a shock. Please believe me when I say....* That was as far as she'd gotten, because she'd known too well that Natalie had every reason not to believe a single word she might say.

Crumpling the paper, she tossed it in the trash can under the kitchen sink, then scooped up the photos. They were six or seven years old, taken the night Natalie had won the prestigious Chaffee Award for a three-part series of articles she'd written. Candace had accompanied her to the presentation, an elegant affair that had given them an excuse for evening gowns, updos and impossibly high heels. Natalie's gown was emerald green—perfect with her wildly curling red hair. Candace's gown was even more perfect—beaded and sequined, formfitting, cut-to-here and slit-to-there, steaming-hot, everybody-look-at-me red.

Even on the biggest night of Natalie's career, Candace hadn't been able to resist the urge to outshine her.

A short time later, she'd destroyed her.

The sound of a powerful engine approaching drew her back from the memories. She stuffed the paper and pictures into a drawer, then hurried to the bedroom, pulling off her T-shirt along the way. She had just enough time to tug a sweater over her head, then run her fingers through her hair, before Josh knocked at the door.

For just one moment she studied herself in the mirror. The sweater was a size too big and made her look almost waifish. There had been a time when everything she'd worn had fitted like a second skin. Maybe that time would come again someday, but right now she relied on baggy clothing to give herself confidence.

The knock sounded again, and she headed for the door. A peek out the window showed Josh waiting, a bag of groceries in his arms. She opened the door, then stepped back as he entered.

"That's an awfully big bag for tomatoes and onions," she said, watching as he set it on the counter.

"I didn't limit myself to that. I said the good stuff. That covers a lot." He unpacked the bag, crowding the contents together in the limited space between cooktop and refrigerator. There were several deli bags, along with a container of potato salad, a six-pack of beer, a jar of dill pickle spears, not just one but three bags of chips as well as two tubs of dip and, for dessert, a coconut-pecan cake. He put away everything that needed to be in the refrigerator, then leaned back against the counter and faced her.

She waited for him to speak, but he seemed content to simply look at her. After a moment she folded her arms across her chest. After another she looked away, glanced back, then smiled uneasily. She combed back a strand of hair that didn't need combing, then awkwardly gestured toward the sofa. "Want to sit down, watch a little television, eat now…?"

He glanced at the couch, then the TV, then shook his head. "Let's go for a walk."

Her gaze slid to the nearest blind-covered window. "It'll be dark soon."

"Are you afraid of the dark?"

"Depends on what's out there."

"Trust me—everything out there is harmless. Besides, you'll be with me."

"And are you harmless?"

He raised one brow, but didn't answer. He was harmless, more or less, to her, because of his family and her intention to leave Hickory Bluff soon and never come back.

But it was the *more or less* that worried her.

He was waiting for her answer, and she knew what it would be. After all, wasn't taking a lovely moonlight walk number four on the third page of her to-do list? And wasn't spending as much time as possible with Josh on her thoroughly and unwisely ignored things-*not*-to-do list?

She put on the jacket she'd removed a few minutes earlier, then draped a gray knit scarf over her shoulders. After opening the door, she descended the steps, then glanced back. He hadn't moved. "Are you coming?"

With a faint smile of satisfaction quirking the corners of his mouth, he shoved away from the counter and joined her outside. When she'd finished locking up, he gestured toward the dock. "Let's go that way."

## Chapter Six

There were trails running all through these woods, and Josh figured he knew every one of them. This lake was where their mother had brought him and Tate to picnic and swim when they were kids, where their Sunday school classes had held wiener roasts and where they'd come to party in high school. He'd fished here, too, whenever he'd had a few hours free and absolutely nothing else to do, and had gotten into all other kinds of mischief here.

The trail starting near the dock curved in and out of the trees, sometimes hugging the lake's shore, sometimes disappearing into the shadows. They crunched over dead leaves and heard an occasional rustling off the trail or the plop of a fish breaking the surface of the water. With all the quiet around and between them, it was tempting to start second-guessing himself again, to wonder what the hell he was doing here, with Candace of all people, and that was an argument he didn't want to have. Not tonight.

He glanced at her in the dim light. Her hands were in

her pockets, and the fringed ends of her scarf fluttered in the occasional breeze. Even with the sky growing steadily darker, with the stars nothing more than distant pinpoints and the moon not yet risen, her hair seemed to almost gleam. Long hair was sexy, he'd told her, but he admitted to himself that short hair was, too. Especially when it had that tousled, just-tumbled-out-of-bed look that hers always did. No matter how often she combed her fingers through it, it always looked ruffled.

And sexy.

She glanced at him, aware that he'd been watching her, and he looked away, shoving his own hands into his pockets. "This isn't so bad, is it?" he asked, just to have something to say. Just to give her something to say.

"No. It's really very nice." The evening dusk seemed to intensify the Southern accent that shaped her words. It made him think of every Southern stereotype he'd ever heard of—beautiful women, honorable men, sultry days and steamy nights, grace, pride, gentility. "I can't remember the last time I took a walk for no reason but to walk."

"Then it's been too long."

"Yes, it has." The trail angled down an incline to run along the lake's edge for a while. She gazed across the water, smooth and still one moment, rippling the next, then asked, "Did you learn to swim here?"

"Yep. I also learned how to roast a marshmallow just right, how to drink beer and cheap liquor without throwing up, how to kiss and how to…" Deliberately he trailed off, trusting her to fill in the blank.

With a grin she did. "What was her name?"

"Vickie Harjo."

"Any relation to Miz Eunice?"

"Her granddaughter."

"So that's why she found it necessary to warn me about you yesterday."

"What did she say?"

"Not much. Just that you're something of a ladies' man. That you dally with one woman after another but never stick around long."

"That's not fair," he protested. "When it's the right woman and the right time, I'll stick. But I'd have to be a fool to try to make every woman the right one. I'd wind up divorced as many times as old Chaney."

"Hey, I'm just repeating what I was told," she said with a laugh. "Don't shoot the messenger."

Oh, darlin', he had things much more interesting than shooting in mind for her, he thought, but wisely he kept it to himself.

Where the path crossed one of the dozen or so creeks that fed into the lake, he moved ahead of Candace, stepped easily from a sandstone boulder on one side to another boulder on the other side, then took a steep step up to the trail again. Turning back, he watched her cross the narrow span of water, then offered his hand. She took it as if they'd done it a thousand times before, when he could probably count the number of times they'd touched on…well, on one hand.

When she was on solid footing again, she pulled free and returned her hand to her pocket. He was sorely tempted to claim it again and slide it into *his* pocket, with his fingers securely wrapped around hers. For whatever reason—temporary sanity?—he didn't.

She glanced around, then spotted a chunk of stone taller than both of them bordering the trail. Leaning against it, she snapped her jacket closed against the evening chill before once more pushing her hands into her pockets. "She also warned me that for you, relationships are just for fun. You must have broken Vickie's heart."

"Probably. As much as a sixteen-year-old's heart can be broken."

She watched him, and he looked back. He was pretty sure she wanted to ask him if it was true—if he did go into relationships with no intention of getting serious. It wasn't, but if she couldn't ask, he couldn't tell her.

When several moments had passed without the question, he moved to lean beside her. "What about your first time? Where did you learn…?"

"My sophomore year in college. In my dorm room. The guy redefined the concept of the quickie. He was finished before I realized he'd started. The whole incident was regrettable. Forgettable."

"Around here, if your first time isn't in the back seat of a car or the front seat of a pickup truck, it hardly counts."

She smiled. "You're really very lucky, you know."

"I know," he agreed, then asked, "For what?"

"Growing up the way you did. Having the experiences you had and the memories to look back on. In spite of the fact that your father's a cold-hearted bastard, you've lived a very fortunate life."

Usually mention of his father by anyone but him raised Josh's hackles, but not this time. He wondered what to make of that. "You're the only person who hasn't had anything to say about him once they found out who he was. No questions, no morbid curiosity."

"Don't forget, I'm a journalist by trade. I have more questions than I'll ever have answers to."

"But you didn't ask any of them."

"I didn't think you wanted to talk about him."

"Uh-uh," he said. "That's not the way it works. I've had more experience with journalists than I ever wanted, and if I've learned one thing, it's that what I want doesn't mean squat to any of you."

"Until this year, that would have been true of me, but not anymore. These days I don't write anything but a few journal entries and some lists. I'm out of the newspaper business, maybe for good."

"Why? What happened this year?"

She glanced at him, her gaze steady and unflinching, then

looked away. She had no intention of answering, a fact she made clear when she gestured across the water. ''Is that light at the campground?''

His look was quick, taking in the lights and darks, the shadows of the woods and the single bright light that shone some distance away. ''No. That's over by the Conways' place. We haven't gone far enough around the lake to see the campground.'' He didn't break the smooth flow of his words. ''Did you quit your newspaper job or get fired?''

She didn't speak.

''I ask because Natalie got fired from hers thanks to you, and it would be some sort of justice if you got fired, too.''

He gave her plenty of time to come up with an answer while he listened to the water against the rocks that lined the shore here, to the hoot of an owl and the distant call of a train's whistle. She was going to ignore him, he acknowledged, which was logical. If he'd betrayed a friend and caused as much heartache as Candace had caused Natalie, he wouldn't want to talk about it, either.

''No,'' she said at last, her voice so soft that it was almost lost in the wind and the water. ''I left because I had no choice, but I wasn't fired.''

So she'd been issued an ultimatum—quit or be fired. As far as he was concerned, that was no better than being fired straight-out.

But he'd been wrong about one thing. It didn't feel like justice.

She moved, putting the width of the trail between them, then faced him again. ''I regret what I did to Natalie more than I can say, and I would give anything to make it up to her.''

''Is that why you're here? To make it up to her?'' The snide tone of his voice made her flinch, and drew a wince from him, but he couldn't make it go away. ''You don't really think that's possible, do you?''

For a moment she stared at him, then abruptly she shuddered, as if an icy blast had blown straight through her. "I need to go home," she said flatly and started back the way they'd come.

She'd taken the big step down, crossed the stream and disappeared into the shadows before he started after her. Though she was walking fast, since she was a good six or eight inches shorter than him, her quickest pace had nothing on his. He caught up with her in no time.

"Hey."

She didn't glance at him, didn't slow her steps or give any hint that she knew he was there.

So he forced her to acknowledge him. "*Hey,*" Catching her arm, he pulled her around to face him.

Though it was too dark to see her expression, he could feel the tension that held her stiff, as well as the little shivers vibrating through her. He released her arm to wrap his hands in the ends of her scarf, then used them to draw her closer.

The tension in her doubled, and so did the rate of her breathing. He pulled her closer still, and caught the faint scent of her perfume—kept pulling her until there was nothing between them but clothing, until the rapid puff of her breathing sounded loud in the evening.

After a long, still moment, she smiled and softly, coolly said, "All right. You've got my attention. What do you want?"

Oh, that was easy—way too easy—to answer. *You. This.* He thought he might have said the words out loud, though judging from her unchanging expression, probably not. What he was about to do would leave no room for doubt.

He bent closer, slowly, giving whatever little bit of common sense he possessed a chance to stop him, and then he brushed his mouth against hers. Last night he'd been satisfied with no more than that—no, not satisfied. He'd settled for no more than that, then spent a restless night regretting it. Any regrets he had tonight would be for things he'd done, not what he hadn't done.

He brushed his mouth over hers once more, then coaxed her lips apart, then her teeth. For an instant she stiffened and would have gasped, he thought, if he weren't thrusting his tongue inside her mouth, stroking, tasting.

His tongue touched hers, and she shivered, then hesitantly brought one hand up to grasp his jacket. He wordlessly urged her to touch him with her other hand, guiding it to his chest, inside his jacket. For the space of a heartbeat, or four or five, her hand simply rested there. Then, with another delicate shiver, she slid it over his shirt, past the open collar, to rest along his jaw, and she began kissing him back, sucking his tongue, pressing for more.

Feeling the effects of the kiss as if it were his first, he slid his hands into her hair, holding her steady while he took her harder, more greedily. She shifted against him, drawing a groan from him when her body rubbed tantalizingly against his. Barely able to think, he backed her against the nearest tree, then turned so the rough bark was at his back. With his feet planted wide apart and his knees bent, he slid his hands to her waist, then drew her between his legs, drew her right up snug until his arousal was pressed against her stomach, until he could feel the heat radiating from her, and still he kissed her. Hungry. Demanding. Needy.

He slid his hand under her sweater, up past her waist, across warm silken skin, and he could feel the fabric of her bra just grazing his fingertips when she stiffened. All the passion, all the heat, evaporated into thin air, and she was suddenly as cool as the night around them.

When she ended the kiss, he wanted to protest, to yank her back and kiss her again so long and so well that she couldn't even think of stopping. But Tate had taught him better than that. No meant no, and Candace had said no as surely as if she'd shouted it at the top of her lungs.

Reluctantly he let her go. His arms felt empty, his body hot, his desire not yet accepting that she was calling it quits. She backed away and he straightened, shoved his fists in his jeans pockets so he wouldn't be tempted to reach for her again, then realized the denim was already stretched uncomfortably tight. Instead, he settled his hands at his hips.

Her manner wary, she unsteadily backed away a few feet. A break in the trees allowed thin moonlight and starlight to touch her face. Realizing that, she returned to the shadows again, but not before he saw the stunned, dazed expression she wore. "I, uh...we—" She cleared the hoarseness from her throat, then faked a careless tone that he knew she didn't feel. "We should get back and have dinner."

He'd rather go back and have hot, wild sex with her, though saying so was unnecessary. With his tongue halfway down her throat, his arousal pushing against her belly and his hand under her sweater, no doubt, she'd gotten the idea. And with her hasty retreat, he'd gotten the clear message that she didn't want the same.

Though she *had* kissed him back. And she'd moved willingly into his arms, between his legs. And for a few sweet moments she'd clung to him.

Maybe it was just too soon. Maybe she wasn't wild about the possibility of having sex in the woods on the hard, cold ground. Maybe—

Maybe it was just plain wrong. Not what she wanted. Sure as hell not what he needed.

She was watching him as if she expected a display of anger or worse. His arousal slowly subsiding, he joined her on the trail and tried to sound totally normal when he agreed, "Yeah, I'm kind of hungry."

Normal. Not regretful. Not disappointed.

The return walk passed quickly and in silence. Josh didn't know what to say and suspected Candace felt the same. She confirmed it for him when they reached the RV and she stopped on the steps, keys in hand. The floodlight shone down on an expression that shifted from awkward discomfort to a blank mask. "You...if you've changed your mind about having dinner with me, I understand."

He moved up one step and fixed an even gaze on her. "Why would I change my mind?"

"Because...well..." With one hand, she gestured toward the woods behind him.

He climbed one more step. "I saw a chance to kiss you, I did, and I got turned on by it. That's no reason for me to change my mind about supper. However, if you've changed *your* mind...."

After studying him a moment, she turned, unlocked the door, then went inside, leaving the door open in silent invitation.

Naturally he accepted.

They washed up, then worked side by side in the kitchen, Josh slicing onions and tomatoes while she took care of everything else. When they sat down to eat, the small table was crowded with food, glasses of ice and cans of pop and their plates. Looking for something innocent and unimportant to talk about, he settled on their surroundings.

"Did you rent and learn to drive this thing solely for this trip?"

She cut her sandwich in two, then carefully lifted a section. "No. I live in this 'thing.'"

"All the time?"

She shrugged. "When I inherited it from a friend earlier this year, I found out real quick that I could afford my apartment or this, but not both. So I gave up the apartment, stored everything I didn't need and moved in."

What did a *friend* have to do to earn a bequest of an expensive motor home? he wondered, disliking the fact that he cared, disliking even more that the caring felt a whole lot like jealousy. He wasn't the jealous type—never had been, never would be. A guy had to either be a nut case or care a hell of a lot about a woman to be jealous, but he didn't fit either category. He was irresponsible, even a little disreputable, but not crazy, and while he liked Candace more than he should—and wanted her way more—it was a short-term thing that would end the day she left to return to Georgia.

None of that managed to keep the hostile edge from his voice when he asked, "What friend?"

Her gaze distant, she ate a bite of sandwich, then scooped a chip into the French onion dip. Once it was gone, the bluest smile he'd ever seen curved her lips. "Her name was Betty. She died about six months ago. Cancer."

Now he felt guilty for the twinges of jealousy and the line of thought that had caused them. With the motor home suddenly feeling too warm, he awkwardly apologized. "I'm sorry."

She didn't say anything but nodded her head in acknowledgment.

Once more he tried to shift the conversation in a meaningless direction. "So what is it like to live in a house on wheels?"

"Not bad. If you ever tire of the view, you can just drive off to a prettier place, and no matter where you go, you never have to leave the comforts of home. Cleaning doesn't take long, and people can tell just by driving past your rental space when you're not home. On the other hand, the drive-throughs at most fast-food restaurants are murder, and as far as decent gas mileage…forget it. This baby guzzles gasoline the way a wino guzzles cheap booze."

"You have a car back in Atlanta, don't you?"

"I used to—a sleek little red Camaro. She was fast and sexy and got admiring looks everyplace we went."

Though there might have been a few people out there who'd admired the car, he'd bet most of them had been looking at its driver. Beautiful, blond and sexy—how could a mere car compete?

"But," she went on with a big sigh, "I sold her. When I'm home, one of my neighbors lets me borrow her car in return for my running errands for her."

"Do you work?"

"After the last year, I decided to take some time off. I don't work regularly, but when I do, it's through a temp agency. Something new every week. I enjoy it."

There it was again—another mention of big changes a year ago. What had happened last year to cause her to give up her job, to make her settle for work as a temp rather than using that college degree she'd worked so hard for? He'd asked out by the lake, but she'd refused to answer, and he doubted her inclination had changed in the hour since. He couldn't help wondering, though—couldn't shake the feeling that it was important.

"Have you ever been married?"

Candace shook her head.

"Never?" he asked skeptically.

"No, but thank you for thinking someone might have wanted me."

His response to her lighthearted words was quick and intense, from the heat pumping through his blood to the tension knotting his gut to the arousal making itself felt in his groin. *He* wanted her. Not for marriage—under the circumstances, that would be impossible—but for everything else…oh, yeah.

"What about you?" she asked, pushing her plate away and settling more comfortably on the bench. "Why don't you have a lovely wife and kids at home, like your brother, or a divorce or two behind you, like your friend, Dudley?"

"I'm only getting married once, so I have to be sure to do it right. Besides, what's the rush? I haven't met all the single women in Oklahoma yet—to say nothing of Texas,

Louisiana, Alabama, Georgia…." Damn, why had he added that?

But she acted as if nothing he'd said could possibly connect to her. With a toss of her head—forgetting, he suspected, that there was no long blond hair to whip around—she smiled as she slid to her feet and began putting away the leftovers. "If you're planning on meeting all those women, you've got to get out of Hickory Bluff, cowboy. Judging from the number of people who have come into U-Want-It the last week just to take a gander at the new clerk, I'd bet you don't get five strangers a year around here."

"You're probably right. And you're the first since Natalie to stay more than a day or two."

Grateful that the refrigerator partially blocked his view of her, Candace paused in returning the sandwich meat and cheese to their plastic zippered bags. Was that the first time he'd mentioned her and Natalie in the same breath without the least hint of derision or hostility?

And so what if it was? It meant nothing. She couldn't *let* it mean anything.

Once the food was put away, she dished up slices of the coconut-pecan cake, took two more cans of pop from the refrigerator, then sat down across from him again. "What's wrong with Theresa?" she asked conversationally as they ate.

Glancing up, he raised one brow in silent question.

"She's pretty. She has long hair." She tightened her fingers around her fork to keep from reaching up to touch the barely there locks of her own hair. "She wants to get married and raise a family. She's happy here. She seems perfect for you."

"Appearances can be deceiving, can't they?"

Absolutely. *She* didn't look like a scheming, manipulative heartless bitch, but she was—or, at least, she had been for the better part of her life. Or should that be the *worst* part of her life?

"Okay," she agreed. "So how about that cute little blonde who worked for Martha before me? I think her name is Sara or Sherry or—no, it's Shelley."

Unfortunately, she'd gotten the name just as Josh took a drink. He managed to set the glass down without spilling it, then coughed so hard his eyes watered. She handed him a napkin, then solemnly went on. "Hmm. I take it that's a no. What's wrong with her?"

"Oh, gee, where should I start? She's a spoiled brat. She's thirteen years younger than me. She used to date my nephew. Or, hey, how about the fact that I can't stand her? Are those answers enough to satisfy you?"

Not by a long shot, Candace thought, but of course she kept the answer to herself. After that kiss out by the lake, who knew how he might respond? And the sad fact was that no matter how he responded, *her* response wouldn't change. Not now. Probably not for a long, long time…if ever.

"Tell me about your nephew." She made the request in an even, casual tone, as if she were asking about the weather or life in general. His hesitation didn't escape her notice—reluctant to tell his sister-in-law's wicked bad enemy anything about their family?—but after a moment he shrugged.

"Jordan's twenty, a sophomore at Oklahoma State. He makes the dean's honor roll every semester and has been one of the standouts on the football team since the first game of his freshman year. He looks a lot like Tate—" as did Josh, Candace silently noted "—and he inherited his uncle's charm with the ladies." He flashed her a grin as if offering an example. "He's a good kid. Some days he's more grown-up than the grown-ups, and some days he seems a lot closer to J.T.'s age than mine."

He sounded exactly like the sort of son Natalie deserved.

And what kind of son would Candace deserve? *Rosemary's Baby?* The incorrigible kid from *Problem Child?* Or how about *The Bad Seed?*

Truth was, even if she found a man to have children with, who knew if she could actually conceive? She was past the midpoint of thirty-eight—already beyond the prime child-bearing years. And there were other factors to consider, as well.

Such as the fact that she needed to meet a man to father the children she might or might not be able to have.

Or the fact that conception could be awfully hard when you were afraid to risk more than a kiss.

It wasn't even eight-thirty when Josh stretched, then stood up. "I need to head home. I didn't sleep well last night, so I think I'll turn in early tonight."

Automatically she wondered why he hadn't slept well, and if it had had anything to do with her, and if he was really going home. But his brown eyes really did look tired, and even as she watched, he hid a huge yawn behind one hand. "Let me pack up your groceries—"

"Keep them. Next time I want a sandwich, I'll know where to go." He pulled on his jacket, then caught her hand and drew her to the door. Apprehension danced through her veins—or was it really anticipation?—and if she'd taken off her shoes, her toes would be curling under. When he slid his free hand into her hair, something warm and comforting seeped through her—relief, maybe. Security. Pleasure.

On the sensuality scale, this kiss fell between the other two. It wasn't nearly as chaste as the first, not with his tongue in her mouth, but not nearly as hot as the last. But it was sweet and carried its own heat, and could easily turn into something even more intimate than the kiss by the lake if they gave it the chance.

"Good night," he murmured when he straightened away from her. "I'll see you."

When he opened the door, the night air rushed in, sending a chilly shiver through her that did nothing to temper the need warming her from the inside out. "Yeah," she replied softly. "See you."

She stood there long after he'd closed the door, then driven away. Finally she twisted the lock, then, hugging herself, turned to look around the RV. There was nothing for her to do but carry their empty glasses and dessert plates to the sink. It would take a few minutes to load the dishwasher, or a few more to wash them all by hand, and then the rest of the evening would stretch out ahead of her with nothing to do but make a check or two on her list.

If she were married, like Natalie, she'd be spending the evening with her family, maybe bathing the kids and reading them bedtime stories before settling in to spend the next hour or two alone with her husband. Maybe they would curl up on the sofa together and watch TV, or tell each other about their day, or go to bed early and make love while the kids slept down the hall.

If she were married, like Natalie, she wouldn't be alone or lonely, and people would count on her and miss her and love her and her life would have meaning in ways she knew nothing about.

But what good did it do her to envy her old friend? Maybe someday, with a lot of work, a lot of making amends, she could at least be more like Natalie, and maybe then she could have the rewards.

Or maybe not.

With a shiver raising goose bumps on her arms, she dug out her legal pad from her purse and sat down at the table.

√Go for a moonlit walk.
√Indulge in a toe-curling kiss.

She gazed sightlessly at the goals listed before her for a long time before flipping to the last page. Two-thirds of the way down she gripped the ink pen tightly, hesitated, then added two more lines.

Tell Josh the truth.
Before it's too late.

Friday dawned cold and dreary, with the temperature steadily dropping throughout the afternoon. It was the sort of day that convinced a person winter was on its way, Candace thought…not that she'd ever lived anyplace where winter was so terribly different from the seasons that preceded and followed it.

She wore a long-sleeved Georgia Bulldogs T-shirt underneath her employee vest and a gray fleece jacket over them both, but the store was still a bit cold, to say nothing of boring. She hadn't had half a dozen customers all afternoon. Presumably the weather was keeping everybody home, though she had no doubt that would change this evening. The Wildcats had another home football game, and the cold this week wasn't likely to keep the fans away any more than the rain had last week.

She wondered if Josh would be there.

She hadn't seen him since Tuesday evening—less than seventy-two hours. No big deal, right? After all, they weren't dating or involved. They were just friendly acquaintances. And even as she thought that, she snorted derisively. Granted, she was more accustomed to people who disliked, disdained or flat-out hated her than with either friends or acquaintances, but she was pretty sure neither friends nor acquaintances kissed the way he'd kissed her that night.

Which brought up an interesting question. What, exactly, were they?

She found no ready answer while she dusted the checkout counter for the third time, or while she fixed herself a cup of hot chocolate with marshmallows or cleaned the nearly spotless soda fountain. Maybe she would ask Josh and accept whatever answer he gave.

Provided she ever saw him again.

She was sitting on a stool near the cash register and drinking her chocolate when a rap on the plate glass caught her attention. Looking over the painted head of the snarling wildcat, she saw a hooded figure waving one red-gloved hand. Wearing a warm grin, Theresa Martin pushed the hood back, waved again, then walked on.

Thank God. Though Candace had liked what little she'd learned of Theresa, the last thing she wanted was another long chat with her. Not when Theresa had dived into a banana split because of the breakup with Josh, while he'd spent the evening with Candace, talking, laughing, kissing her till her toes curled. Under the circumstances, even the slightest friendly gesture, like that wave, would make Candace feel guilty.

The shrill ring of the phone echoing around the store practically startled her off her seat. Sliding to the floor, she picked up the wall-mounted phone and offered a cheery greeting. "U-Want-It. Can I help you?"

There was a moment's silence, then... "Is Martha there?"

Her fingers tightened around the receiver, and the butterflies that normally resided in her stomach swooped down to her toes. It was Natalie. She knew the voice too well to ever forget it.

Her throat closed up, and she coughed to clear it, giving her voice a ragged edge. "Uh, no, she's over at her mom's. She'll be in first thing in the morning, though. Would you like to leave her a message?"

"I just wondered... Who is this?"

Candace wanted desperately to hang up without answering, and just as desperately to give her name, then let loose a torrent of apologetic words so Natalie would hear at least some of them before she managed to hang up. She settled for the middle of the road. "I-I'm Martha's part-time clerk."

"Obvious—" After an abrupt pause, Natalie spoke again. This time her voice was flat and heavy with animosity. "It's you. Candace."

Candace held her breath, waiting for the slam of the phone. No, that would have been her own style in the past. No matter how angry she was, Natalie's style was to hang up without a sound. She didn't slam doors, either, or throw things when she was mad. She was better mannered than Candace was. Better raised. Just plain better.

Straining to hear, Candace picked up the distant sounds of a child's voice. "Natalie?"

"Why aren't you back in Georgia where you belong?" This time the voice was so cold and stiff that Candace never would have recognized it.

"I came here to talk to you, and I can't leave until..." Until she did. Or until she gave up.

"Are you the one who keeps calling and hanging up?"

Heat flooded Candace's face. "You hung up on me a time or two," she unwisely pointed out.

"It's my phone. I'm allowed to do that."

The door opened and the damned fight song started to play. Candace forced a smile onto her face and nodded politely at the man who'd come in. He didn't respond but headed toward the back of the store. When she judged he was out of earshot, she said, "I just need to talk to you. If I could come out to the ranch tomorrow morning—"

"No. I don't want you here."

It was irrational, but that hurt. Candace tried to hide it, though. "Then maybe you could meet me in town...."

"Why? I've already told you—you couldn't possibly say anything of interest to me. So just get the hell out of Oklahoma and leave me alone."

"Natalie, please—"

She'd been wrong earlier. The phone was slammed down so hard it made her ears ring.

Still holding the receiver, Candace closed her eyes and rubbed away the tension gathered in her forehead with her free hand. It wasn't until the phone started emitting loud, harsh beeps signaling the receiver was off the hook that she realized her customer had returned and was watching her from the opposite side of the cash register.

With a weak smile she hung up, shrugged in place of an explanation and picked up the items he was purchasing— shaving cream and a five-pack of razor cartridges. She sneaked a glance and saw that they were indeed needed. He looked as if he hadn't shaved in a week, though she had to admit, the heavy stubble added a certain appeal to the dark-dangerous-desperado air about him.

He was also buying a box of laundry detergent, a bottle of bleach, a box of fabric softener sheets and a twelve-pack of condoms.

Inside she cursed the blush warming her cheeks. It wasn't as if she hadn't dealt with condoms before—she was thirty-eight and single. Enough said. And it was no surprise to her that the store carried them—she dusted them every time she cleaned. She just hadn't actually seen anyone buy any. She'd figured Hickory Bluff being the small town it was, the men and especially the boys bought their protection elsewhere. After all, Martha was no slouch in the gossip department.

But this man didn't look as if he gave a damn what anyone said. His eyes were so dark a brown they were nearly black, and bloodshot to boot. His face was lean, the lines and angles hard, and his mouth was compressed narrow and flat, a stranger to smiles or soft kisses—but probably intimately familiar with rough, raw passion.

"You're new in town." His voice sounded rough and raw, too, and greatly underused.

"I'm Candace." She rang up the condoms as if they

were no more interesting than a box of bandages, then read out the total.

"Cal."

It took her a moment to realize that the grumbled sound was his name. When she did, she smiled. "Nice to meet you, Cal."

His dark gaze drifted to her left hand, then back to her face. "You married, Candace?"

"No." But he was. The band on his left hand gleamed enticingly against the bronze of his skin.

"You in the mood for a private party?"

"What? Just you, me, a bottle of booze and these?" She tossed the box of condoms in the air, then bounced them from her palm into the bag.

"Actually, I was thinking two or three bottles of booze...unless you don't drink."

"I don't. At least, not so anyone would notice. Can I give you a bit of advice, Cal?" When he nodded, she tapped one fingernail on his wedding band. "Why don't you find the woman who gave you that and patch things up?"

"Some things can't be patched."

Natalie was slowly driving that message home to Candace. But the only thing at stake there was a friendship—the best friendship she'd ever known, but still just that. Cal was risking a whole lot more, and if his demeanor was anything to judge by, it was killing him.

She was seized by the desire to wrap her arms around him, pat him on the back and tell him it would be all right. Insane. He was a foot taller and a whole world tougher than she was, and the last thing he wanted from a woman, she suspected, was motherly comforting. Even if it was the first thing he needed.

After counting out his change, she slid the shopping bag across the counter to him. "Listen, Cal, I close up at five. How about we forget the booze and the condoms, and go down to Norma Sue's and have a bowl of her wonderful chili to chase away the cold?''

''I have a better idea. How about we forget the chili and go to your place and chase away the cold in bed?''

He was a handsome man, she thought, and in another time and place, she would have accepted his invitation without a second thought. She would have used him, just as he would have used her, and in the morning...well, things would have looked different, if not brighter.

But it wasn't merely a matter of time and place. She was a different person now. Less casual about sex. Less willing to take risks. Less confident about herself as a woman.

''Sorry. I don't have sex with strangers...and I don't think you do, either. Besides, I'm willing to bet you could use the food much more than the sex.''

For a long moment he watched her, then the corner of his mouth slowly quirked into what might have been a smile. ''Sorry, darlin'. You'd lose. But what the hell. I can always get laid later. Let's go to Norma Sue's.''

Candace checked the time—a few minutes before five. By the time she balanced the cash register and locked up, closing time would have come and gone.

She worked quickly, and within ten minutes was standing outside, locking the door while Cal left his purchases in a pickup truck that had seen better days. When he rejoined her on the sidewalk, they headed for the diner down the block.

''You know Natalie Rawlins?'' he asked after a time.

Her last words before she'd realized he was standing at the cash register had been ''Natalie, please.'' Hickory Bluff being such a small town, it was no surprise that he knew Natalie, too.

''I used to. A long time ago,'' she replied, shivering as wind gusted down the street. A glance at Cal showed that he didn't seem to notice the cold. Was that because he had more liquor than blood pumping through his veins, as his bloodshot eyes suggested? Or was he numb from the inside out, thanks to his absent wife?

"You know Tate and Josh, too?"

Her lips pursed, she looked inside the store windows they were passing, uncertain how to answer. Obviously Josh didn't want anyone to know that they were anything more than acquaintances, but she hated to lie about it. Still, she didn't even know Cal. What did it matter if she misled him?

"Josh has come into the store a time or two. I've never met Tate."

"They're good people. Good friends." He opened the door to Norma Sue's, then added, "Though Natalie doesn't appear to want to be friends with you."

No more than your wife wants to be married to you, she thought uncharitably, then immediately felt guilty. Obviously, she knew nothing of the problems in his marriage, but it was clear he was suffering over them.

She went inside, then headed for the booth at the rear, where Josh had found her the day she'd gone to the ranch. She'd been in several times since then, and no one besides her ever seemed to sit there, not even when the place was crowded.

As it was this evening. Green and gold streamers encircled the front windows, and matching pennants hung on the walls. Virtually every customer, as well as the staff, was dressed in the Wildcats' colors. Most of the men wore Wildcats caps, and two tables near the front were occupied by the school's cheerleaders.

Man, were they going to get cold tonight, she thought.

"You didn't answer about Natalie," Cal pointed out once they'd ordered two large bowls of chili.

"You didn't ask a question. You made an observation."

"So why doesn't Nat want to be friends with you?"

Candace idly watched as a couple of cheerleaders approached. In the uniforms that showed their midriffs, and way more thigh than she would have thought acceptable in high school, they looked athletic, amazingly young and vivacious. Veering to the left, they disappeared through a door marked Rest Rooms, and she finally turned her attention back to him. "I'll make you a deal. You tell me all the sordid details of your marriage gone wrong, and I'll share my history with Natalie with you."

The look that crossed his face was part anger, part anguish. Then his expression went blank. "Forget I said anything." But in the next breath he brought it up again. "Is that why you're here?"

After a moment she nodded. "I had this crazy idea that I could make things right with her. Only, as you so kindly pointed out, she's not interested."

That odd quirk of a smile returned. "So forget about her. Spend the night with me. I'll show you a good time."

"No, thank you."

"You're hurtin' my feelings."

"Oh, yeah, I can see that," she teased as the waitress brought their meal.

"Then the least you can do is go to the game with me."

"I thought you were planning a private party."

He shrugged negligently. "There's time. Besides, my first choice turned me down. I'll have to find someone else, and in Hickory Bluff the only place to find someone on a Friday night with a home game is at the game."

Candace glanced again at the pretty young cheerleaders, the parents, the grandparents and supportive citizens, all decked out and buzzing with excitement. Sure, it was cold, but she could go home and change into warmer clothing. Hell, she even had a gold sweater she could wear. And what would she do if she turned him down? Watch TV? Read? Listen to her tapes? Whatever she did, she would do it alone.

Sit home alone or experience all the fun of a small-town football game. Talk about a no-brainer.

She smiled. "All right, Cal. You talked me into it. I'd be happy to go to the game with you."

*Chapter Seven*

The football stadium, located near the high school, was lit up like a spaceship when Josh finally found a space to park. There were a few dozen other places he'd rather be on a cold night like this, but his mom had assumed they were all attending the game, since Jordan and Michaela were home, and so here he was. He wore a long-sleeved thermal shirt under his chambray shirt and had brought a shearling-lined jacket and gloves, as well as the wool blanket Lucinda had thrust into his arms, but he was still going to freeze his butt off.

The things he did for family, he thought with a grimace as he got out of the truck.

"Dad's parked over there," Jordan said, gesturing as he slammed his door. "Man, it's cold."

"Big college football players aren't supposed to notice that."

"Yeah, well, this one does. I'm gonna have to find some-one to help keep me warm."

That had been Josh's preferred method of surviving frigid games all those years when he'd come to watch first Tate and then Jordan play. A pretty woman, a blanket, a spot on the bleachers fairly distant from his family…not a bad way at all to spend a few hours. Too bad that lately only one pretty woman seemed able to hold his attention, and the odds of her being at the game were somewhere between slim and none.

The rest of the family, plus Michaela and Arthur Scott, were waiting for them by Lucinda's car. J.T., bundled up like a pint-size snowman, climbed on Josh's shoulders for the two-block walk to the stadium gates, and Lucinda took his arm.

"Arthur pointed out on the drive into town that you might have had other plans tonight," she commented.

"Nope. Not at all." Except thinking about Candace. Maybe going to see her. Definitely kissing her again—and, if he was lucky, a whole lot more.

He'd wanted to see her Wednesday night, enough that he'd made himself stay away. If he'd known his entire Thursday night was going to be spent dealing with a couple of sick calves, he wouldn't have been so determined to stay home Wednesday.

"I hear you and that Martin girl broke up."

He glanced at his mother, trying to identify the emotion in her voice. Resignation? Disappointment? Censure? He couldn't tell, and her serene expression offered no hints.

"The trouble with you, Josh, is women come too easily to you. All you have to do is smile, and they swoon at your feet. You've never had to really work for a relationship."

"Hey, I like women, and they like me. That's not a crime. Besides, what's so great about having to work? If it's meant to be, it'll be."

"Not necessarily. I thought my relationship with Tate's father was meant to be, as well as the one with your father. I was wrong."

She said the last words so calmly, acceptingly, when Josh knew it hadn't been that easy for her. Tate's father, a rodeo cowboy who'd forgotten to mention the fact that he was married until Tate was on the way, and Josh's old man had both left her brokenhearted and pregnant. It had taken her more than thirty years to even consider getting involved with another man, and she was still taking it very slowly.

Too bad, because Arthur Scott was nothing like the two bastards she'd first hooked up with. Arthur was as honest and decent as the day was long, and he made Lucinda happy enough that she didn't often interfere in Josh's love life. Nothing would make her butt out entirely, but Arthur came close.

Josh removed one hand from J.T.'s knee and slid his arm around his mother's shoulders. "Don't be so impatient for me to tie myself down like Tate," he teased. "What if I decide to follow your example and wait until I'm fifty—ah, older to settle down?"

"I already had you two boys. Waiting was an option for me. It's not for you. I want more grandbabies." She gazed up at him as they joined the end of the line outside the ticket office. "I want you to be happy and whole."

"I am happy, and last time I looked, I was whole, too."

"You know what I mean. Like Tate and Natalie. Like Calvin and Darcy."

"Be careful what you wish for. Cal came home from a rodeo, and Darcy was gone. Took everything she owned and left a note saying her lawyer would be in touch." Josh had heard the news just that afternoon when Cal's older brother, Caleb, had come over to look at the cantankerous bull Josh and Tate had decided to sell. The ornery creature liked to tangle with everything from other bulls to barbed-wire fences to unsuspecting cowboys. Wednesday the un-suspecting cowboy had been Tate, and though he'd proven he was faster than the bull, he'd insisted he was fed-up and wanted to be rid of him.

According to Caleb, Cal was kind of an ornery creature these days, too—drinking too much, brooding too much and as prickly as a cactus. Sort of the way Tate had been during his one rough spot with Natalie. Someday he'd probably change his mind, but at the moment Josh would rather do without those rough patches.

They bought their tickets from Mrs. LaFortune, the coach's mother-in-law, then walked through the stone archway that separated the two locker rooms. The concession stands and bathrooms, sharing a building at each end of the field, were also built of stone and had withstood everything from rowdy championship celebrations to a tornado or two. Lucinda had spent her share of time working concessions during Tate's high school career, and in another dozen years or so, Natalie would do the same. Would there be another Rawlins wife and mother to follow?

Being a Hickory Bluff native and a teacher, Theresa would be a natural for such duty, as would most of the women he'd dated. He wondered, though, how Candace would fare. City girl or not, she would probably do just fine.

As long as Natalie and the rest of the family wasn't around.

The southside bleachers were home territory for Wildcat fans. Holding J.T. firmly by the knees, Josh brought up the rear of their group as they negotiated the crowded ramp. At the top he got cut off by a trio of budding juvenile delinquents racing for the ramp, and waited impatiently for the chance to catch up with the family.

When it came, he didn't take it. Instead, he found himself face-to-face with Candace. Standing behind her, with his hand resting on her shoulder, was Cal Bridger. Josh looked from her to him, then back again. "Well…isn't this interesting."

Candace wore a long gold sweater over black pants, with gloves and a quilted green vest. Her cheeks were pink from the cold, and wisps of her hair curled over the edges of a knitted green cap.

Cal wore an in-search-of-trouble look, and Josh was suddenly more than willing to give it to him.

"Hey, Josh," she said quietly. Her gaze shifted above him to J.T., then even higher, to the bleachers where Natalie was settling in.

He ignored her greeting. "What are you doing, Cal?"

"Same thing you and me always did at football games. Looking for a quiet place to cuddle up with a pretty woman."

Someone behind him complained and Josh moved to his left, leaving a narrow lane for traffic to pass and placing himself that much closer to Candace. "Do you know he's married?"

Before she could answer, Cal slid his arm around her from behind and tugged her back. "That doesn't mean anything to Darcy, so why should it matter to Candace and me?"

"Uncle Josh, c'mon, let's go sit down," J.T. called, bouncing on Josh's shoulders. "Ever'body went on without us. *C'mon.*"

Candace pushed Cal's arm away and down to her side, keeping him from hugging her again with her grip on his hand. "We're just going to watch the game, Josh, with everyone else in town. When it's over, I'm going home and Cal's going to party."

"Unless I change her mind."

The smile Cal gave her was familiar to Josh. It was the same one *he'd* given countless women over the years when he was at his charming best. Just how susceptible was Candace? he wondered darkly, trying to judge her expression. He couldn't guess.

"Can I talk to you a moment?" he asked.

Candace shrugged.

Turning, Josh scanned the bleachers until he spotted his

family, then took a quick look at the people coming up the ramp. "Hey, Pastor," he said when he saw the minister of the church the other Rawlinses attended more regularly than he. "Could you do me a favor and deliver J.T. to his mom and dad? They're right up there."

"Sure thing, Josh."

Josh swung J.T. down from his shoulders and handed him over, then caught Candace's hand and started down the ramp. At the bottom, he turned toward the locker rooms, then ducked into an alcove where outcroppings of rock shielded them from anyone not directly in front of them. He maneuvered her against the wall, then stood in front of her. As slender and short as she was, no doubt he blocked her entirely from view.

For a moment he couldn't think of anything to say, but finally he blurted out, "Cal's still in love with his wife."

"I know that."

"Sleeping with you isn't going to help him. You'll both regret it tomorrow."

Her smile was faint and less than amused. "Tell me, Josh, is that a comment on how irresistible Cal is? Or how easy I am?"

"God knows you're not easy," he said without thinking, then winced. "I didn't mean— What are you doing with him?"

"He needs a friend, and I thought maybe I could be one, at least for the evening." That smile came again. "It's not as if I have so many people clamoring for an hour or two of my time."

Whether she intended it or not, Josh felt a flush of guilt. He should have called her, gone to see her or...or something. He shouldn't have just kissed her good-night, then gone home and forgotten about her until they happened to meet again. Not that he'd *really* forgotten about her. Not for one damn second. But she didn't know that.

"For the record, Josh, I have no intention of sleeping

with Cal, and he knows it. The fact of his marriage may not mean much to Darcy, but it does mean something to me. I came with him this evening because he's a nice guy who's having a tough time, he's friendly, and he's not ashamed to be seen in public with me.''

Her last words struck him with the impact of a slap across the face. He stared at her as the color in her cheeks deepened, as the anger inside him built. ''You think I'm *ashamed* of you?''

She shrugged awkwardly. ''We went to dinner in Tulsa, where you weren't likely to run into anyone you knew. You've come to my place a couple of times, where you definitely won't see anyone you know. When you're in the store and there's someone else there, you pretend you don't know me. It was a complete surprise that you bothered to speak to me this evening. But then, if anyone noticed, they would assume you were talking to Cal and I just happened to be there.''

Josh leaned closer to her, right in her face. ''We went out to dinner in Tulsa because the toy store and the bookstore were there. The first time I went to your place, you invited me, and the last time, you didn't seem interested in doing anything else. And as for acting like I don't know you…''

For the first time since leaving his truck, he wasn't freezing, thanks to the guilt that sent a wave of heat through him. He turned away and dragged his fingers through his hair. When Miz Harjo had come into the store on Monday, he'd remained silent until she'd disappeared into the back, and he had deliberately chosen to pick up Candace for the trip to Tulsa at the campground to avoid being seen leaving town with her. He'd ignored her, too, when he'd walked into the store the next day and seen Theresa there, but that didn't count…did it? With Theresa being upset and thinking he'd come looking for her, ignoring Candace had seemed the better idea.

But what would it have hurt if he'd just said hello? *Hey, Candace, how are you doing?* He said that, or something similar, to virtually everyone he saw in town. It wouldn't have meant a damn thing to Theresa…but it would have to Candace.

He faced her once more. "You're right. I don't want anyone in my family to know that I've spoken to you or even seen you since the day you showed up at the ranch. You can blame me for that, but it's not like I have a hell of a lot of choices."

"I know it's my fault," she quietly admitted. "I'm not blaming you for anything. But…it's just a nice change that Cal isn't afraid."

Meaning that *he* was. Josh resented the implication…at the same time he admitted it was at least partly true. But, damn it, his family were the most important people in his life. How could he betray them for someone who wasn't?

"So what do you want me to do?" he asked hostilely. "Walk out there with you? Take you up in the bleachers to sit with Natalie and Tate? Make sure everyone in the damn stadium sees us together?" Wistfulness appeared in her blue eyes and made him feel like a bastard when he killed it. "Because that's not gonna happen. I'm not going to cause Nat any more pain over you. You're a beautiful woman, Candace, and I want you—I *like* you—a lot. But not enough to put you ahead of my family. They've stood by me for thirty-three years, and I'm not going to jeopardize that for an affair with someone who'll be gone before I know it."

He breathed deeply to ease the tightness in his gut, but it didn't help. He had the damnedest feeling that the next few minutes were seriously important, far more than he wanted to admit. He wanted to shut up and walk away, or shut up and kiss her, but he couldn't do either. Not yet. "If you don't mind keeping a private 'relationship'—" he hated that word, but he'd caught her flinch when he'd called it an affair ''—private, okay, fine. But if you're looking for someone who will take you out in public, to football games, Norma Sue's or Frenchy's, you'd better stick with Cal. He can do that. I can't.''

Some things were better left unsaid, Candace thought as she gazed at Josh, and that line about Cal not being ashamed of her was one of them. If only she'd kept her mouth shut, she could have enjoyed Josh's display of jealousy, harmless as it was, and maybe even gotten a kiss or two from him.

Instead, she'd talked herself into an ultimatum. A clandestine relationship with Josh or no relationship at all. Because she'd meant what she said. The fact that Cal was married mattered to her. She didn't dally with married men. In the past she'd considered them too much trouble, but the new, improved Candace really did believe marriage should equal monogamy. She couldn't force Cal to remain faithful to his wife until the divorce was filed, but she certainly wouldn't be the one he was unfaithful with.

But this was about Josh, not Cal. If she had any pride, she would tell him what he could do with his secret proposition.

Actually, she did have pride and plenty of it. She also had common sense. The details of her relationships had never been open to the public. Why should this one be different? Why should she make him choose between her and his family when she *was* going to be gone before he knew it? When they weren't going to fall in love, when marriage wasn't a remote possibility, when even sex didn't seem likely?

Deep down inside she knew the answer—because she'd never been that important to anyone, and she needed to be, just once.

But not at the cost Josh would have to pay.

Sheesh, she'd been such an awful person that a simple friendship with her could come between a man and the people who loved him. If she had died all those times she'd thought she would in the past year, that could have been her epitaph. A good reporter, but a sorry excuse for a human being.

"Well?"

Fighting the unfamiliar urge to cry, she forced a smile. "Okay. In town you don't know me, but at the campground we'll be best buds."

"Candace—"

She interrupted his warning tone. "I'm kidding. But, yes, I'll agree to your terms."

Now he looked irritated. "You make it sound—"

She took his hand and he fell silent. His gaze dropped to their hands, and she tried to remember if this was the first time she'd touched him. Not brushed against him or handed him something or gotten tire changing or chopstick holding help from him, but really touched him.

"Look, Josh, I'm sorry I started all this. I understand why things have to be this way, and I don't mind, honestly." That was a lie. "I was just feeling a little...difficult." That wasn't a lie, if *difficult* could also mean hurt. Blue. Ashamed of herself for giving him little choice but to keep what was between them secret.

Unable to think of any way to settle the issue definitively without losing her pride by pleading that she would take any bit of his time he was willing to give her, she suggested, "Let's just forget this conversation took place, okay? We'll go on just like we have been. Nothing has to change. Okay?"

For a long time he simply looked at her, making her worry for an instant that he was going to say, No, forget it, I can't see you again. But finally he nodded, though his expression was far from certain.

She smiled as if she hadn't noticed his reluctance, then turned him toward the bleachers. "You'd better go find the others before they come looking for you."

He glanced back. "Candace—"

"Go on. I'll see you...." Blinking once to clear her eyes—it was the cold, of course, making them water—she repeated the words. "I'll see you."

He kept glancing back until he was out of sight. Candace turned her back to the stadium, leaned one shoulder against the cold stone and hugged her arms to her chest. If she could go back an hour or two in time, she would refuse Cal's invitation to the game and thereby avoid this damned conversation with Josh, and she would feel so much less confused and hurt.

But, hell, why stop with an hour or two? If she could turn back the clock a few years, six or twelve or twenty, if she could go back to when she was an innocent child—for surely even she had been innocent at some time in her life—she could make different choices and become a different woman.

Even though she was beginning to like a few things about the woman this past year had turned her into.

"So Josh has come into the store a time or two, and that's all."

Before she even thought to look over her shoulder at Cal, he was wrapping his arms around her from behind and holding her snugly to him. The idea of pulling away didn't cross her mind. Instead, she relaxed against him, and considered how *good* it felt to be held by someone who offered only comfort.

"I won't ask what's going on between you two—"

"Good, because then I would be forced to ask what went wrong between you and Darcy."

"—but for whatever it's worth, Josh is a good guy."

"I know. He's not the problem here."

"Then what is?"

She opened her mouth to answer, then closed it again as the Hickory Bluff High School marching band burst into song. That was what she'd come for tonight—the music, the crowd, the excitement, the spectacle. Not to cry on the shoulder of a man she'd met just a few hours earlier.

Twisting away, she pasted on a cheery smile. "Nothing, really. Did I mention that this is the first high school football game I've ever been to? Let's go find a seat. I don't want to miss a thing."

Even with the extra leaves in the dining table, Tate and Natalie's table was crowded Saturday evening for dinner. J.T. sat in the seat of honor with his mom and dad on one side, his grandmother and Arthur Scott on the other. Lucinda's parents came next, across from Jordan and Michaela, and Michaela's dad, Matt, and Josh were squeezed in at the end.

While they ate a dinner of hot dogs, baked beans and spaghetti—menu courtesy of J.T.—Josh studied the others. Tate and Natalie were about as happy as a couple could get without becoming disgusting, Theresa had teased, and it was true. Lucinda and Arthur still held hands and sneaked kisses like teenagers in love for the first time. As for Gran and Grandpop…Josh wasn't sure how AnnaMae had put up with the old man for fifty-some years, but she'd not only managed but even seemed to enjoy his company. Even Jordan and Michaela made one hell of a couple. Of course, they'd never been seriously involved, just best friends from the cradle. But they still looked and acted as if they belonged together.

Which left Josh and Matt as the odd ones out.

Apparently, the same thought was on Matt's mind. He leaned close and murmured, "Have you ever noticed that you and I are the only ones who never manage to pair up with someone for these get-togethers? I wonder why that is."

"The fact that you haven't even considered dating in the fourteen years since your marriage broke up might have something to do with it," Josh remarked.

"As well as the fact that you refuse to get serious about any of the dozens of women you've dated," Matt retorted.

Josh felt a hawkish stare on him and looked up, then away, but not in time to avoid Grandpop's gaze. To say the two of them didn't get along was an understatement. The worst time of Josh's life was the weeks he'd spent at their place helping out when the old man had broken his leg. Tate had stayed here, pretended to be Josh and gotten interviewed by that nosy reporter, Natalie, for Chaney's biography, and had thought he'd gotten the worst of the deal. No way. From the moment Josh had driven onto Grandpop's property until the time he'd driven away, he hadn't done a single thing right, to hear the old man tell it. He couldn't even take a breath without getting criticized for the way he did it.

"We figured maybe you'd be thinking of settling down by now," the old man said, a note of censure in his voice.

"I've been thinking about it—about how to avoid it."

Ralph gave a shake of his head that set his shaggy white hair in motion. "By the time I was your age, I'd already built that ranch out of nothing, made a home and a living for my family and got your mama half-raised. And you've…what? Been arrested a few dozen times? Had a few dozen girlfriends? Spent a lot of time partying and having fun?"

"Grandpop, don't start," Tate said, but the old man gave no sign of hearing him.

"For the record," Josh said evenly, "I doubt I've spent more than fourteen, maybe sixteen, nights in jail in my life—and there have been a *whole* lot more than a few dozen girlfriends."

"No more than fourteen, maybe sixteen, nights in jail. And you say it like you're proud of it." A familiar expression—part disdain, part sneer—crossed Ralph's face. Josh couldn't remember a time when his grandfather hadn't looked at him like that, and he knew why. Tate might have been illegitimate, but at least his father had been a cowboy, someone Ralph could relate to, and at least Tate had turned out responsible even if his father wasn't. Hell, until he'd married Natalie, Tate had always acted a good twenty years older than he was, even when he was a kid.

But Josh... Not only was he illegitimate, but his father was a politician, always in the spotlight and almost always caught up in some scandal or another. On top of that, Josh was impulsive, willful, brash and disrespectful to boot. It had never mattered to the old man that Josh worked as hard as Tate did, but Ralph had always found fault with the fact that he played as hard as he worked. He'd always found fault with everything.

"I'm not proud of getting into trouble," Josh said, knowing his words would aggravate Ralph and saying them anyway. "But I'm not ashamed of it, either, and I'm sure not going to lie about it."

Grandpop snorted and opened his mouth to continue, but Natalie stalled him. Gathering dirty dishes, she paused behind Josh's chair and wrapped her free arm around him. "Leave Josh alone, Grandpop," she said in the stern voice reserved for responding to J.T.'s tenth *let me stay up just ten more minutes* of the evening. "We love him exactly the way he is." She brushed a kiss to Josh's cheek. "And there will be no more harsh words to disrupt J.T.'s birthday dinner. Understand?"

"Any man deserving of the name shouldn't have to count on a woman to stand up for him," Ralph grumbled. "It's a sad day when I can't make a simple comment to my own grandchild without being accused of disrupting things. But all right. I'll just give my attention to my other grandchild and my two great-grandsons."

That suited him just fine, Josh thought darkly.

His grandfather ignored him, and vice versa, through the cake and ice cream, the opening of J.T.'s presents, and the conversation afterward. When everyone else moved into the living room, Josh helped Jordan and Michaela with the dishes. "Safer in here than with the old man, isn't it?" Jordan had teased. When that was done, he got his jacket, but instead of saying his goodbyes and escaping, he went outside onto the deck that joined Tate's house to their mom's.

He was standing at the rail, gazing into the darkness, when the door behind him opened. Whispering a quick prayer that it wasn't his grandfather, he turned to see Natalie.

"It isn't fair," she said as she came to stand beside him. "Grandpop's forgiven your mother for having Chaney's baby, but he hasn't forgiven you for having Chaney's blood."

"It doesn't matter." Oh, when he was a kid, he'd wondered why his grandfather preferred Tate to him, what he'd done to earn Ralph's disdain. But he'd long ago accepted that nothing was ever going to change, and he really didn't care...most of the time.

Natalie slid her hands into the oversize jacket she wore—Tate's, he realized. "It does matter. He's been hard on you all your life for something you had no control over. What about when you have kids of your own? Is he going to punish them for having Chaney's blood, too?"

"If he is, then I'll have to count on you to keep him in line." And he had no doubt she could do it. Natalie had a way of making the men in the Rawlins family do what she wanted, and thinking it was their own idea from the start.

"I don't care if he is older than God, I'd smack him. And that crap about how he raised your mother—" she made a derisive snort "—he no more raised her than I did. 'Raisin' young'uns' is women's work in his world. He raised cattle and horses and hell, and your grandmother did everything else."

He gently bumped one shoulder against her. "Aw, he's an old man. Let him remember it his way."

They stood in silence for a moment, arms barely touching, the quiet between them comfortable. He'd often teased Tate that if he'd known four years ago that the reporter pestering him for an interview was so pretty, he would have been more than happy to meet her…and marry her. It was just teasing, though. He loved Natalie dearly, but like a best friend or the sister he'd never had.

That was why he had to open his mouth three times before he managed to say what he wanted. "I, uh…saw Candace Thompson at the football game last night."

Natalie stiffened, then drew away and faced him. The porch light showed the tension lining her face and the way her mouth had flattened into a thin line. "What was she doing there?"

"Cheering on the Wildcats?" he suggested lamely.

"I wish she would just go home and leave me alone. How many times do I have to tell her I don't want to talk to her? What could she possibly say that would mean anything after what she did to me?"

"What did she do?" Josh asked the question quietly, but Natalie heard. He knew from the shift in her breathing, from the sad, distant look that crossed her face.

"She was the best friend I ever had," she said at last. "I loved her more than I ever loved anyone…and she set me up, then knocked me down. She used me and betrayed me and broke my heart." Her voice stronger now, underlaid with anger, she went on. "I can't believe her arrogance, to think that she can just come here and say, 'I want to talk you,' and I'll agree. Though I don't know why I'm surprised. She always thought if she wanted something she should have it, no matter who she hurt in the process. I wonder what she wants now, and what my role is in her getting it."

"Maybe she wants her best friend back."

Natalie gave another of those derisive snorts. "She never thought of me as her friend. I was the means to an end.

She was ambitious. She wanted out of Montgomery—wanted to go someplace big like Atlanta—and she was too impatient to earn it. So she took a few shortcuts, and she succeeded. She got everything she wanted. And all she had to do was play me for a fool, then give me the shove that ended my career and made my father disown me.''

Josh was having difficulty reconciling what he knew of Candace with what Natalie was saying. His Candace— Mentally he drew back from his phrasing, started to change it to *the Candace he knew,* then, remembering Cal's arm around her the night before, decided he'd been right the first time. His Candace worked for minimum wage in a five-and-dime and lived in a motor home. She meditated and read self-help books and offered a sympathetic ear to people who needed it. She wasn't ambitious, arrogant or calculated.

She was sweet.

His gut tightened, and in a flash he found himself wishing he'd left as soon as the dishes were done and driven the seven or so miles to the lake. Jeez, when was the last time he'd found being sweet a turn-on?

''Maybe she's changed,'' he suggested hesitantly.

''Yeah. And maybe the bull that chased Tate into the bed of the pickup the other day has become as docile as a lamb. People like Candace don't change, Josh. They can't. They're too selfish and greedy and self-absorbed. She's used and manipulated people all her life, and she'll continue doing it until the day she dies.'' She started toward the side door, then turned back. ''Even if she could change, so what? She destroyed every good thing I ever felt for her, including—especially—my trust. And without trust, nothing else matters.''

When she reached the door, she extended her hand to him. ''Come on. We'll put duct tape on Grandpop's mouth and spend an enjoyable evening with him for once.''

''Nah, let him talk. I think I'm gonna head out.''

. Natalie smiled her amazingly womanly smile, the kind that could make every male who didn't see her as a sister grateful to be a man. "I notice you didn't say 'head home.' Got a date?"

"Nope. Just thought I'd catch up with everyone over at Frenchy's." As he voiced the lie, guilt swept over him. Damn it, he hated lying, but after the conversation they'd just had, how the hell could he tell her he wanted—needed—to see Candace?

"Be careful. Don't drive if you drink too much. And if you get thrown into jail, we'll let Grandpop spring you. That'll give him something to harp on for the next five years."

"I'd rather rot behind bars than let the old man have the satisfaction. I'll see you guys tomorrow. Tell J.T. happy birthday for me again."

He waited until she'd gone inside, then headed across the yard to his truck. He did drive by Frenchy's and, when he caught a glimpse of a convertible parked on the side, drove through the parking lot. The car wasn't a rental, though, and carried three Wildcats bumper stickers. Feeling more relieved than he wanted to admit, he pulled back onto the highway and continued to the campground. The convertible he was looking for was parked outside the RV, and though the curtains were drawn, there were plenty of lights on inside.

He parked in his usual spot, crossed the yard to the door and knocked. A moment later, a curtain fluttered, then the door opened.

Candace wore a sleeveless blue leotard with a pair of filmy black shorts, as if it were midsummer and not well into fall and approaching winter, and she looked incredible. For a moment he just took it in—the shape of her breasts, her narrow waist curving into womanly hips, and legs that were damn fine even if they were short. Just like the first time he'd come here, her feet were bare, with the silver ring still circling one toe, and just like the first time, he found that oddly sexy.

Of course, these days he was liable to find everything about her sexy.

"Hi," she greeted him, before picking up the remote and muting the television.

He glanced at it and saw a woman in leotard and tights twisted in ways the human body wasn't meant to twist, then smoothly unfolding, stretching, rising to a standing position. "Am I interrupting?"

"No. I can finish later."

*Go ahead and finish now*, he wanted to say. *Don't stop on my account.* But God knows how turned on he would get if he watched her make those slow, graceful, controlled moves—probably enough to embarrass himself.

She rolled up a mat she'd spread on the floor in front of the kitchen sink and stowed it in a closet, then pulled a sweatshirt over her head. It was way too big—courtesy of an ex-boyfriend?—and made her look like a child playing dress up.

After she sat down on the sofa, he took a seat in the captain's chair next to the couch. "Did you enjoy the game last night?"

Her smile was quick and bright, reminding him again of Natalie's assessment of her—ambitious, arrogant and calculated. It just didn't jibe. Maybe the whole experience had been so traumatic for Natalie that it was exaggerated in her memory, or maybe Candace really had changed her ways. Either way, it was as if they knew two different women.

"It was fun. It was the first football game I'd ever gone to, you know, and I really enjoyed it."

He couldn't help scowling. "You would have enjoyed it more with me."

"Yes, but you didn't ask. Cal did."

He didn't respond to that. He couldn't. "What did you guys do after the game?"

"Let's see...we stopped at the drive-in for a real old-fashioned black walnut malt, and he showed me where Darcy grew up, and then he took me back to my car and followed me home. He didn't walk me to the door, though. I guess his mother doesn't have the same expectations of him that your mom has of you."

"Mrs. Bridger's got eight kids, every one of them a hell-raiser. She was happy if she knew which county lockup they were each in at any given time."

Candace's only response to that was a faint smile. She fiddled a moment with her sweatshirt, rubbing at a spot near the hem, then met his gaze. "What did *you* do after the game?"

"I dropped Jordan off at a party."

"And then?"

He shrugged. "I stopped by Frenchy's for a beer." At least, that had been his excuse. Truthfully, he'd wanted to make sure she wasn't there with Cal. It was probably a good thing she hadn't been, because considering the mood he'd been in, he probably would have gotten his ass thrown in jail, and then Grandpop would have really ragged on him.

"Then what?"

"I went home."

She opened her mouth, closed it, then opened it again. "Alone?"

For the first time since he'd walked into Tate's house and found Grandpop there, Josh truly relaxed. She'd sounded pretty cool and controlled, but she was jealous. She didn't like the idea of him with another woman any-more than he wanted to think of her with another man.

He moved to sit on the couch, closer to her but not close enough. "Would it matter if I said no?"

For a moment she looked as if she wanted to bluff, to carelessly reply that she couldn't care less, and for that moment she seemed years younger than thirty-eight, and amazingly unsure. She glanced at him, shifted awkwardly, hugged her knees to her chest, then glanced his way again. "Yes."

It was a good answer—exactly the one he wanted. But before he could say so, she surged to her feet. "I'm going to change clothes. I'm a little cold. There's water, pop and the rest of your beer in the refrigerator. Help yourself."

Josh watched her until the closing bedroom door blocked her from sight. She'd moved so quickly he hadn't had the chance to make the obvious response—*I can keep you warm.* Somehow he doubted it would have changed the outcome.

After getting a beer from the refrigerator, he stretched out on the couch and used the remote to flip through the TV channels. When he found a movie that he remembered as passable entertainment, he set the remote down and half watched it, half waited.

When she returned, he would have guessed it had taken her fifteen minutes or more to change clothes, but a glance at the clock showed it really had been less than six. She still wore the sweatshirt, but underneath it now was some kind of sports bra—one wide multicolored strap showed where the shirt slipped off her shoulder—and instead of tiny little shorts she wore navy sweatpants. She'd added a pair of thick white socks, too.

She was about to sit down in the chair when he patted the sofa cushion in front of him. "Come over here."

"I don't want to crowd you."

"I want to be crowded. Come on."

Her steps were halting, as if she really didn't want to share the couch with him but couldn't think of a reason to refuse. Or maybe it was because she *did* want to share the couch with him but thought she shouldn't. Either way she finally sat down on the edge of the cushion and let him draw her back until her head rested on his shoulder. He pulled her nearer until they were fitted snugly together, then he wrapped his arms around her, clasped his hands together and rested them on her stomach. After a long, still moment, she laid her own hand over them. It was a simple act, but it felt like a victory to him.

Then they watched television. He couldn't stay focused on the movie, though. He kept thinking about how comfortable it was—a quiet evening, the TV on, nothing really happening, just him and Candace together—and about how good she felt and smelled, and whether he wanted to just enjoy it for what it was or do his best to see what it could be.

The movie ended and a news broadcast out of Tulsa started, but neither of them reached for the remote. She shifted, touching him in places that felt incredibly good, then quietly asked, "How was your nephew's birthday?"

"Pretty good for him. Not bad for me."

"What would have made it better for you?"

"If my grandfather hadn't come, or if he'd ignored me the entire evening instead of just part of it."

She glanced up at him. "You don't like him?"

"Nah, I like him fine. He just doesn't care for me, and he makes sure everyone knows it. Sometimes it's real hard for me not to reciprocate."

"Why doesn't he like you?"

He smiled faintly. The last time he'd had this conversation with a woman he was dating, she'd laughed and insisted he was exaggerating. Why, *of course* the old goat liked him; Josh was his *grandson*. He was grateful Candace had accepted him at his word. But then, she understood better than most that blood relations didn't always count for a lot. "He thinks I'm my father's son."

"And he doesn't like your father."

Josh shifted onto his side so he could better see her. "I can't blame him for that. I don't like Chaney, either."

"But you're nothing like him. Well, except for your fondness for having a good time. And you both have a fine appreciation for the fairer sex. But that's where the resemblance ends.''

''You think so?''

''I know so.'' Releasing his hand, she reached under a couple of magazines tossed onto the table and drew out a book—Chaney's biography. An emery board marked her place about halfway through.

He wasn't sure whether he was flattered or annoyed. Immediately after the book was published, word had gotten out that he was included, however briefly, and for weeks it had been impossible to go anywhere without running into people who had a million questions about it. Up until that time, only one book could be found in virtually every house in the county, Lucinda had declared—the Bible. Chaney's biography had made it two.

The Lord and Boyd Chaney together in Hickory Bluff. That was a scary thought.

''When did you get that?''

''This morning. I checked it out of the Hickory Bluff Public Library. They wouldn't give me a card on my say-so, but after Martha vouched for me, they couldn't sign me up fast enough.''

''Are you learning anything new?''

Slowly she turned onto her side, too, and made him wish the couch was just a few inches narrower. Though her legs were pressed against his, and her hand rested on his ribs, there was still space between her breasts and his chest, and her hips and his. Of course, even if they got rid of that space, there was still the matter of their clothes.

''Actually, yes,'' she murmured. ''Turning his back on your mother and then you was the kindest thing Boyd Chaney could have done. He's the poorest excuse for father material I've seen.''

Ducking his head, he kissed her once—nothing impressive—then grinned at her. ''That's your prize for being so perceptive and accurate.''

Then he kissed her again, coaxing her lips apart, sliding his tongue between her teeth, pulling her close enough that they touched from head to toe and holding her there like he was never gonna let go.

For putting up with Grandpop tonight, for watching her with Cal last night, for the thirty-three years he'd waited for her....

This was *his* prize.

## Chapter Eight

The sun was shining. Water lapped against the lakeshore. The boom box sitting on a tree stump softly played an instrumental CD—lots of flutes and harps and keyboards giving tune to songs arranged to relax. A light breeze drifted through every now and again to take the edge off the eighty-degree temperature, and occasionally wood smoke floated on the air, subtle, distant, its fragrance teasing, then disappearing.

It was, Candace decided, an absolutely perfect moment.

It was another Saturday, a week after J.T. Rawlins's birthday, and she'd seen Josh almost every evening. He didn't stay long—the work he did and the hours he did it required getting to bed earlier than most people she'd known.

Still, the time they spent together was…special. Precious.

And it had to end soon.

She'd been in Hickory Bluff for three weeks now. Natalie still refused to take her calls, and Wednesday morning, when Candace appeared on the Rawlins doorstep uninvited, Natalie had refused to answer the door, even though she was obviously home. The television had been audible through the door, along with a little boy's voice asking, "Mama, can I see who it is?"

After knocking repeatedly, ringing the doorbell and calling loudly, Candace had given up. Fearful that Josh might come back unexpectedly, find her there and get angry, she'd gotten in her car and left.

Since then she'd been working on *The Letter*. That was how she thought of it, capital letters, italics and all. It was that important.

And that impossible.

"You sure do brighten up that patch of grass," Patsy Conway called.

Candace opened her eyes, then sat up and spotted the owner of one-half of Conway Campground and Church Camp—4Cs for short—coming out of the woods. The woman was old enough to be retired from her job of driving a tractor-trailer rig between Tulsa and just about every major city in the country and some that weren't. She had three children, eight grandchildren and two great-grandchildren, she'd told Candace the first time they'd met, and she got possession of every blessed one of them come summer and all holidays. Candace couldn't even begin to imagine how it would feel to have a family like that.

"What are you doing out in the woods on such a pretty day?" Candace added.

"Can you think of a better place to be?" Patsy glanced around, spied the aluminum lawn chair Candace had bought on her first trip into U-Want-It and brought it to the edge of the quilt. "I'd join you down there and soak up the sun, but the way my arthritis has been acting, it'd take you and Dub both to get me back on my feet." She settled into the chair, the nylon webbing straining under her weight, then gave a sigh. "I've been to Maine and Oregon, down Highway 1 in California and the Blue Ridge Parkway. I've climbed Pike's Peak and sat on the beach down in the Florida Keys, and I spent so much time in Montana and Wyoming that I started to talk like those folks. But nothing I've ever seen compares to Oklahoma in the fall. This is a beautiful place."

Then her eyes twinkled. "'Course, it has to be, because it's just durn ugly in the winter. All the trees lose their leaves, except those ornery old blackjacks. They hang on to their dead, brown remains until spring comes around again. Nope, without snow it's not a pretty sight around here from November through March. But the rest of the year there's nothin' better." She directed her gaze at Candace. "You must like it. You've certainly stayed more than the week or so you'd planned on when you came."

"I do like it," Candace replied, half-surprised at hearing the words. She'd lived her entire life in cities, with a stereotypical, born-of-ignorance, big-city disdain for rural small-town life. But she *did* like Hickory Bluff—and not just because Josh was there. The people were friendly, and they were part of a community the likes of which she'd never known. This was a place, Cal had sourly told her, where it was damned hard to get left alone. Everybody knew everybody else, and they all thought they had some sort of stake in each other's lives.

Under better circumstances it was a place where she could stay and make her first-ever home for herself.

But not with Natalie hating her and Josh wanting her but not loving her.

Not that she loved him, either, she hastened to assure herself. And not that she wanted him to love her. It was just that…if he loved her, they could go to Norma Sue's or Pepe Chen's for dinner instead of having to drive twenty miles to Dixon or even farther to Muskogee or Tulsa. They could go to his house for a change, or she could go with him to the Halloween party in town tonight. If he really, truly cared for her, he would tell his family and quit hiding out here in the woods with her.

"What's wrong, hon? All of a sudden those clouds in the sky don't have nothin' on the one crossing your face."

Candace automatically glanced at the sky. While it was still warm and sunny at the lake, in the distance storm clouds stretched to the horizon. "Is it supposed to rain this evening?"

"Rain, sleet, snow…nobody knows for sure. I swear, I wouldn't mind a job as a weather person in Oklahoma. You can be wrong 100 percent of the time and nobody cares. Nothing's ever absolute with them. It *might* rain, or there's a *chance* of thunderstorms, which also means it might *not* rain and there's *no* chance of thunderstorms, so they're right either way. And if they do happen to miss the forecast entirely, then they blame the weather for being unpredictable."

Candace shifted into a yoga position, bringing the soles of her feet together, and contemplated the possibility of sleet or snow. On a day like this, it seemed much more an *im*possibility. "The weather here is certainly changeable."

"That it is. If there's one thing you can count on in Oklahoma, it's that you can't count on anything." Patsy chuckled, then corrected herself. "Now, that's not really true. It's almost a sure bet that as soon as my peach trees blossom in the spring, we'll get a hard freeze. And within twenty-four hours of my watering that big ol' yard of ours in August, we'll get some rain. A drought's usually followed by a flood, and a flood's usually followed by another one. If we wear shorts to Christmas dinner one year, the next we'll have snow in April."

"And you always get tornadoes."

Patsy sobered. "Yes, ma'am, we always get those. I can't say that I've ever actually laid eyes on one myself, though. When the sky turns green and the hair on my arms stands on end and I hear that freight train rumbling, I head for the storm cellar, like an intelligent woman. Dub, on the other hand, grabs the camera and runs outside to take pictures. I keep telling him that someday he's gonna be swept away and he *ain't* gonna land in Kansas, but he doesn't listen, the crazy man.''

The distant sound of an engine drew Patsy's attention to the lake. Candace turned to look and saw the aforementioned crazy man putt-putting their way. As he steered a small boat to the dock, Patsy stood up with some effort, folded the chair and returned it to its place near the door.

''We're gonna take a spin around the lake and make sure everything's as it should be. It'd be a tight fit, but you're welcome to come along if you'd like.''

''No, thank you,'' Candace said politely. *Tight fit* was an understatement. The boat was narrow, with only two planks for seating, one of which was occupied by Dub. That meant she and Patsy would have to share the other, and while Patsy was many things, slender enough to share that seat with anyone else was not among them. ''Have a good time.''

Patsy glanced back over her shoulder. ''Hon, I'm goin' with my husband of forty-two years. How good a time can I have?'' Then she winked and grinned lasciviously before turning to maneuver into the boat.

As they pulled away, Candace rolled onto her stomach and cupped her chin in her hands. If she got married this very moment, to spend forty-two years with the man, she would have to live to be eighty years old. What were the odds of that? Better than they'd been a year ago. Not as good as they'd been before that.

But it was too perfect a day to think about dying. Besides, who needed all that negative energy? She was a big believer in the power of the mind, both good and bad. She wasn't about to risk the consequences of the bad.

Lying flat, she rested her head on her arms. Between the

sun, the breeze and the music, she was more asleep than awake when a tickle near her left ear made her shiver. She drowsily brushed it away, then it came again, barely there, a flutter against her cheek. She swiped at it again before turning her head to the opposite side. Just as she felt herself sinking deeper into sleep, something warm and moist touched her right ear. She forced one eye open and saw nothing out of place—forced the other open and tilted her head back and saw Josh leaning over her.

"Was that your tongue?" she asked sleepily.

"You tell me."

"Do it again."

He bent closer and touched the tip of his tongue to her ear, tracing along the curve, making her shudder again. With delicious hunger swirling and twisting deep inside her, she rolled onto her back and smiled at him. "What are you up to?"

He was stretched out beside her, leaning on his elbows, watching her from behind a pair of dark glasses. "Looking for something to do and someone to do it with."

"Well, have you tried Theresa?"

"Not interested."

"Um, how about that waitress at Norma Sue's? She seemed to like you the first time I was in there."

"Really?" His grin took about ten years off his face. "Did she say something to you?"

"No, but when you left in an obvious temper, she practically threw my food at me."

"In an obvious temper?" he repeated. "That sounds so girly. I wasn't in a temper. I was pissed."

"Oh, of course. So…how about her?"

He removed his sunglasses so she could see the glint of amusement in his eyes. "Nope."

"Do you even know which one I'm talking about?"

"Nope, but I'm not interested in her, either. Guess that just leaves you."

"Oh, gee, lucky me. Don't sound too happy about the prospect." She sat up and stretched, then hugged her knees to her chest.

"I like your silver heart."

She gazed down at the toe ring, then wiggled all ten toes. "Thank you. It's supposed to be sexy."

"It works for me." He sat up, too, facing her, and put the shades back on. "So what have you not done in the time you've been here that you would like to do?"

Her obvious answer—talk to Natalie—remained unspoken. But there were other options. She'd discovered just this morning that she would like to go for a boat ride, just leisurely putt-putting around the lake with the sun keeping her warm, and maybe a picnic in a basket.

And she would like to go on a real date with him—dress up, see a movie or go to a club, share a lovely meal. Someplace, of course, where they wouldn't see anyone he knew.

Or she would really love to see the ranch where he spent his workdays, to meet his horse and see the cattle and ride over the land. All out of the question, of course, since the people who most definitely couldn't see them together all lived there.

"Well?" he prompted.

"I-I'd like to see— If it's possible without— I'd like to see where you live."

Reluctance crossed his face, then disappeared as quickly as it had appeared. Hastily, before he could say anything, she rushed on. "It's okay if you don't want to. I mean, I don't even know *where* you live."

"My house is on the south end of the ranch, about three-quarters of a mile or so from the main house."

"Oh. Never mind."

He frowned. "Is that a problem?"

Her smile was as quavery as the leaves in the breeze. "My first day in town, a handsome cowboy told me that if

I set foot on the ranch again, he'd have me arrested. I'd like to keep my nonexistent arrest record nonexistent.''

A flush warmed his cheeks and turned them the faintest pink under his tan. ''Yeah, well, he likes you better today than he did then. Come on. Get some shoes on.'' He pulled her to her feet, then shook out the quilt, punched the stop button on the boom box, and carried them both to the RV.

In her bedroom Candace pulled on a long-sleeved shirt over her tank top, tied the tails at her waist, then rolled up the sleeves. In deference to the heat, she chose sandals instead of sneakers or boots. Hey, a man couldn't find a toe ring sexy if he couldn't see it, now, could he? Adding her own shades and a baseball cap—good for camouflage—she grabbed her purse, then followed him to his truck.

They drove right through downtown Hickory Bluff—an act of defiance on Josh's part, she thought—then picked up the highway heading west out of town. Country music played on the radio, and the windows were down to let in the sweet autumn air. It was such a pleasant way to pass the time that she was about to tell him to forget about the ranch and just keep driving when he slowed and turned onto Rawlins Ranch Road.

''Must be nice having a road named after you,'' she teased.

''The name was picked by the commissioner for our district who happened to be sweet on my mom. It didn't do him any good—she still wouldn't go out with him. Nah, around here you can get a street named just about anything. In town we've got a Lois Lane—the only person who lives on it is Lois Faye Wickham—and an Easy Street.''

''Now living on Easy Street would be nice,'' she said with a laugh.

They'd gone little more than a mile when he slowed and turned onto a narrow dirt road. Without being asked, she got out and opened the gate, waited until he drove through and secured it again. As she walked ahead to the truck, she couldn't ignore the faint queasiness settling in her stomach. She knew it was silly—if there was any risk of running into his family, he wouldn't have brought her here—but she couldn't help it. She didn't want to be the cause of problems between him and them.

Josh watched her settle in the seat again and fasten her belt. With that baseball cap, she looked more Jordan's age than his. He wondered if it was supposed to be something of a disguise in case they were spotted by anyone. Odds of that were slim. No one came to his house without being invited except his mother, whose every-other-month clean-out of his refrigerator wasn't due for another six weeks, and occasionally Jordan, who'd brought a pretty little girl home from college with him this weekend and wasn't likely to have a thought for anything but showing her off to all his buddies.

He drove the remaining half mile to his house, parked in front and shut off the engine, then looked at Candace to judge her opinion. Most of the women he brought here were pleased enough, though more with the potential for changes than with what was already there. It wasn't fancy—he wouldn't like living in a house that was—but it was comfortable, and at the end of a long day that counted for an awful lot with him.

"This is great," she said as she climbed out. "The color, the windows, the porch, no yard to mow…and it fits perfectly here, with all the trees. I'm impressed."

Easily so, he thought. But her next words would be, *But wouldn't a flower bed look great along the porch?* Or, *All it needs is a cute little railing and a glider for cool spring evenings.* Or, *If you cut down just a few of those trees, you could let in some sunlight. A dozen or two should do it.*

But she didn't say anything at all as she followed him onto the porch, then inside. He propped open the screen door, unlocked the door, then stepped back to let her enter first.

The front door opened directly into the living room. Every woman who saw it insisted the focal point of the room should be the big stone fireplace, his one extravagance. Okay, so he couldn't decorate his way out of a paper bag, but he couldn't watch movies in the fireplace, while he could on the TV diagonally opposite. But if Candace agreed with the others, she didn't say so.

And if she preferred carpeting, she didn't mention that, either. The floors were wood everywhere except the kitchen, separated from the living room by a broad counter, and the bathroom, where he'd settled for vinyl. He had wood because he hated vacuuming, and it was dusty wood because he hated sweeping, too.

"I've lived in the motor home—and before that, apartments—for so long that I'd forgotten what it was like to actually have room." Candace walked around the sofa, past the dining table and into the kitchen, and he trailed along behind her. Because the place was small—just one bedroom—the only hall was a short one on the other side of the fireplace. It connected with the kitchen in back and opened into the bathroom and the bedroom on the right.

She looked into the bathroom with its claw-foot tub and old-fashioned pedestal sink, both rescued from a remodel of his grandparents' house years ago, then gave him a sly look. "Tell me your mother comes over and cleans for you."

"She'd smack me if I even hinted at it—though she does come over periodically to remove anything growing fuzz from my refrigerator."

"So you're this neat."

"You're neat, too."

"I *have* to be. I live in a motor home."

Her last stop was his bedroom. A pair of stained and ripped jeans were on the floor, the dust seemed heavier in there, and his bed wasn't exactly made. He'd just pulled the comforter up over the rumpled sheets when he'd gotten up that morning. But it wasn't bad.

"This is nice," she said, giving him a smile.

"Yeah?"

"Yeah. Especially this room. I like the colors. They're great."

The comforter and sheets were a Southwest pattern in rust, tan, turquoise and green, and the walls were painted Terra Cotta Dust. Theresa had been pretty sure they could be saved with a sponged-on coat of Creamy Ecru, and the woman before her had wondered why he hadn't had the good sense to go with plain white.

He was glad he'd had the good sense not to settle down with either of them.

Candace walked over to the pine dresser and studied the pottery lined up there before picking up the central piece. It was a four-legged creature made of clay and painted turquoise, with round black eyes. She turned it over and read aloud, "T J F J. Does that translate to something?"

"To Josh, from Jordan. He made that for my birthday when he was in first grade."

"And you've kept it all this time." Gently she returned it to its place, then remarked, "So the love-'em-and-leave-'em cowboy is sentimental at heart."

"Is that a bad thing?"

"No, not at all. You'll make a great father someday."

She continued around the room, looking, touching. He wished she would look at him. Better yet, he wished she would touch him.

Finally she completed her circuit and stopped in front of him. He was blocking the door, but she didn't say anything and he didn't volunteer to move. Why would he, when he had her where he wanted her? Well, *almost* where he wanted her.

"You have a very nice home."

"You sound so prim and polite."

Her smile was shy and sweet, and it made him want to kiss it away. He touched his fingertips to her mouth, and the smile somehow got shyer and sweeter, and her lips parted just enough so he could feel the warmth of her breath on his skin.

"I'm not prim," she disagreed, dislodging his fingers.

"But you are polite. Southern girls like you say *please* and *thank you* and *may I* all the time, don't you?"

"When it's to our advantage."

"But you never say it to me." He moved closer, brushed his mouth across her ear and made her shiver, then trailed kisses along her jaw and down her throat. Her pulse quickened beneath his kiss, and his own increased in tempo as he claimed her mouth.

She was ready for him, hungrily sucking at his tongue as if she might devour him. Sliding his arms around her waist, he held her tight against his erection and felt the heat where her hips cradled his. In some small part of his brain where logical thought remained possible, he tried to remember not to get too caught up in this. She was more likely to turn him down than to fall into bed with him. But could he help it if he wanted her more than any woman he'd ever known? If just one kiss was enough to make him hot and hard and greedy as hell?

"Please," she whimpered, and he thought how damnably erotic that one polite little word could be, and then she repeated it, her voice stronger. "Please...Josh, don't... don't...."

By the time he realized what she was pleading for, she'd twisted out of his arms and turned her back to him. He felt a moment's anger, then it turned to disappointment. Of course she had the right to stop. He would never even consider forcing her to continue. But damn it, what was missing here? How could he want her so damn bad when she didn't want him at all?

No, that wasn't true. She wanted him. He'd kissed too

many women to miss the signs. She wanted him. She just didn't intend to have him.

"I...I'm sorry." Her voice was little more than a whisper, and she wouldn't look at him. Keeping her head down, she slipped past him and returned to the living room.

Dragging his hand through his hair, Josh took a deep breath. Too bad they weren't at the RV. Then he could just walk outside and jump in the damn lake. The next best thing would be a cold shower, but he didn't want the next best thing. He wanted the *best* thing.

Candace. In his bed.

He stood there a while, wanting to punch or kick something, to swear, to take out his frustration somehow. But his pine bed was solid enough to break any bones that came into contact with the wood, patching holes in drywall was one of his least favorite jobs, and swearing wasn't going to help. Neither was being frustrated or losing his temper.

Finally he left the bedroom and walked as far as the doorway into the living room. She was standing in front of the fireplace, studying the photos crowded on the mantel. Though she didn't acknowledge his presence, he knew from the uneasiness of her movements that she was aware of him.

He leaned one shoulder against the doorjamb. "Funny, isn't it? How we can go from having our tongues in each other's mouths to not even able to talk to each other in just a couple minutes."

Her hand shook as she returned the frame she was holding to the mantel. "I...I'm sorry."

"Yeah. Sure."

"I don't mean to...to—"

"Tease?"

Her cheeks turned pink. "I just...forget good sense when you...when you kiss me."

Well, that was something. It just wasn't enough. Why was not making love with him good sense? Why—

A shrill whistle split the air, making her stiffen guiltily, making them both turn toward the open front door. Outside Josh could see a familiar paint—Jordan's—and the head of a second horse, no doubt ridden by the cute little girlfriend. He pushed away from the door frame and headed in that direction. "Why don't you wait in the bedr—in back?" he suggested, and she nodded, then fled.

He walked out onto the porch, stopping at the top of the steps. "Hey, Jordan. I figured you'd be in town catching up with old friends."

"Keely wanted to do some riding. She hasn't been able to since she was home in Virginia over the summer."

Josh shifted his gaze to the girl. She was very pretty, very sophisticated, very feminine, and she had Jordan wrapped around her little finger. Her name was Keely Rayescroft—how could you trust a woman with a name like that?—and she'd grown up in Washington, London and Paris, thanks to her father's State Department job. Why she was going to college at Oklahoma State instead of Radcliffe, Brown or Yale was anybody's guess. Jordan clearly didn't care why. He just considered himself very lucky to be the center of her attention.

"Hey, Keely."

She gave him a warm, eyes-only-for-him sort of smile and said, "Hello, Josh," in the same sort of voice. Though most of his nephew's friends called him by his first name, most of them didn't make him feel a little creepy when they did it. Maybe it was because she'd been raised a diplomat's daughter and was too polished and...well, diplomatic for a girl her age. It could be because she intended to go into politics, and God knows, thanks to his old man, he didn't think any too highly of politicians. Or maybe it was because he suspected she was the biggest phony he'd ever met. Whatever the reason, he didn't like her, and he was pretty sure she felt the same about him.

"You goin' to the Halloween party tonight?" Jordan asked.

Every year on the Saturday before Halloween, Hickory Bluff had a town party, with all ghouls invited. In good weather, three blocks on Main Street were shut down to traffic and the celebration took place there. Bad weather moved it into the high school gymnasium—and tonight's forecast was calling for bad weather.

"Have I ever missed one?"

"You dressing up?"

Josh gave him a dry look. "Do I ever?"

"You're turning into an old man, Uncle Josh." Jordan gave a mournful shake of his head, then changed the subject. "You got company? I thought I saw someone else inside when we first rode up."

"Yeah. I've got company."

Jordan grinned. "A woman? Can we meet her?"

"'Fraid not. She's got a thing for younger men. I don't want to tempt her with you."

Keely reached across to clasp Jordan's hand. "Jordan's temptation-proof when I'm around, aren't you, Jordy?" she asked sweetly.

*Jordy?* Give him a freakin' break. And his nephew didn't even have the sense to look embarrassed. He just grinned at her like some lovesick sap. Feeling particularly annoyed, Josh leaned against one of the posts that supported the roof. "Aw, anyone can be tempted, darlin'," he said in an exaggerated drawl. "You just have to give 'im a good enough reason."

Though Keely's smile didn't waver, confirmation of her feelings for Josh passed through her cold blue eyes. "We should go back now, Jordan. I don't want to spend too much time in the saddle or I'll be too sore to enjoy the party tonight."

Josh had a pretty good idea how she intended to enjoy it—making snide little insults cloaked as innocent remarks, skillfully and subtly putting down anyone who threatened to take Jordan's attention from her, and developing an urgent need to leave long before the celebration was over.

Thank God he'd never been that young and gullible—or, if he had been, at least he'd never met the woman who could capitalize on it.

Though he knew at least one woman he would probably let succeed, if she would just try.

He waited until they were well out of earshot, then went back inside. "You can come out now."

Mere seconds later Candace appeared in the kitchen. "You should be ashamed of yourself—telling that boy I have a thing for younger men."

"Hey, I'm younger, remember? And you've got a thing for me. Sort of. Except when it comes to sex. Why is that, Candace? Why won't you let me make love to you?"

It was odd, Candace thought, how the same words that brought her desire back to life so quickly could also stir up a whirl of apprehension and fear. They made her want to take him to the bedroom, to seduce and be seduced, and at the same time she wanted to run outside and all the way home, to lock herself inside the RV and drive away.

Of course, she did neither. "Josh—"

Holding up one hand palm out, he scowled at her. "You can stop there. If you were going to say anything I wanted to hear, you would have started with sweetheart or darlin' or something. Not 'Josh....'" He mimicked her tone, though she was certain she hadn't sounded nearly so…whatever.

"I'm not an endearments sort of person," she said apologetically.

"No endearments. No sex. No physical anything except a few kisses."

She moved farther into the living room, stopping when only the sofa separated them. His hands rested on the back, clenched so tightly on the fabric that his knuckles had turned white. She wished she could uncurl them and hold them tightly in her own hands, but at the moment, touching him didn't seem wise.

"Josh," she began gently, "we both knew from the start that there was no future to a relationship between us. I'll be going home before long. Your family hates me. We have to see each other in secret. Just now I had to go hide in the bathroom so your nephew wouldn't see me. Being friends in these circumstances is tough enough. Being anything more is too big a risk, especially when there's no future to it."

And there was the other no-future, no-win possibility. A year ago her body had betrayed her and done its best to destroy her. There had been times in the months since that she'd honestly thought dying must be the better choice. She'd survived once, but now she was at a higher risk of having to go through the whole miserable ordeal again, and the second time, she knew from her research, was usually harder, psychologically if not physically. There was no future—especially for him—in that, either.

That was assuming he was still interested after she told him everything—an awful big assumption. He might decide he was better off without her. He might find the idea of being intimate with her repulsive. He might damage her confidence beyond repair.

She couldn't risk it.

"Let me get this straight," he said. "Someday you're going to leave here, but until then it's okay for you to spend all this time with me and kiss me and make out with me, as long as you stop short of having sex with me. That way you won't miss me so much when you're gone. Is that it? Did I get it right?"

Unable to meet his dark gaze, she shrugged. He could sound as sarcastic as he wanted, but it made sense. As long as they weren't having sex, they could be just friends, and friends didn't break your heart when they weren't around any longer. Oh, sure, you missed them, but you got over it. Whereas absent lovers…

She feared Josh might be the one lover she would never get over.

"You're wrong, Candace." His conviction was so strong his voice practically hummed with it. "Either you're as insincere and full of bull as Natalie says, or you're dead wrong."

Her theory *did* make perfect sense…*in theory*. In practice, though, she was afraid she *was* wrong. In her weeks in Hickory Bluff, she'd come to know him better than any other man in her life, and he knew her better than every other man. If she followed her panicked instincts and drove away right now without a look back, his absence would create a huge emptiness inside her. Regardless of whether she had sex with him, that fact wasn't going to change.

She tried to smile to ease the tension but knew she didn't pull it off. "So…you've been talking to Natalie about me." Flippantly she tossed the question he'd asked her last week back at him. "Did you learn anything new?"

"Yeah. She said you were arrogant, ambitious, greedy, self-absorbed and manipulative."

Though it felt as if something were crushing her chest, Candace managed a smile anyway. "Natalie always was great at detailed descriptions."

"She also said she loved you and you broke her heart."

That hurt even more than the insults. It propelled Candace to the screen door, then out onto the porch in an effort to expend some of the energy that she thought just might burst inside her.

Josh followed. "You don't deny that."

"No." Jerkily she turned to face him. "I wasn't a good person back then. I haven't tried to hide that from anyone. But I *have* tried to change."

"Natalie says people like you can't change. She says

even if you could, it wouldn't matter because she could never trust you. She wouldn't want to.''

Candace reached the end of the porch and, hugging her arms to her chest, she stared off into the woods. Sometimes in her worst moments, she'd fantasized about a clearing so deep in the forest that no one could find her, where she could live in utter isolation. With no human contact, there would be no one she could hurt, and no one who could hurt her. There she could live out the rest of her life with whatever peace she could find within herself, whether it was a few years or decades.

Was it really living, though, when she was all alone? Or just surviving?

She knew by the creak of the floorboards that he had come closer, but she didn't face him. ''And what do you say, Josh? I know you think I'm worth sleeping with, but what about the other? Do I deserve Natalie's forgiveness? Am I worth a second chance?''

A particularly loud board right behind her alerted her to his movement, but not in time for her to evade when he grabbed her arm and pulled her around to face him. His brown eyes were hard, glittering like ice, and a muscle in his jaw throbbed with the control necessary to restrain his anger. ''I think you're worth 'sleeping with'?'' he repeated harshly. ''I like kissing you, I like holding you and spending time with you, and yes, God forgive me for being such a selfish bastard, but being around you arouses me. I want to make love with you. I want to…to physically express what I feel for you. Is there something wrong with that? Isn't that what men and women do when they—when they care for each other? Or do people do things differently in Georgia?''

She grabbed hold of the annoyance stirred up by his snide tone on that last question and used it to keep her voice cool and steady. ''I imagine you would know more about what people do than I. After all, unlike you, I haven't slept with every single person who would give me a tumble.''

Hurt flashed through his eyes, and he abruptly released her arm and took a step back. After searching her face as if he could find an explanation there, he shook his head, then softened his voice. ''What are you afraid of, Candace? Getting hurt? That doesn't have to happen.''

''I'm leaving soon to return to Georgia,'' she said through clenched teeth.

''But you don't have to go.''

''It's my home.''

''It's where you live, but it's not a home. What's back there for you?''

Candace's eyes were stinging with tears determined to fall, her throat was so tight she could hardly swallow, and she was terribly afraid she was on the verge of complete emotional meltdown for the first time in her life. That— and the need to escape so it could happen in private—was the reason she looked him in the eye and coldly, mercilessly, answered his question.

''The same thing that's here for me. Nothing.''

He backed off another step and stared at her. Twice he opened his mouth, but no words came out. When he did manage to spit out a brief statement—a curse—it was vulgar and coarse with loathing. Then he turned on his heel and stalked away.

A tear slid down her cheek as she watched him go. Angrily dashing it away, she turned to face the woods again as a second tear escaped, then a third. She heard his pickup door slam, the engine turn over, then the sound of tires spinning on dirt. An instant later he was gone and she was alone. At his house. Miles from her own home.

And it was one damnably blue place to be.

## Chapter Nine

He was one sorry bastard.

It was barely seven o'clock on a rainy Saturday evening, and Josh had already managed to piss off Candace, whom he'd left alone at his house with no way to get home; Cal, whom he'd finally thought to call and ask to give her a ride; Tate and Lucinda, neither of whom had been happy to find him on his way to oblivion before the sun had gone down, particularly on an evening when he had family obligations; Natalie, Jordan and J.T., whose Halloween celebration he was missing....

Was there anyone else important to him that he hadn't yet ticked off? His grandmother, but she was a hundred miles away. Besides, Grandpop was always mad enough at him for two or three people.

Yep, he'd covered all the bases.

Instead of attending the annual Halloween celebration, he sat alone in a booth at Frenchy's, his mood as dark as the walls around him. It seemed he'd drunk a hell of a lot, but it hadn't been enough. He could still remember…still feel…and he felt terrible.

The crowd was average for a Saturday night, and the noise had leveled out just under earsplitting. It drowned out the sounds of the storm outside, but from time to time lightning flashed while the door was open, and the thunder vibrated right up from the ground. He neither knew nor cared if a tornado warning accompanied the storm. Short of a storm cellar, Frenchy's was probably the safest place in town to be in a tornado.

While a motor home was a pretty lousy place to be. A good strong wind gust could turn that sucker on its side. A couple of them could probably roll it into the water. Not that it was any of his concern. She'd made that painfully clear.

He'd hoped Cal would drop by the bar—because he was a pretty good drinking buddy, he insisted. *Not* because he wanted to be certain Cal wasn't still with Candace. *Not* because he'd neglected to ask Candace if her no-sex rule applied to all men around here or if he was the only lucky guy—because she liked him so much, of course. Well, she had a damn funny way of showing it.

"Hey, Josh."

He blinked twice, then stared at the girl who'd just sat down opposite him. "What the hell are you doing here?" he demanded. "You're too young to be drinking."

Michaela Scott held up her can so he could see the soft-drink name. "I figured you'd be at the Halloween party."

"I didn't want to go." He scowled and repeated his question. "What are you doing here?"

"I'm kind of on a date. Dinner at the Dairy Delight, drinks here." She grimaced, then shrugged—her opinion, presumably, of both the date and the idiot who'd planned it.

He blinked again. "When did you start dating?"

"I'm twenty years old," she said dryly. "I've been out a few times."

"So where is this guy?" Maybe he needed to have a talk with the kid, like any good almost-uncle, and warn him to behave. No doubt her father had already done that, though, and probably her granddad, too. Besides, who was he to be giving warnings? In his younger days he'd always been the one fathers did their talking to.

"He's losing this week's paycheck to Dudley Barnes over at the pool table."

"Dudley?" Josh practically choked on his whiskey. "Jeez, he must be the worst player in the county."

"I could beat him one-handed, but he doesn't play girls," she said disdainfully.

Yeah, he only played *with* them. Josh knew the type. Maybe he would have a word with him, after all.

"So why aren't you at the party?"

"I'd rather start my quantum physics paper over from scratch than spend one more minute in the company of Kee—" Abruptly she broke off and blushed. "Anyway, Todd wanted to come here, and I..."

"And you *really* wanted to work on the quantum physics paper."

Her only response was a half smile and a quirk of one arched brow.

"How's college?" he asked.

"It's fine. How's Miss Martin?"

"I imagine she's fine, too. For the past week or two, she's been fine with someone else."

"If regrets are in order, I'm sorry." Michaela wrinkled her nose as if regretting the formality of her statement, then curiously asked, "If you and Miss Martin have broken up, why are you here alone?"

"I'm here because I'm working at getting drunk—and so far failing. And I'm alone because..." The only woman he cared about, the one he wanted, the one who tormented his sleep, had told him he was *nothing* to her.

That had been quite a jolt to the old ego.

To say nothing of the old heart.

He realized Michaela was watching him, her gaze steady and solemn, waiting for him to finish. It would be easy to forget that she'd been like a nephew to him, to confide in her and ask her opinion. She seemed so much more grown-up than he felt, and being a woman—even if just barely—she might be able to explain Candace's reasoning to him.

Then he caught himself. Confiding his woman troubles in *Mike?* She was a kid. He'd changed her diapers and watched her grow up. He damn sure wasn't going to her for advice, no matter how mature she seemed.

He shrugged. "Don't worry about me. My social life's never dull." Rarely smooth, either, at least since Candace had come into it.

For a time they sat in silence, Michaela looking around the bar, Josh looking at her, amazed at how much she'd grown up. She was delicately pretty, and could do so much better than any of the guys in Hickory Bluff—his nephew included. Jordan was a great kid, but when it came to girls, he had a regrettable fondness for phony Barbie doll clones like Shelley Hawkins and Keely Rayescroft. Maybe someday he would open his eyes, see what he could have in Michaela and chuck all the pretty dolls for good...but Josh doubted it.

Or if he did, she wouldn't want him anymore, or would hold his previous women against him or count him as nothing. She would confuse the hell out of him and leave him smarting and wondering why he even cared, and...

Thunder vibrated through the building, near enough and loud enough to startle both him and Michaela. Someone propped open the front door, and gradually the sweet, cool scent of rain drifted in on the heavy air.

"That feels good," Michaela said.

Josh gazed out into the rain. Only a few weeks ago he'd been out in it, helping Candace change a tire and, later, coming damned close to kissing her. Practically ever since, he'd been kissing her a lot…and that was all she wanted. Hell, maybe more than she wanted.

But he'd sure thought differently. Wouldn't his buddies get a kick out of that—Josh Rawlins reading a woman wrong? And wouldn't all the women he'd once dated enjoy knowing that the one he got serious about was the one who didn't feel the same? Who didn't want him at all?

A heavy sigh drew his attention to Michaela again. "I think I'm going to find Todd and see if I can talk him into getting out of here. I really do have a lot of work."

Josh glanced across the room to the pool tables, where two games were going strong. Dudley was obviously winning, though if he ran true to form, he'd blow his earnings on drinks for the house or buy into a game of poker, which he had even less talent for than pool. "Nah, let Dudley bleed him dry. I'm not sticking around. I'll give you a ride."

She leveled her steady, cautious gaze on him. "Are you sober enough to drive?"

The question shamed him. She was like a neph—a niece to him, and a niece shouldn't have to ask that question of the uncle who'd changed her diapers and watched her grow up. "Yes," he said quietly. "I'm sober."

While she went to say goodbye to the idiot who thought leaving her to amuse herself in a trashy bar was an ideal date, Josh settled his tab, then waited by the door. He hoped the kid was caught up in his pool game and didn't decide to prove how stupid he could be, because the last thing Josh wanted tonight was a fight with someone little more than half his age. When he heard raised voices coming from the area of the pool tables, he swore silently, then turned in that direction.

Before he'd taken more than a couple steps, Michaela caught his arm. "Come on, let's go."

He looked over his shoulder as she pulled him out the door and saw Dudley bending some kid over the pool table and…er, educating him on the finer points of something. It was a lesson young Todd wouldn't soon forget. And neither would Josh. Next time he and Dudley played pool, he'd let the big guy win for once.

They ran through the downpour to his truck. Just as they settled inside, another rumble of thunder shook the earth, followed by a crack of lightning that lit up the night. "Damn," Michaela said, shaking her head and sending raindrops flying. "They said this system would move right through, but it doesn't seem to be going anywhere."

Josh gave her a sidelong look, that *damn* echoing in his head. Yep, she'd grown up a lot. Dating, swearing, going to bars…why, before long, she was going to be having sex and everything.

And that was something he couldn't bear to think about.

The drive to the Scott ranch took twice as long as usual, thanks to the rain standing inches deep on the pavement and spilling from overflowing ditches to cover the dirt roads. They talked little—Michaela wasn't a chatter, especially with most males—but when he pulled up to her door and reached to turn off the engine, she smiled politely. "Don't bother getting out. It's just a few feet, so there's no need for you to get wet. Thanks for the ride."

"Anytime."

She started to get out, then hesitated. "Are you okay?"

His breath caught in his chest, and he had to force the grin that usually came so easily. "I'm fine. Honest."

"Okay. Well…good night."

He watched as she ran up the steps and inserted her key in the lock. Abruptly, her father opened the door, stepped back so she could enter, then raised a hand in a friendly wave to Josh.

At the end of the half-mile drive, he sat idle for a moment, debating his choices, then headed back toward town. The best thing for him to do was go home, get out of these wet clothes and get something to eat. He knew that as sure as he knew the worst thing he could do, but he didn't turn around.

He drove to the campground, cursing himself every mile of the way. Just before the road rounded a curve and the RV became visible, he switched off the truck's headlights, took the curve and came to a sudden stop.

The RV looked fine, and so did the convertible parked next to it. So did Cal's pickup, parked next to that.

Aching way down inside, he backed around the curve, turned around and headed back the way he'd come. At the highway he turned the headlights back on, and he went home.

Saturday afternoon and Sunday—and the storm that just hadn't given up—had lasted at least a week or more, by Candace's calculations. She'd been so lonely and miserable that she was sure the clock moved backward twice for every time it ticked forward. Thankfully the storm ended just before dawn on Monday, and the sky had turned a clear, peaceful blue. She was more grateful than she could say to get out of the RV and go someplace.

The only problem was, until her shift at work started at noon, there was no place to go, no one to visit, nothing to do. Oh, she could stock up on groceries, like that was a big thrill. Or she could go by the library, as if she hadn't already examined virtually every book in the small, one-room structure. Maybe she could drop by U-Want-It and chat with Martha without looking too pathetic.

Or maybe she could drive out to the Rawlins ranch and let both Natalie and Josh throw her off their property.

She stepped outside to gauge the temperature, then

grabbed a jacket and her purse. She wasn't sure where she was going—just that she was.

She'd made it to her car and was unlocking the door when a faint noise sounded in the woods behind her. Turning, she scanned the area, but saw nothing out of place—a lot of trees, bushes, sandstone, soggy brown leaves carpeting the ground, some limbs broken in the storm. Once more she started to go, but once more she heard the noise, a distinct whimper.

Apprehension tickled down her spine. Being a woman on her own, she knew better than to give in to fear, or it would rule her life. But there was definitely something—or someone?—hidden over there in the woods, and she was all by herself with nothing more deadly than her handbag for a weapon.

"Hello? Is someone there?"

When no response came, she laid her purse on the car seat—sorry, but she wasn't using a four-hundred-dollar indulgence to slug some dirty creature—and took a few halting steps toward the tree line. When she got closer, she could hear rapid breathing, followed by a whine—most definitely a canine whine.

Breathing a great sigh of relief, she picked out the clump of bushes from which the whine had come. "Hey, puppy," she called, crouching a fair distance back. "Come here, sweetie. Come on."

For a moment there was no response, then the bushes rustled and the most pathetic, bedraggled four-legged creature she'd ever seen crept out into the open. Eyes wide and wary, the dog came to her, one step forward, two steps back, until finally he was crouched just out of arm's reach.

"Well," she remarked as they studied each other. "You haven't had an easy time of it, have you, puppy? You're wet, hungry, dirty, scared and all by yourself. Gee, why do I relate?"

Slowly she got to her feet, then backed away from the

dog. Returning to the motor home, she unlocked the door, went in and grabbed a bag of sliced ham from the refrigerator, then took a seat on the steps. The dog was still watching her alertly. It took a few minutes to coax him closer, a few more to persuade him to come up and take the meat from her. Once he'd decided he could trust her that far, he scarfed down a half pound of ham in practically seconds, then turned around and vomited it all up again.

The look he gave her was so woeful that she half laughed, half cried. "Oh, puppy, I can *so* relate. It's hell when you're hungry but can't keep anything down, isn't it? Believe me, I understand. But we'll take care of that."

And that was how she found herself driving the most pathetic, bedraggled four-legged creature she'd ever seen to the local vet.

In the next hour that passed, they waited, then the puppy was poked, prodded, given shots and thoroughly examined. Now he sat on the exam table, leaning against Candace as if she were his mama.

"Are you going to keep him?" The vet, a slender black woman with long hair and the rather musical name of Nicolette Dorsett, looked up, her pen poised over the dog's chart.

Keep him? He was just a puppy, and she lived in a motor home. She had a job and would have to leave him alone half of every day. Puppies chewed, didn't they? And needed housebreaking and regular checkups and cuddling and obedience training. They were a commitment—not just days, but years.

She didn't have the right to make a commitment that ran into years.

"If you want him, our groomer would be happy to clean him up for you. If you don't, we can try to find a home for him," Nicolette said, "but I doubt we'll have much luck. Folks around here get more than their share of unwanted pets dumped on them."

Candace bit her lip. Whether she took him or someone else did, he was in dire need of grooming. And who knew? Once all that dirt was washed off—and all those ticks were picked off—there might be a good-looking animal under there. Probably not, but she was nothing if not optimistic.

"Go ahead and turn him over to the groomer," she said at last, "and I'll...I'll decide by the time he's done."

She wandered outside, stared up at the sky for a time, then took her cell phone from her purse. The number she dialed was stored in memory, for months the number she'd called most frequently. She went through voice mail, then a receptionist and a nurse before finally reaching her target. "Hey, Doc, it's Candace Thompson. How are you?"

"That's supposed to be my question."

"I'm fine."

"Glad to hear it. Me, too. Next question—*where* are you?"

"Oklahoma."

"Still marking goals off that list?"

"Yep."

"Coming back soon?"

A lump appeared in her throat at the thought of how dearly she would like to answer no to that question. But how could she not go home? There was no place else for her to go, no place else where she was wanted. "Of course I'm coming back. It's home, isn't it?" No matter what Josh insisted. "Hey, I've got a question for you. I found a puppy today that apparently no one wants. Should I take him?"

"That's why you called? Jeez, I don't know, Candace." He sounded perplexed. "Do you like dogs?"

"I don't really know. I've never had one. But he's a cute puppy." Honesty forced her to amend that. "Well, he's so ugly he's cute. He's a mixed breed and, no kidding, his feet are bigger than mine."

"If you like him, then take him."

"But…he's a baby. Puppies can live a long time—eight, twelve, fifteen years."

"Ah. And you're afraid you won't." There was a moment's silence, filled only by the sound of his pen tapping on his desk, a habit he indulged whenever he was thinking. When the pen stopped, he said, "Take the puppy, Candace. Enjoy him. Grow old with him."

A lump formed in her throat, and her eyes teared up. "Really?"

"Really. Have fun with him. Teach him to fetch your slippers—or, better, not to eat your house."

"Thanks, Doc. I'll see you when my next checkup comes around." She disconnected the call, returned the cell phone to her purse, then took a couple of long, deep breaths. Could she do this? Could she commit to the responsibilities that came with the puppy? Could she do the dog justice?

It wasn't rocket science, she thought with a rueful smile. *Anyone* could be a good dog mama—a three-year-old kid or a ninety-year-old granny, rich or poor, educated or not, living alone or part of a large family. There was nothing to it—teach him to do his business outside, feed him a few times a day, don't let him run wild and scratch his tummy when he needed it. She could handle that.

And if she could succeed at this commitment, who knew what else she might do?

Josh wasn't having one of his better days when he parked in front of U-Want-It Monday morning. The weekend's thirty straight hours of rain had turned the ranch into one huge mud pit, and around 2:00 a.m. a tree limb had come down on and partly through the roof right above his bedroom, startling him so badly that he'd fallen off the sofa where he'd gone to asleep.

Then, on his way to Tate's to get supplies for a temporary fix, his pickup had gotten stuck in the pasture, leaving him to slog his way to the barn, then return with the tractor to pull it loose. On his way back to Tate's after patching the roof, he'd run into a half dozen of their neighbor's buffalo, made antsy by the storm and far enough from home to mean they'd gone through at least three fences. He'd roused Tate, who'd roused ol' Vern, and while they were trying to round up the scruffy beasts, one of them had tried to go through *him*. He'd gotten out of its way in time, but he had the aches to show for his quick escape.

Thanks to Candace, he had more aches than he'd ever known.

He'd done little but think about her—miss her, hurt for her and because of her, and damn her and Cal both to hell—for the past forty-eight hours, but he still didn't have a clue what to do. The wise thing, he suspected, was to keep his distance, stay away from the store when she was working and from the campground and Frenchy's and anyplace else he might run into her. Soon enough, she would tire of waiting for Natalie's attention or forgiveness or whatever the hell she wanted from her, and she would go back to Georgia, and he would be that much farther along on the path to forgetting her.

Yeah, like that was ever gonna happen.

The next wisest course would be to settle. Settle for whatever she was willing to give him, for being friends with her, for a few kisses and embraces, and accept that there could never be anything more because she didn't want anything more from him. And while he was at it, why not train his horse to kick him in the head every hour or so? It couldn't be any more painful.

Or he could try to change her mind. Apologize for Saturday morning, take her flowers or chocolate or some sort of gift, maybe invite her someplace for a long weekend and do his damnedest to seduce her. Even though he knew she didn't want to be seduced.

Hell, he didn't know *what* to do.

That was why he'd changed his planned afternoon trip

into town to this morning. He had to buy shingles, roofing felt and everything else necessary to fix his roof, and Lucinda had asked him to stop by Martha's. He'd wanted to say no, but that just wasn't done. As far out as they lived, no one made a trip into town without offering to make whatever stops were necessary. Besides, if he had tried to refuse, his mom, as well as Tate and Natalie, would want to know why, and he would have no reason to give them.

So he'd said sure, okay, he would be happy to pick up thread to match the fabric swatches in his pocket, and then he'd left three hours earlier than he'd originally planned. Better to deal with Martha than with Candace, especially when he didn't know *how* to deal with Candace.

When he walked in the front door, the University of Oklahoma fight song was thankfully silent. "What's up?" he asked Martha, who was sitting on a stool behind the counter. "You mourning the Sooners' loss this weekend?"

"They wuz robbed," she said emphatically. "Unlike your Cowboys, who oh, so politely handed a win to Kansas."

"And your Sooners who…oh, yeah, fought, kicked and screamed and *still* lost thirty-six to six."

"At least we scored," she pointed out as she petted the animal in front of her. Josh looked, then did a double take.

Sitting on the counter as if it was the most natural thing in the world was the ugliest mutt he'd ever seen. The dog's coat was black and brown, coarse and thin in places, his skin was too big for his body, and the white and red bandanna tied around his neck—some sort of badge of courage given those who survived the groomer at the vet's clinic—was just plain undignified. "That's one pitiful lookin' animal. Man, look at those feet. They're as big as my horse's."

"Give him a year or so, and *he* might be as big as your horse."

Josh reached out to touch one of the massive paws, and

the dog lifted it and laid it in his hand. "Friendly, huh? Now I know this isn't your dog, Martha. George would never let this guy come around his purebred coonhounds."

"No, he's not mine. He belongs to—"

Before she could finish, the mutt's owner came up from the rear of the store, a half dozen collars in her hands. She stopped short when she saw him, a wary look in her eyes, then continued as if he were just any customer.

It hurt to know that in her opinion, apparently, he was.

She looked beautiful, of course. He doubted she could pull off anything less no matter how she tried. Her jeans were faded and worn to the point where they were as comfortable as a second skin, and her plain white T-shirt was tucked in, the sleeves neatly cuffed. It was about as simple as an outfit could get, but on her it looked incredible.

She stopped with as much distance between them as she could manage without making it obvious to Martha that she didn't want to come closer. That hurt, too, but damned if he was going to back away because she couldn't bring herself to get within touching range.

"What do you think, puppy?" she asked, holding the collars out for the mutt's inspection. He sniffed them, decided they weren't one of the major food groups, and disinterestedly started scratching himself.

She laid down all but one collar and tried to fasten it around his neck, but it was way too big. She adjusted it, put it back on, adjusted it again, then frowned.

"You need a choke chain," Josh said at last.

She didn't look at him. "I don't want to *choke* him."

"It only chokes when you pull on it. Besides, none of those are going to fit him."

Acting as if she hadn't heard him, she tried one more and was reaching for a third when Martha said, "He's right, hon. Those are all the same size—too big. Besides, even if they did come close to fitting, he could wiggle right out of 'em. I'd recommend a chain, too. Let me see if we've got one in his size.''

Once she left the stool, Candace went behind the counter and cupped the puppy's face in her hands, scratching under his jaw and behind his ears. The dog's tail beat a rapid rhythm on the cash register, underscored by soft grunts of pleasure.

I know how you feel, buddy, Josh thought. If she would get that close to *him* and touch him, rub him, scratch him, anywhere, he'd be vocal about enjoying it, too.

None too proud that he was feeling jealous of a stray dog, he cleared his throat and said the first words that came to mind. "I'm sorry about Saturday."

For an instant she stopped petting the dog until he nudged her hand with his nose. Her gaze locked on the animal, she absently started again. "You have nothing to apologize for."

He wasn't sure of that, though at least he'd done nothing to deliberately hurt her. She couldn't say the same. It didn't matter, though. He wasn't smart enough or strong enough to keep his distance from her, and he wasn't wild about settling for whatever she would give him or trying to seduce her against her will. But he knew one thing for sure—he couldn't just walk away.

The dog turned toward him, sniffing him all over, and Josh raised one hand to scratch him and keep him away from the edge of the counter. "I've missed you."

Her gaze darted up from the mutt, then down again. "Nothing's changed, Josh."

Meaning she still didn't want to make love with him. Maybe it wouldn't be so bad if he knew why. She wasn't a virgin—she'd told him her first time had been regrettable and forgettable. Maybe she'd called a halt to sex outside marriage. Maybe she had some serious hangups about sex, or suffered from some sort of sexually transmitted disease that prevented her from indulging.

Or maybe he just wasn't her type. Forget that he wanted her more every time he saw her. Maybe she just didn't feel the same. No sparks, no hunger, no lust, no need. Maybe the only guy around here she felt that way about was Cal.

That was too painful an idea to bear.

"Tell me you haven't missed having me around the past couple days."

Finally she met his gaze head-on. "So what if I have? What difference does it make? My time here is still limited. Your family still hates me. And I'm still not interested in a sexual relationship."

"Is that a sexual relationship, period, or a sexual relationship with *me?*" When she didn't answer immediately, he recklessly went on. "You can tell me, Candace. Is it just me you don't want to sleep with? Are you open to other guys, like…oh, I don't know—maybe Cal?"

Her cheeks reddened with anger, not a blush, and her blue eyes turned cold. "I told you before—I have no intention of sleeping with him."

"Or me, either."

"I don't want a sexual relationship with anyone. Period." Her expression was defiant, her mouth set in a stubborn line, and her manner was prickly. It was about as clear a statement as he could ask for, but…

"I don't believe you," he said stubbornly.

"And what do you know about it?"

"Hey, darlin', that's me you've been kissing the past couple weeks. I know a hell of a lot about it." He took a taut breath, then softened his voice. "I know you're afraid, and I wish to God you'd tell me why so I can help you deal with it."

She started to answer, but Martha's return delayed her. The older woman looked from him to Candace, then back again, curiosity bright in her eyes. "That looked like one intense conversation I interrupted."

"Not at all," Josh replied, his gaze on Candace. "I was just asking her what she planned to name the mutt."

"He's not a mutt," Candace said, her tone flat, her defense automatic.

"Yeah, right. He's got so many different breeds in him, I bet Nicolette couldn't identify even one of them."

"You're wrong. He's part German shepherd."

His chuckle sounded unnaturally forced. And why the hell not? He wasn't in a laughing mood. "Yeah, part shepherd, part horse. Did she tell you how big this dog is going to get? He's gonna outweigh you before his first birthday."

"He *is* going to be a big boy," Martha said as she formed a loop in the chain she carried, then slid it over the puppy's neck and checked its fit. "But that's probably a good thing for a woman who lives and travels alone. He'll keep you company and make critters of the two-legged variety think twice before bothering you." Running her finger between the chain and the dog's neck, she asked, "What do you think, Josh? Should we go up one size?"

"First rule—no bandanna without a cool pair of shades to go with it." He pulled the fabric over the dog's head and tossed it on the counter, then checked the chain. "That should be okay for a few months. If you get it too big, he can get it caught on something and choke himself."

"So what *are* you gonna name him?" Martha asked.

Candace pursed her lips for a moment as she studied the pooch, then she smiled smugly. "He kind of looks like a Josh, doesn't he?"

Martha laughed. Josh smiled. "So from now on, you'll be spending your nights snuggled close to my namesake."

"Actually, I think he looks more like a Luther," Candace announced. "What do you think, puppy? You want to be Luther?"

He stood up, placed his monster front paws on her shoulders and licked her jaw.

"Okay, Luther it is."

With a shake of her head and a roll of her eyes, Martha nudged Josh with an elbow in the ribs. "Hey, I heard you got a rude awakening in the middle of the night. Vern says the roof fell in on your bed."

"Yeah. It's a good thing I was sleeping elsewhere at the time." He gave Martha a wink and a grin, and was rewarded by the twitching of a muscle in Candace's jaw. Part of him—the macho male that was alive and well inside every man—hoped she was wondering where he was and with whom, and regretting that he hadn't been with her. The responsible adult part, though, hoped she knew it would take a hell of a lot more than one argument to make him turn to someone else.

Yeah, just like he'd had so much faith in her.

"Hmm, that sounds intriguing," Martha said. "I'd ask where you were, but I know you're too much a gentleman to kiss and tell." Then she added hopefully, "Aren't you?"

"Yes, ma'am." He grinned again. "My lips are sealed."

## *Chapter Ten*

Dear Natalie, I know my showing up here has been something of a shock. Please believe me when I say I don't want to cause you any pain, or bring back bad memories, though I'm afraid that's probably already happened. I certainly don't want to disrupt the life you've made for yourself. I just want...

Candace reread *The Letter*, then sighed, put down the pen and crumpled it. *I, I, I*—that seemed all she was able to say. She wasn't the important one here. She was the bad guy, not the victim, and yet she was certainly making it about her.

When she sighed again, Luther, curled up on the couch, opened one eye to look at her. "I thought we came to an agreement about you and the furniture," she remarked. It was nice, hearing the sound of her own voice and knowing someone else was hearing it, too. Granted, Luther wasn't

' much of a conversationalist, but at least he pretended to listen—though he then did what he wanted, anyway.

She slid to her feet and crossed the short distance to the kitchen. In honor of Luther's arrival in her life, she was splurging on dinner—no sandwiches or canned soup, but an honest-to-goodness real meal of a chicken, mushroom and wild rice casserole. It wasn't often she bothered to cook for just one, but hey, if she had any leftovers, she was sure Luther would do them justice. So far, he'd eaten his puppy food, a piece of toast she'd absentmindedly turned her back on, a few pages from a magazine and the rubber soles of her house slippers.

"But that's our secret, right, puppy?" she reminded him as she pulled the throwaway casserole pan from the oven. "Martha warned me about leaving you here alone while I was at work, but I insisted that you'd be fine. So for the record, you *were* fine, okay?"

He lifted his head, sniffed, then jumped to the floor. She would have accepted it as a compliment to her cooking if he hadn't made a beeline for the door with a low growl rumbling in his throat. A moment later a knock sounded, sending him on a fit of barking that sounded much too big and threatening for such a baby.

She peeked around the edge of the curtains, then drew back. It was Josh, no doubt wanting to be friends again, or...or something. She could pretend she wasn't here—as if she had any place to go besides the bar he'd passed on his way here, or any way to get there besides the car parked next to his truck. Or she could politely but firmly tell him through the door that this wasn't a good time.

Or she could grab hold of Luther's collar and open the door and...and *deal* with him. Wasn't that what he'd wanted this morning, when Martha interrupted them? *I know you're afraid, and I wish to God you'd tell me why so I can help you deal with it.*

He knocked again and earned more frenzied barks for

his efforts, so she did the logical thing—the thing she wanted to do. She grabbed hold of Luther's collar and opened the door.

Josh stepped inside and closed the door behind him, then studied her. He wore jeans, boots, a chambray shirt and a brown leather jacket, and his brown hair was windblown, and just the sight of him made her knees go weak.

Finally he shrugged out of his jacket and hung it over the back of a chair, then crouched to pet the dog. Looking up at her, he said, "For future reference, if you're thinking about pretending you're not home, you should park your car on the other side of the RV."

"I wasn't—" Dismissing the lie before she finished it, she shrugged. "We were just getting ready to eat. Want to join us?"

"I've already had supper, but I'll sit with you."

She dished up a plate, grabbed two soft drinks from the refrigerator, then returned to her place at the dining table. With a few grunts Luther managed to pull himself onto the bench, then headed for her plate, but she pulled him back. "Hey, we talked about this, too, didn't we?" she scolded. "Your food is in the bowl over there by the sink—or would be if you hadn't inhaled it in one breath. Anything on a plate is *mine.*"

Across from her Josh didn't quite stifle a snort. "You're trying to reason with a puppy."

"And what would you have me do?"

"Tell him no in a firm voice, then put him on the floor."

She looked from him to Luther, then shook her head. "He's just a baby, and he doesn't like firm voices."

"Hey, this baby is going to be about the size of a pony when he grows up. Train him now, while you've got a chance. How'd he do on his first afternoon alone here?"

"He was fine, weren't you, puppy? He and the RV both survived completely intact." Candace ignored the flush warming her face. It wasn't a lie—he and the RV *had* survived. She was under no obligation to mention the house slippers and the magazine that hadn't. Just to be safe, though, she changed the subject. "How was the Halloween party?"

"I didn't go. I wasn't in the mood."

"I thought you'd never missed one."

"Yeah, well, Saturday wasn't one of my better days."

Thanks to her. He didn't say it and nothing in his manner even hinted at it, but she knew she was to blame. "So what did you do?"

He shrugged. "I had a few drinks at Frenchy's, then took a beautiful girl home."

She remembered his comment at the store that he hadn't been in his bed when the limb crashed through. In her heart she *knew* he hadn't spent the night with another woman, but some part of her couldn't help but wonder....

"Her name is Michaela Scott. Her family lives down the road from us, and she and Jordan have been best buds all their lives. She's twenty, which is *way* too young for me, especially since I like older women...you in particular."

Heat slid along Candace's skin. It was such a simple statement, and it made her feel about twenty herself, seriously infatuated and seriously inexperienced.

"Michaela's mother left the family when she was six, and her dad just sort of raised her as a boy. Everybody called her Mike. She grew up knowing nothing about fixing her hair or wearing makeup or any of that girly stuff—but damned if she couldn't fix any engine, rope any steer or castrate any bull around. Then Natalie came and helped turn forgettable Mike into gorgeous Michaela. Unfortunately, too many of the guys around here don't seem to notice the change."

"They will. Give them time." Candace ate the last bite of chicken from her plate, then pushed the leftover rice into a neat mound with her fork. After playing with it for a moment, she looked up. "Are you ever going to ask me about what I did to Natalie?"

He shifted uncomfortably. "Do you want to tell me?"

She considered it a moment, then nodded. "Yes. I do." Then she smiled without mirth. "Don't worry. You'll still be able to give 100 percent of your loyalty and support to her. She was definitely the victim, and I was definitely the villain."

He didn't say anything, and for a moment neither did she. She wasn't even sure why she was doing this. She wanted to be sure he knew every detail? She wanted to show him how brutally honest she could be in contrast to how appallingly *dis*honest she'd once been?

Or did she need to know that he could know and want her anyway?

"I was very ambitious. That ambition got me out of the projects, into college, into a good job. I wanted to be like Natalie's father—one of those rare journalists who has respect and prestige…and fame and fortune, as well. But being the best takes time, and I didn't want to wait. I'd devoted myself to being *somebody* from the time I started first grade, and I was tired of working so damn hard. I wanted some reward. I wanted a shortcut.

"When I went to work in Montgomery, Natalie was already occupying the position I was after. If I wanted to advance, to fulfill my ambition, I had to move her out of my way. So I befriended her. I knew a lot about her. She'd grown up with money, and all the privileges that bought, but emotionally she had been as neglected as I was. She needed a good friend, and I knew how to act the part."

She stared off into the distance, thinking back to that time. "It wasn't all acting. I truly liked Natalie, as much as I was capable of liking anyone. Having a friend was as much a novelty to me as it had been to her, and I really did value her support and companionship and friendship. Just not as much as I valued my career."

Realizing that she was clutching the fork tightly enough to bend it, she forced herself to put it down, then stretched her fingers a couple of times before continuing. "I went to her one day with a story about bribes and corruption in both government and charitable agencies that were supposed to be providing assistance to the poor in Montgomery. I'd already done most of the research, but I told her I was too close to it because of how I'd grown up. I thought it would have more impact if she wrote it. I talked her into it, and she did a three-part series that won one of the more prestigious awards in our industry. The only problem…"

She risked a look at Josh, but his face was impassive. Whatever he was thinking, whatever he was feeling, she couldn't begin to guess. The test would come when she was done. If he got up and walked away without a word to her, then she would know. It might break her heart, but she'd know.

"The only problem was…I falsified most of it. Then *I* broke the story that exposed her for a fraud. She lost everything—her job, her friends, her reputation. Even her father disowned her…but he helped *me* get a job in Atlanta." She shook her head numbly. "I remember thinking, *This is the only friend you've ever had.* But I did it, anyway." She bit her lower lip, then softly repeated, "I did it, anyway."

One long moment crawled past, then another, and still she didn't have a clue what he was thinking. Her nerves were stretched taut, and she was on the verge of demanding some response from him—of pleading for some forgiveness from him—when he exhaled loudly.

"Well…you told me you weren't a good person back then, and you were right. But if this is supposed to scare me off, Candace, it's not gonna work, because you also told me that you'd tried to change, and I believe you have. I don't believe you're that woman anymore."

For an instant she thought she might collapse on the

bench where she sat. He wasn't walking away. He didn't hate her for what she'd done.

Oh, God, she loved him.

Unable to force any words past the lump in her throat, she slid to her feet, then carried her dishes to the sink. After covering the leftovers with foil and sliding them into the refrigerator, she turned...and found Josh standing directly behind her. A nervous smile quavered on her lips. "You move quietly for a big man."

"It's my natural grace," he teased. Hooking his fingers in the waistband of her jeans, he drew her closer. "I've missed you."

"So you said. But you still stayed away."

"I wanted to come back before I even left."

"Then why didn't you?"

He ducked his head to brush his lips along her jaw, and slid his arms around her middle to cradle her against him. "A man's got to have some pride. When a woman tells him he's nothing, he can't just stay around and wait for another kick in the head."

There was no harshness or rancor in his voice, but she felt the ache—and the shame—anyway. Raising her hands to his face, she gently cupped his cheeks. "I am so sorry. I'm not very good at...at caring for someone, and I was upset, and I'm so sorry, Jos—"

Before she could whisper his name, he was kissing her, his tongue thrusting inside her mouth, his hands pulling her closer, harder, against him. His erection was impressive, strong and unyielding against her thigh, and his kiss was persuasive, making her heart flutter and stirring heat and hunger deep inside her. She was dimly aware of Luther trying to force his way between them, barking a time or two, and then she wasn't aware of anything but Josh...wanting him...needing him...aching for him in ways she'd thought she'd forgotten.

He moved until the refrigerator was behind her, giving

the support her trembling muscles couldn't provide, and he moved against her, rubbing, thrusting, sending heated little shocks through her. She tingled every place they touched— between her thighs, her belly, her chest, her mouth. When had his hands slid under her shirt? she wondered dazedly. Not that it mattered. His fingers were warm, his skin callused, and they were sliding up to cup her breasts—

The panic came in a rush, despite her best intentions, and she twisted free, first her mouth, then her body. She didn't try to escape completely, though, but turned her back. He wrapped his arms around her from behind, trapping her snugly between the refrigerator and his body.

It was a sweet place to be.

"Aw, babe, you're killing me here," he murmured in her ear, his voice guttural and unsteady. "I want to make love with you, and I know you want me, too. You can't deny it. Please, sweetheart…"

"Every single woman in this county wants you," she whispered.

"I want *you.*"

"You don't know what you're asking for."

With one hand he forced her chin up and around so he could kiss her again, a hard, greedy demand. His mouth so close to her ear that it made her shiver, he replied, "I know exactly what I'm asking for—you. All of you."

Once more she pulled free and she studied him for a long moment. "Are you sure?" she whispered.

"Honey, I've been sure for days now."

Her hands trembling, she began undoing the buttons that fastened her shirt. She slipped the shirt off and let it fall to the floor, then reached behind her to undo the hooks of her plain white bra. He was watching her with a sweet, amused smile that disappeared the very instant she pulled off her bra.

"Okay," she said, trying to sound challenging but coming off teary instead. "It's your lucky day, Josh. You got

what you wanted—all of me. Or, at least, all of me that the
cancer didn't take. Isn't it a lovely sight?''

She didn't let her gaze slip from his face for one second.
She knew how she looked—she'd seen herself plenty of
times. A lot of smooth, creamy skin, indentations above her
collarbones, one perfectly shaped breast…and one thick-
ened, puckered scar where her right breast was so obviously, so obscenely, missing.

His face turned a few shades paler, and his eyes darkened
with…pity? Revulsion? Withdrawal? She couldn't tell because the tears she was furiously blinking back blinded her.
Then he reached for her, pulled her to him and enveloped
her in his arms, rocking her slightly from side to side. ''Oh,
babe…I'm sorry. I'm so sorry.''

No one was as sorry as she was—sorry she'd come here,
sorry she'd let him get close, sorry she'd wanted him even
closer. Most of all she was sorry that one way or another
he was going to break her heart.

But before he did, she was going to absorb every second
of being in his arm . She was going to imprint the feel and
the smell and the heat of him in her very soul, to savor the
strength of his body, the tenderness of his caresses, the
husky, soothing sound of his voice. She was going to remember this moment and this safe, secure, peaceful feeling
forever.

After a while he cupped her face in his palms and gently
forced her head back so he could see her face. ''Are you
okay?''

Instinctively she knew he meant not right then but in the
grand scheme of things. Was she a survivor, or was her
future destined to be unnaturally short? ''My doctor says I
should live long enough to see Luther grow old.'' She
wiped her eyes with the back of one hand, though none of
the tears that had gathered there had managed to fall. ''I
think the more pertinent question is are *you* okay. With me.
Looking like…like this.''

He grinned his usual cocky grin, but this time, somehow, it was gentler. "Am I okay with you looking beautiful? I think I can handle it. I prefer homely women, you know— they take less attention away from me—but since you *are* gorgeous, I have no choice but to try not to mind."

She frowned at him, or at least tried to.

"Truth is, darlin', I'm not a breast man. My weaknesses are legs…nice hips…a shapely behind…blue eyes…blond hair." He pressed a kiss to the top of her head, then grew serious. "But if you mean am I okay with this…"

His palm rested gently on her chest, covering the scars and the flat nothingness. She'd been touched there before, by doctors, nurses, therapists, even by the sales clerk who'd fitted her prosthesis, but that was all so different. Impersonal, asexual. This was intimate, and it made her breath catch in her lungs and her skin tingle with unbearable heat.

"I'm sorry as hell that you had cancer, Candace. I'm sorry you had to go through all that fear and pain and uncertainty, and I'm sorry you lost your breast, and I wish I could make it all right. But do I still want to make love with you? Absolutely. Do I still think you're beautiful? You bet. Do I still think I'll go crazy if I don't get naked with you? No doubt about it."

Then he kissed her and lifted her hips against his so she could feel for herself that he wasn't all talk. His mouth was hot and greedy, and his arousal was even more impressive than before.

He really did want her, no faking, no fooling. He wasn't repulsed or turned off. He wasn't making a speedy getaway.

Finally two of those tears broke free and rolled down her cheeks.

She freed her mouth from his and for a long time simply stared at him. He stared back, so intense, so solemn.

"Tell me what you want, babe," he murmured.

She stared a moment longer, nerves knotting in her stomach, then whispered, "You. All of you." And like that, the tension inside her disappeared. The fear, the anxiety—all gone, replaced by the warm, quivery sensations of arousal mixed with anticipation mixed with a heady feeling of release.

With a grin he swung her into his arms—swept off her feet, Candace thought, just as Miz Harjo had predicted— and carried her into the bedroom. As soon as he laid her on the bed, though, and followed her down, the grin faded. "You're so beautiful."

For the first time in too long, she *felt* beautiful.

For long lazy moments he kissed her, touched her, giving her a chance, she suspected, to become intimately familiar with his caresses, letting her touch him. Though he was powerfully aroused, he didn't rush her, but before long, she was half wishing he would. Her muscles had gone taut, her nerves quivery, and every stroke of his tongue, every caress of his hands, set off a million tiny explosions throughout her body. Her skin grew damp, her breathing ragged, as she pleaded silently, with her hands and her body and her whimpers, for more.

When she was certain she couldn't bear any more, he slid her jeans and panties down her hips, her legs, off her feet, leaving a trail of hot kisses along her skin. As slowly as he'd eased hers off, he shucked his own clothes in a heartbeat, tossed a couple of plastic-wrapped condoms from his pocket onto the bed, then joined her again—literally. Moving between her legs, probing, sliding inside her, filling her. *Filling* her.

So many times in the past year she had despaired of ever doing this again—had thought she might never have sex again, might never feel pretty or womanly or whole again. Truth was, she couldn't have done exactly this again, because she'd never done it before. Not with a man who mattered.

Not with a man she loved.

He teased her, tormented her, made her plead, and when

she was absolutely certain she was beyond bearing any more, he pleased her. Made her toes curl and her blood hot, made her lungs stop working and her brain stop functioning, made her shatter again and again.

Quivery, shaky, raw and achy, she was more *pleased* than she'd ever been in her life.

The RV's bedroom was about as functional as a room could get—a queen-size bed, a closet on one side and a night table on the other, and a smaller closet in one corner. A lamp on the table created as much shadow as it did light, and the open blinds at the side window let in just enough illumination from the street lamp to cast more shadows.

Not that he really gave a damn where they were, but Josh half wished they were at his house, in his bedroom. Plunked down in the middle of its rust-colored walls, massive pine bed and Southwest-patterned bedding, Candace would look like an exotic little plaything. And he would dearly love to spend…oh, at least the next few years doing nothing but playing with her.

He turned onto his side to look at her. She lay on her back, her head on the pillow next to his, her eyes closed and her breathing finally settled again in a normal rhythm. She looked as if she was peacefully sleeping, but she wasn't.

Slowly his gaze moved from her eyes over her pert little nose to her mouth, the corners twitching occasionally as if she was trying not to smile, across her stubborn jaw and down the long, elegant line of her neck to her chest. Her breast. Her scar.

It wasn't as bad as he might have expected, if he'd ever given a mastectomy scar any thought. He hadn't. If any of the women he knew had had breast cancer, they'd kept it quiet. He thought of it as a disease for people older, more mature, more grown-up, than him. It scared him that he was involved with someone who'd had it.

The scar started under her arm, curved down her side,

then halfway across her chest. But it wasn't what was there that troubled her so much as what wasn't, and he had to admit, it was unsettling to look and see one breast—nicely rounded, smooth, topped with a soft pink nipple—and on the other side, nothing but the scar.

As if she knew he was looking, she rolled onto her side to face him, then folded her arms across her chest. "Did you get your roof fixed?"

"I got a start on it. I've got some guys coming in to-morrow to put in a skylight."

She opened one eye, then both. "A skylight?"

"You've heard the saying, When life gives you lemons, make lemonade? Well, when a storm gives you a hole in your roof, make a skylight."

"It'll be nice for you to lie in bed and see the stars up above." She hesitated, then asked, "Where were you when it happened?"

He'd made a deliberate effort that morning in the store to make her jealous, and the cautious tone in her voice told him he'd succeeded. He grinned his best grin. "I was asleep on the couch, all by my lonesome—and I *was* lonesome without you."

"Good."

Silence settled between them, easy, comfortable. Before it got too comfortable, though, he broke it. "Do you mind talking about it?" He didn't need to define *it*. It had stood between them from the moment they'd met, and was such a momentous thing, he suspected it would always be there, like a dark cloud stalled low in the sky.

"I don't know. I never had anyone to tell." With a shrug she wiggled under the bedspread, tucking it under her arms, then asked, "What do you want to know?"

"Everything."

For a time her gaze was fixed somewhere in the distance, her expression somber, the corners of her mouth turned down. Was she looking for her own definition of *everything,* or just trying to figure out where and how to start?

When she'd found the *how,* she began, her tone conversational. "Most people are average, you know? They work the same kind of jobs as everyone else, make the same kind of money, go to the same schools and churches, take part in the same leisure activities. All my life I wanted to be different—one of the elite few rather than the everyday average masses.

"There's a reason for that saying, Be careful what you wish for. Did you know that only 20 percent of all breast lumps are cancerous, and less than 5 percent of those occur in women under the age of forty?" She made a sound that might have been a chuckle if she'd let it fully form. "I wanted to be one of the few, and damned if I didn't get my wish. Too bad it was the wrong few."

At the foot of the bed, Luther was snoring. Candace's breathing was steady, and his own...hell, he was hardly breathing. His chest was so tight he had difficulty squeezing out his next question. "How did you find out?"

"About a year ago, Eric, the man I was seeing, discovered a lump in my breast. I went to the doctor, had a mammogram and an ultrasound, then a biopsy, and found out it was cancer."

She smiled ruefully. "*Breast* and *cancer* in the same sentence may be the most terrifying words a woman can hear. They certainly scared the devil out of me—literally. One of the first things the doctors asked me about was my support system—spouse, lover, parents, siblings, friends. I had to tell them there was nobody. No one to be with me at the hospital or to understand the answers to questions I could barely ask or to help me when the therapy made me sick. No one to care if I died. That's when I realized that if I survived, I had to do it as a different person."

"What about Eric? Why wasn't he there?"

She laughed softly. "Oh, we weren't dating, not really.

Mostly we were just passing time with each other until one of us got bored or met someone new. I told him I had cancer, and he told me he didn't have time for a personal crisis, especially someone else's. End of affair.''

"Bastard."

"Actually, I understood. If he'd been the one who'd gotten sick, I can't honestly say I would have stuck around, either." She gave him an apologetic look. "I told you, I wasn't a good person then."

That sounded like the Candace Natalie knew. But she'd done such a good job of turning herself around that he still couldn't picture her as the manipulative bitch both she and Natalie agreed she'd been.

"So you had surgery."

"My surgeon recommended a lumpectomy. I insisted on a mastectomy. I felt like I had been betrayed by my own body, and I wanted the breast gone. If I missed it, I could always have it reconstructed later. No problem."

A sudden, shaky breath made her tremble, made him slide his arm around her protectively. "After the surgery, I underwent eight weeks of radiation therapy and six months of chemotherapy. Sometimes I was sick as a dog—" She listened to Luther snore, then laughed softly. "Don't get any ideas, puppy. Most of the time I was so tired I had trouble getting out of bed. I worked as much as I could, because I needed the insurance, but it was tough. A reporter at a smaller paper who knew I had cancer asked me once where someone interested in my job should apply. I believe my response was physically impossible, but I was hoping she would give it a try, anyway.''

Josh couldn't imagine facing a life-threatening ordeal all alone. He'd always had his mother, Tate, Jordan and his grandmother and, in a crisis, he was pretty sure his grandfather would come around. On top of that he had friends, and plenty of them.

And she'd had no one. She looked so fragile, but to get

through the past year all on her own, she must be tougher than he'd ever thought about being.

"I know it sounds silly, but the worst time for me was when my hair fell out. Some women don't lose their hair at all—some don't get sick from the treatment at all—but I did both. I'd just started chemo, and I was throwing up and exhausted and having hot flashes and nausea and taking medicines to try to control it all. Then my hair started falling out—a few strands here, a handful there. By my third treatment, I was bald. The day the last of it came out, I sat down on the floor in the shower and cried until the water ran cold. It was the only time I cried."

She sniffled just talking about it, then grinned. "But it wasn't all bad. I didn't have a bad-hair day for months, and I didn't have to shave my legs, so getting ready for work didn't take as long. And I saved a ton of money not having to get my hair done or my eyebrows waxed."

His mother had long preached looking on the bright side of things, and he figured she knew what she was talking about. She'd loved two men dearly and had been left by both of them, pregnant and on her own. She'd gone through problems with her parents—one out-of-wedlock pregnancy could be explained away as an accident, but two looked more like carelessness or loose morals. She'd raised two boys alone and shouldered most of the responsibility for the ranch until Tate had been old enough to take it over.

She would like any woman who could find the slightest reason to smile about having cancer.

Someday soon he would have to introduce them.

"Eventually I completed my treatment," Candace went on, "and I quit my job. I didn't like the woman I was when it came to work, and there were so many more important things I wanted to do, like walk on the beach or watch the clouds or go to a football game. I didn't want to get to the end of my life, however long that might be, and have no memories to look back on. My doctors recommended that

I wait until I had the reconstructive surgery done because I couldn't afford it on my own. But I couldn't bear the thought of having more surgery right away, of more doctors, hospitals, pain and hassle, and I...I *needed* to start my new life. I didn't know how long it would last. I couldn't wait. Of course—'' she shook her head ruefully ''—I thought the odds of any man besides my doctors seeing me naked were somewhere between slim and none.''

''You thought wrong, darlin'. I've wanted to see you naked since right after we met.'' He cupped her breast through the bedspread, rubbing his thumb over her nipple, making it swell and pucker. The ready response made his voice turn husky and stirred a similar swelling in his groin. ''In fact, I'd really like to see you naked again right now. Right here. On top of me.''

She gave him a narrow look, started to lift the spread away, then shook her head. ''I don't think so.''

She was reluctant to be on display, he guessed. As if he hadn't already looked at her, touched her, kissed her. Catching her hand, he drew it to his erection and molded her small, delicate fingers around him. ''Aw, come on, darlin','' he coaxed. ''I'll make it worth your while.''

''Uh-uh. You come over here.''

In one swift movement, he was leaning over her, shoving the cover away, then bracing his weight on his hands.

''I like a man who holds out for what he wants,'' she teased.

''Either way, babe, I get what I want—me inside you— so I win.'' He shifted to his knees, unrolled a condom into place, then lowered his body to hers again and slowly, slowly filled her. When he'd gone as far as he could, when he felt her body, hot and moist, clenching his, he closed his eyes and focused on the sweet pleasure of it. No doubt about it. This was *exactly* what he wanted.

When Candace awoke Tuesday morning, she felt better rested than she had in months, though it took her drowsy mind a moment to remember why. The shifting of a warm body behind her brought back all the memories from the night before—Josh, getting naked, telling him everything, making love, then doing it again.

Smiling, she shifted beneath the covers to face him…and instead found herself nose to cold, wet nose an instant before a sloppy kiss made her draw back. "Luther!" she exclaimed, not sure whether she was greeting the puppy or scolding him. He bounded up and placed his front paws on her chest, then tried to give her another lick that she dodged by ducking her head under the covers. That was his signal, apparently, to jump into the game with all four feet and mouth. Biting at the lumps she presented under the blanket and barking loudly, he was having a ball until she finally wrestled him down and held him away from her face.

"Where's Josh?"

He answered with an excited bark.

Sliding out from under him and to the floor, she grabbed her robe from its usual spot on the night table, pulled it on and left the bedroom. The water wasn't running in the shower, and the bathroom door was open, showing an empty room. There was no sign of Josh in the living room/ kitchen, either—as if there were someplace for him to hide, she chastised herself.

In fact, if not for the facts that she was naked, deliciously tender between her thighs and relishing the sensation of having been truly and well made love to, there was nothing to suggest that he'd even been there. No, wait—there was his leather jacket, practically out of sight where it had fallen from the chair back where he'd left it. He must have been in some hurry to leave without it.

It was no big deal. Ranchers had to get to work early, and it was already eight o'clock. The storm damage to his house had meant taking time out of his regular schedule, and that had to be made up sometime. He'd needed to get back on that schedule so his family wouldn't suspect he had a few secrets. No big deal.

As hard as she tried to believe that, she was incredibly relieved when she picked up her shirt and bra from the table and found a note underneath.

Hey, babe,
I took Luther out before I left, but he'll probably need to go again soon. Gonna be busy today. Can you meet me at Pepe Chen's for dinner? About six-thirty? Luther found your clothes before I did. Sorry about the teeth marks. J.

Smiling foolishly, she held up the shirt and found dirty smudges, then checked the bra. It was okay, but the prosthesis had a couple of doggie teeth impressions. Fortunately, it was okay, too. She had no desire to go through the fitting for another one.

So Josh was actually going to appear with her in public—and right in downtown Hickory Bluff, no less. She could only assume that the rest of his family didn't like Mexican or Chinese food or figured, as she had when she'd first seen the place, that there were better places to get both.

But it wasn't a date, she counseled herself. That would involve his asking, her accepting, dressing up at least a little, getting picked up here at the house, being brought back afterward and maybe taken to bed.

No, this was just having dinner together. In public. Where anyone could see them. Where word could get back to his family.

It was even *better* than a date.

√Share a romantic interlude.
√Be wicked.
√Have *incredible* sex.

\* \* \*

The interior of Pepe Chen's was just as...er, unusual as its name and menu. Chinese fans shared wall space with sombreros, serapes and giant, faded, crepe paper flowers. A fountain in the center of the dining room held koi, the neon beer signs on the wall were in Spanish, chopsticks were wrapped with forks in the red napkins, and the fake cacti scattered around the room sat in black lacquered pots.

Candace wore blue jeans, starched and pressed, along with a deep purple sweater and Josh's leather jacket, and she sat alone in a booth, a frozen margarita in front of her. Before the cancer she'd been a social drinker, but since then she rarely indulged. Tonight, though, waiting alone in a restaurant filled with couples, groups and families, she felt the need for fortification—also her reason for wearing his jacket.

She had hoped he would call her at work, just to say hello or he missed her or he'd had fun the night before, but he hadn't. He'd said he would be busy...but too busy to take a sixty-second break? She understood heavy workloads. She wouldn't have kept him long.

Oh, Lord, she sounded needy, didn't she? And she'd always been *so* above that.

Sipping her drink, she looked over the menu, divided into Mexican specialties, Chinese and combos that made her stomach a bit queasy. Guacamole, queso and sweet and sour sauce? Or how about a chimichanga with a side of General Tso's chicken?

Six-thirty came and went. Six-forty. Six-forty-five. The teenage waitress stopped by twice to ask if she wanted an appetizer while she waited. By seven o'clock the girl had come by twice more. A few minutes after seven, she returned, looking as if she were the bearer of bad news.

"Are you Candace?"

"Yes, I am."

"We, uh, just got a message for you. Josh can't make it."

For a moment Candace didn't grasp the significance of the words. They'd had a wonderful time last night. He'd made love to her and slept holding her in his arms. He was meeting her for dinner in front of his friends and neighbors. He couldn't cancel like this. He couldn't stand her up.

But he *was*. She knew it in the emptiness suddenly spreading through her. "Is that it? He didn't say anything else?" No explanation? No excuse? He didn't even have the decency to ask to speak to her and blow her off in person?

"He described you, then said, and I quote, tell her I can't make it. And then he hung up. He didn't even say he was sorry or he'd call you. Jerk. You're better off without him. So…you wanna go ahead and order?"

Candace wasn't sure where the smile came from and didn't care. She was just happy it came. "Uh, no. No, thanks. I'll just finish my drink."

But when the girl left, she didn't pick up the heavy glass. Her hands were trembling in her lap, and she had a really sick feeling that wasn't going away.

Okay, so he hadn't shown much finesse in canceling their dinner. There could be a dozen reasons. Maybe he hadn't had enough privacy to hold the phone while the waitress located her. Maybe there were problems at home with the cattle or the skylight or the buffalo or the fence. Maybe something had happened to his mother or his brother, to Natalie or one of his nephews.

Or maybe he'd decided in the bright light of day, when his arousal was satisfied for the time being, that an affair with a one-breasted freak really wasn't his idea of a good time.

The trembling that made her hands unsteady was spreading into her legs and throughout her body. She dug a ten-dollar bill from her purse, slapped it on the tabletop, then

left the restaurant before she burst into tears right there and
scared the little waitress half to death.

The night was cold and helped cool the embarrassed
flush that burned her skin. She crossed the parking lot to
her car, put the top down and turned the heat on high, then
headed south out of Hickory Bluff. Going nowhere in particular, she cranked up the volume on the stereo and sang
along so she wouldn't have to think or worry, so she
wouldn't feel so hurt and ashamed.

So she wouldn't have to face the fact that after making
love with her, after seeing her in all her glory, Josh suddenly couldn't even be bothered to have dinner with her.

Angrily she swiped at a tear. Singing along with the radio
wasn't doing a very good job at stopping her from thinking
or hurting. Instead, she shoved in one of her visualization
tapes. She'd always found the tapes calming, soothing, and
truly believed they'd helped with her recovery.

And this tape helped tonight. By the time she reached
the interstate, then drove all the way back to Hickory Bluff,
she was calmer. Cooler. More angry, less hurt. Angry
enough that when she looked up at the four-way stop sign
just north of town and saw Josh's pickup parked in front
of Frenchy's, she didn't hesitate to pull in beside it.

The bar did good business regardless of the day of the
week, and this Tuesday night was no exception. She
stopped inside the door to look around and found Josh in
a booth halfway to the back. For a moment she remained
where she was, trying to talk herself into leaving. If he was
so put off by her physically that he could stand her up
through a teenaged, braces-wearing waitress, then she
should follow his lead. Forcing him to face her would only
mean more pain for her.

But when she moved, it wasn't out the door. She made
her way around tables and customers, walking with her
head up, her shoulders back, her jaw clenched. Maybe she

was wounded beyond words inside, but damned if she would let it show.

She was only a few feet from his booth when she realized he wasn't alone. Of course he wasn't. Hell, this was Josh, and the trouble with Josh was he liked women, who always liked him back. The woman of his choice tonight was so young she made Candace feel ancient. So pretty Candace felt plain in comparison.

She stopped next to the table and waited. He glanced up, clearly expecting anyone else in the world but her. Stiffness shot through him and an ashamed look came over him. Then he looked away without a word.

She couldn't say one, either. If she could force anything out past the lump in her throat, it would be a sob, and she couldn't let that happen. Instead, she shrugged out of the leather jacket, laid it on the table and walked away.

By the time she got home, she was numb, both inside and out. She went inside the RV, immediately came right back out with Luther, then locked them both inside once he'd done his business. When her stomach got queasy, she ate a sandwich to settle it, then she curled up on the sofa with Luther, a book and another of her imagery tapes. She couldn't read, though, couldn't cry, couldn't concentrate on the tape. All she could see was Josh's shame, and all she could hear was his silence when he'd turned away from her.

She was on the fourth tape when a sharp rap at the door made her jump. "Candace, it's me," he called. "Open the door. I want to talk to you."

As Luther burst into fierce barking and leaped to the floor, she lay motionless, as if—as if what? If she was still enough, he might think she wasn't home? Her car was parked not ten feet from the door. He might think she was asleep? This early? With all the lights on?

"Come on, Candace, please. I'm sorry about tonight. I didn't mean... Come on and open the door."

His words were indistinct, as if he'd had too much to drink. How could he be stupid enough to drink, then drive? It would serve him right if she called the sheriff and they arrested him. In fact, that was what she would do.

She slid from the couch and padded to her purse, on the chair just inside the door, to get her cell phone. When he banged hard on the door right beside her, she gave a start, then clamped her hand over her mouth so he wouldn't hear any noise she might make.

"I know you're upset, Candace, and if you'd just let me…let me explain…please…just…let me…"

For a moment everything went so quiet that she thought he might have passed out. She was seriously considering opening the door when another voice filtered through— softer, sober, very definitely feminine. "She doesn't want to talk to you, Josh. Let's go home."

"But I wanna tell her…"

"You'll have to do it later. Come on. Don't make me call Tate."

Candace tiptoed to the nearest window and peeked out. The girl from the bar was steadying him as they slowly made their way to his pickup. It took a couple of tries on her part as well as Josh's to get him into the passenger seat, then she climbed in behind the wheel and drove away.

After turning off the damned upbeat *Yes-You-Can* imagery tape, Candace curled up on the couch again, cuddled Luther close, buried her face in his coat and wept.

## *Chapter Eleven*

Josh wasn't the most respectable man around, and everyone who knew him agreed he could use some lessons from Tate about behaving responsibly. In fact, not many would argue with the opinion that he was something of a screw-up.

But he'd never screwed up this badly.

He'd hurt Candace. He didn't even need to close his eyes to recall the image of her standing beside the booth there at Frenchy's. The look on her face…the wounded disappointment in her eyes…they'd made him feel lower than a snake in a ditch, and he didn't know what to do about it.

Hell, he didn't know if he *should* do anything about it. Maybe the best thing he could do for her was stay away. Let her meet someone else who wouldn't give a damn what other people thought of her, who wouldn't let a little thing like cancer scare the hell out of him. Let her find someone who could handle the prospect of loving her and maybe losing her in six, eight or ten years, someone willing to take that chance. She'd be happier with some guy like that, and he wanted her to be happy, more than he could say.

He *needed* her to be happy.

God, was that statement true, in both of its forms. He needed for her to be happy, and he needed her in his life to be happy himself. So why was he making them both miserable?

Because he was the biggest, lowest coward ever seen.

"Hey."

Tate's voice through the open pickup window startled him and made him realize that they'd reached their destination—apparently some time ago, because Tate had already stripped off his work shirt, and the smell of wood smoke hung heavy in the air.

"You gonna sit there all day or come out here and help me?" Tate asked.

Josh glanced around and realized they'd were in the southwest section of pasture where he'd bulldozed down about five acres of timber last spring. Some of it he'd cut for firewood, but the rest of the trees he'd dozed into a big pile for burning. Tate had already lit the fire.

He got out of the truck and walked to the rear, where Tate was filling a cup with water from the cooler. "Can I ask you something?"

Tate shrugged.

"Four years ago…if you'd known that something… something was wrong with Natalie and…and that she might not live very long, would you still have married her?"

His brother frowned at him. "What does one have to do with the other? I didn't marry Natalie because she was healthy and destined to live to a ripe old age."

"But you have a reasonable expectation that she *will* live to see old age. What if you didn't? What if she was dying?"

Tate gestured impatiently. "Jeez, where do you come up with stuff like this?"

"You said I could ask."

"Yeah, but I thought you meant about something like how do you choose between two beautiful women when you like sleeping with both of them, or what's the best way to dump someone because she's got kids and you don't want 'em."

He'd thought it would be something selfish and shallow—kind of like Josh himself. Josh wished it was.

Tate sat down on the tailgate and watched the fire for a moment. "We're all going to die, Josh. It's just a question of when. And most of us don't know that. We can't live our lives waiting for them to end."

"Yeah, but..." Josh focused on the fire, too.

Everything had seemed so *possible* Monday night. So Candace had had cancer. So what? She was alive and well, and he loved her, and he was pretty sure she loved him, too. She was strong, and so was he. They would handle it.

All that had been easy when he was in her bed, when she was lying naked in his arms and he was feeling protective and damn lucky to have her and willing to do anything to keep her safe. But practically from the moment he'd driven away, the doubts had set in.

Cancer. *Breast* and *cancer* in the same sentence may be the most terrifying words a woman can hear, she'd told him. Well, they were pretty damn terrifying for a man, too, especially when he'd just fallen in love for the first time in his sorry life. People *died* from cancer. It was a horrible disease, and she'd had it, which meant she was at higher risk for having it again. How the hell was he supposed to *handle* that?

"What's this about?" Tate asked.

Josh imagined answering honestly—*I know we're all supposed to be hating her, but I've fallen in love with Candace Thompson and I want to spend the rest of our lives*

*together, only hers might not be more than a few years,
and how can I do that? How can I make a future with
someone who might not have a future?* Instead, he settled
for asking another question. "Would you have had J.T.? If
you knew Natalie might not be around to help raise him,
that you might be doing it by yourself?"

"None of us has any guarantees, Josh. Okay, yeah, Natalie could die of some awful disease. But I could get kicked
in the head by a bull, or the tractor could roll over on top
of me, or I could just drop dead of a heart attack. Or we
could both live to be a hundred. The fact is, I would have
married her and had J.T. with her even if I'd known beyond
a doubt that she would die the day after he was born. Do
you think not being married to her would make me miss
her any less? Do you think it would hurt any less?"

Probably not, Josh admitted. But Tate was a better man.
He was stronger and more responsible and had already
raised one child to adulthood without help from any woman
but their mother. Josh was pretty sure he couldn't do that.
He was too immature and irresponsible.

He was too scared.

"When she brought you home last night, Michaela said
there was a woman at the bar. Is that what got you thinking
about this?"

Josh nodded dumbly.

"This is someone you've been seeing?"

He nodded again.

"Who is she? Anyone I know?"

Josh shook his head until he realized he was doing it
again—betraying her by denying her. He'd done that long
enough—hell, way more than long enough. "Her name is
Candace Thompson," he said quietly, and felt a rush of
relief at having told the truth at last.

Tate stared at him. "Candace Thomp— The woman who
cost Natalie her job? The one who tried to destroy her reputation and her family and her life?"

"The scheming cold-hearted witch," Josh agreed. "At least, she used to be. Now she's just a nice, sweet woman who's trying to be a better person and to make things right."

"Oh, man." Tate walked away, then swung back around. "Tell me you didn't go and fall in love with the one person Natalie hates most in this world."

Josh thought his best answer was no answer at all. He fully expected his brother to be angry. Wasn't that part of the reason he'd kept his family in the dark from the start about Candace? He couldn't even blame Tate. If he'd ever had an enemy, and Tate had wanted to bring her right into the family…

Josh swallowed hard. That was exactly what he wanted to do—bring Candace into the family. If she was healthy. If she would stick around and not go off and die, damn it, and leave him all alone.

"Damn." Tate dragged his hand through his hair. "You're gonna have to tell Natalie about this yourself. And don't say I didn't warn you, but she's liable to take your head off." He walked over to lever a tree more fully into the fire, then came back. "Is she sick?"

All Josh could do was shrug.

"Is she dying?"

"Not at the moment. But she came close before, and could again."

"From what? Does she have some kind of disease like cancer or—" Staring at him, Tate broke off, then swore quietly.

"Don't tell Natalie that. It's not my place— I shouldn't have—"

"So that's why she's here."

Josh nodded. "She promised herself if she survived, she'd…" He exhaled loudly, then shrugged. "She'd be a better person. That includes apologizing to Natalie."

"If she'd tell Natalie—"

"What?" Josh interrupted. "Nat would feel sorry for her and would listen to whatever she has to say? That wouldn't mean anything to either of them."

"No, probably not." Tate sat down beside him again. "Well, hell, little brother, you've always had a knack for getting yourself into and out of trouble. You're gonna need it this time."

Josh thought of the cowardly way he'd chosen to stand her up the night before, and swallowed a groan. He wasn't the only Rawlins known for having a knack. Tate was known for always being right. This time Josh was afraid he was so damn right, and it was going to hurt so damn bad.

All in all, it hadn't been quite the trip she'd imagined when she'd planned it, Candace thought Thursday afternoon. She hadn't kidded herself. She'd known things with Natalie might not work out—had prepared herself for exactly that outcome. But she'd thought she would make the effort and, win or lose, she would go back to Atlanta in no worse an emotional state than she'd left—better, in fact, for having tried.

Yeah. Right.

She was sitting cross-legged on a quilt in the yellowed grass. It was a snappy fall day, chilly enough to require a jacket, though Luther didn't seem to notice. He was amusing himself as well as Candace, running nose-down through fallen leaves, barking fiercely at shadows until they retreated and chasing the occasional bird that flew nearby. What he would do with it if he caught it, of course, was open for debate. .

She'd gone by U-Want-It a few hours earlier, apologized to Martha and quit her job. She had a call in to the car rental agency in Muskogee to pick up the convertible this afternoon, and she'd notified Patsy Conway that she would be over first thing in the morning to settle up her bill.

She was going home.

Correction: she was going back to Atlanta. It was where she lived, but it wasn't home. No place had ever been as much home as this one—her secondhand motor home, parked in a third-rate campground. Was that pathetic or what?

Before she had to answer that question, the sound of a vehicle approaching distracted her. She called Luther over—she didn't want to find out just now how he might behave around cars—and cradled him in her arms as she watched a car follow the loop of the dirt road around to her space.

The driver let out his passenger—the friendly young man from the car rental agency—and drove off again. Luther bristled for a moment, then tumbled out of Candace's arms and went chasing after a butterfly.

"You picked a pretty place for your visit," the man—Rich, or was it Rick?—said as she stood up. "Did you get a chance to do any fishing?"

It was one of the things she would have liked to try. He'd learned to fish on this lake, Josh had sai— Well, it was something she would have enjoyed at least once. "No. I'm afraid I like my fish in aquariums." Digging the car keys out of her jeans pocket, she held them out.

"Yeah, I have to admit I'm not much on fishing. It's not a bad pastime when they're biting, but it's pretty darn boring when they're not. It's just easier to go to Red Lobster." He accepted the keys, then turned his attention to the clipboard he held. After doing a walk-around inspection of the car, he unlocked the driver's door and bent in to copy the mileage. When he straightened again, he made a couple of notes as he spoke. "So you're heading back to Georgia before cold weather sets in."

"What can I say? I'm used to warm sunshine."

"Did the car do okay for you?"

"Oh, yeah, it was great."

"I'm glad we had good weather for you—well, at least most of the time. That was some storm last weekend, wasn't it?" He came around the car and offered her the clipboard, indicating the places she needed to sign. When she handed it back, he tore off a copy, folded it and handed it to her. "Well, Candace, I hope you enjoyed your visit. And if you ever come back and need my services, give me a call. I'll do my best."

With a wink and a smile, he got in the car, put the top down, then drove off, calling, "Goodbye," over his shoulder.

"Goodbye," she murmured. Once he'd driven out of sight, she returned to the quilt with a melancholy sigh. She was leaving tomorrow and would never return, but she couldn't say goodbye to the two people who mattered most. Natalie didn't want to hear anything, not even goodbye, from her, and Josh…

Apparently, he felt the same. She was just guessing, but then it seemed a pretty good guess, considering she hadn't seen him since Tuesday evening.

But that was okay. She'd tried, and she'd marked off plenty of items from her to-do list. That counted for something, didn't it? And she would continue to fulfill all those little wishes and dreams. One failure—one broken heart—didn't mean she would give up trying.

She'd just settled on the ground again when the sound of another vehicle broke the quiet. Did Rich or Rick forget something? she wondered, but almost immediately saw the answer was no. It was a pickup coming around the bend in the dirt road—not, she realized with a rush of hope followed by a bigger rush of disappointment, the late-model black truck she was used to seeing out here, but a beat-up faded green one that looked about as old as she felt.

The driver parked where the sun glinting off the windshield made it impossible for Candace to see inside. Her eyes narrowed against the glare as a chill ran up her spine.

For just one moment the reminder raced through her brain that the campground was terribly isolated, but immediately she banished it. She hadn't been afraid the entire time she'd been staying out here, and she wasn't going to be now. Besides, it wasn't as if she were alone. Luther was somewhere nearby, crackling leaves under his paws. If he sensed any cause for alarm, he would surely be barking his fool head off.

Then she smiled faintly. What did Luther know about alarm? He was a baby.

Her mystery guest shut off the engine, then, a long moment later, climbed out of the truck.

Oh, God, it was Natalie.

Candace stared at her as if a lifetime had passed since she'd last seen her. She was dressed casually—faded jeans, scuffed boots, a plaid shirt over a thermal T-shirt—and her long red hair was pulled back and caught in a clip that allowed curls to cascade down in a controlled sort of fall. Her only jewelry was a wristwatch and a wedding ring, and her makeup was minimal, as well. And she looked ten times prettier, healthier and happier than the sophisticated woman Candace had known.

"Natalie."

"Candace."

Were those the last civil words they would speak to each other? Candace wondered. Her first impulse was to launch into a rapid-fire, no-breathing-till-it-was-over apology to ensure she got to say everything she wanted before Natalie turned away. Truth was, though, she couldn't think of a thing to say.

Finally realizing they had company, Luther trotted over, sniffed in a circle around Natalie, then returned to his play.

"Cute puppy," Natalie commented.

"Thanks." Stupid answer, Candace chastised herself. As if she were somehow responsible for Luther's being cute? "Um…would you like to—" She looked around for her folding lawn chairs, then remembered they were already stowed in a closet inside. "Would you like to go inside?"

Natalie shook her head as she sat down on a sandstone boulder only a few feet from the quilt. "I understand you've been seeing my brother-in-law."

Candace's breath caught in her throat. "He told you that?" She wasn't sure whether that emotion in her chest was shock or worry or sweet relief that he cared enough about her to tell—

"No. He told Tate, and Tate told me." Natalie stretched out her legs, crossed her ankles, then shoved her hands into her pockets. "Tate also told me that no one had come between him and Josh ever in their entire lives, and he wasn't letting that change, so I'd better settle things with you one way or another."

Slowly Candace sank to the ground. When Luther climbed into her lap, she scratched him in all of his favorite places. "It will be settled tomorrow," she said quietly. "I'm going home first thing in the morning. I won't be back."

"Does Josh know that?"

Candace shrugged. "He knows that's been my plan from the beginning."

"So why did you come here?"

Gazing past her into the woods, Candace took a mental picture of the red, scarlet and gold leaves while at the same time considering how unfair life was. She had always loved words—had known how to use them to persuade, arouse, anger or mollify people. She knew how to twist them to her advantage, how to build with them as well as destroy. But right now when she needed the most persuasive and eloquent words of all, they refused to come.

Finally she forced her gaze back to Natalie. "I wanted to tell you how sorry I am for the things I did, the person I used to be and the ways I hurt you. That's my official reason. Unofficially…I was hoping that you could forgive me and we…we could be friends again.'' She said that last in a whisper, as if not voicing it aloud could somehow protect her from the obvious response. It would take a very special person to forgive what she'd done, and not even Natalie, she feared, was that kind. She had a family who loved her and friends who would never dream of betraying her. What use could she possibly have for someone like Candace?

Natalie's blue gaze was as cool and unclouded as the lake beside her. ''You think it's that easy? You say you're sorry and that wipes away the betrayal, the lies and all the hurt?''

''No, I don't think it's easy at all. I'm not sure it's even possible.'' Maybe, to some extent, she'd thought so when she'd first come here, but she had learned a lot since then about caring, emotion, hurt and healing. Until a year ago she'd never felt anything deeply but ambition—had never loved, never hated, never cared much at all about anything at all except being the best. Now she knew what a difficult, complex thing caring was, and how difficult and complex that made forgiving.

''What about Josh? Were you just amusing yourself with him while you waited to see what happened with me, or was he somehow part of your plan? Was he supposed to manipulate me into talking to you, or did you intend to hold him over my head like some kind of threat?''

Candace knew she deserved Natalie's suspicions, but they still hurt. She wasn't like that anymore, she wanted to protest, but the woman Natalie had known was exactly like that. She could be forgiven for still seeing her in that way.

''I didn't pursue Josh,'' she said quietly. ''We ran into each other a few times in town and…something…clicked.''

''You're five years older than him.''

''I know.''

''You could break his heart.''

"For whatever it's worth, I think he's already broken mine, so you don't have to worry about that."

"As usual, you're wrong, Candace. I *do* have to worry. Josh is family, and anything that affects him affects us."

Candace's eyes misted over. "Well, like I said, I'm leaving tomorrow, and I won't be back. I promise."

"You never did keep your promises," Natalie said scornfully. "Except once. It was a few weeks after you came to work in Montgomery, and we went out for drinks one Friday evening. You said you'd have my job within two years, and then you laughed and said you were just kidding. But you weren't. And, in fact, you had it in half that time…at least for the few weeks it took you to worm your way into my father's life and convince him to get you a job in Atlanta."

"If it's any consolation, he quit returning my phone calls a year ago." Candace knew it wouldn't be. Natalie had lived most of her life seeking her father's approval and love, and all in vain. Knowing that Candace had fallen out of favor with the great Thaddeus Grant wouldn't make her own rejection any easier to bear.

"I know the apologies and the excuses are inadequate, Natalie, and I know there's no reason why you should even listen to me, much less forgive me. But…I had to make the effort, for my own peace of mind if nothing else."

"Why? Why now? Why not two years ago, or three or five? Why bother at all?"

Candace stared at the lake, its surface rippling with tiny waves stirred up by the breeze. There was a huge part of her deep inside—the part that was feeling raw and sore— that wished she'd left for Georgia this morning so this conversation never could have taken place. Look how many of her goals she'd accomplished. She could have handled one failure.

But she hadn't failed, not really. So things weren't going well, and Natalie clearly had no intention of being friends with her again. But she'd done her best, and no one could ask more of her than that.

"A year ago I was diagnosed with breast cancer," she said without looking at Natalie. "You might say the experience gave me a new perspective on life and the way I'd lived it."

"So you promised to become a good person and do good deeds and right old wrongs." Natalie's voice was sharp with sarcasm. "It doesn't look like you've done a very good job of it so far."

Nope, definitely no renewed-old-friendship hiding in there. Pain twinged through Candace—but not surprise. Natalie had always been pretty up-front about her feelings. If she liked you, you knew it, and if she didn't, you knew that, too. Someday Candace would like others to think of her as being that open and honest, too.

"I'm sorry you think my becoming a different person is so impossible," she said quietly. "But I'm doing the best I can."

"Bullshit."

Candace's head swiveled around so she could stare at Natalie. Thaddeus had cursed like a stevedore on a three-day drunk, but coarse language from his daughter had been forbidden. Sure, she'd sworn occasionally—when he was in a different state—but always fairly mild curses. "I beg your pardon."

"You heard me. You say you're trying to make apologies and right old wrongs and change the way you live, but look at yourself. You don't have a regular job. You don't have a regular home. You don't have any friends who were around last month or will be around next month, and you're still using men as you need them, then dumping them. I don't see a damn thing to suggest that you're doing your best at anything."

Her stomach was tied in knots, her jaw hurt from clenching it, and her throat burned from the desire to curl up somewhere and cry. "Josh certainly talks a lot for someone who's keeping secrets."

"Josh isn't in the habit of keeping secrets. He doesn't do things he's ashamed of, so he has no reason to hide them."

Wrapping Luther's leash around her hand, Candace got to her feet and called the puppy. When he bounded over, she attached the leash to his chain, then stiffly said, "Excuse me. I have to take Luther for a walk."

As they passed Natalie, Candace gave her a wide berth. That didn't stop the other woman from standing up and calling, "Go ahead and run away, Candace. Ignore the trouble you've caused here, run all the way back to Georgia and tell yourself you did your best. And because your best is so pathetic, there won't be anyone around to call you a liar."

Candace and Luther reached the edge of the woods and the trail she had walked that night with Josh before she abruptly turned back. "I don't have a regular job because I don't know how to do anything besides be a reporter and I don't want to do that anymore. And I live in a motor home because it was a gift from a dear friend whose cancer killed her the second time around, and I can't afford both it and an apartment, and it allows me to make trips like this one. I don't have many friends yet, but that will change, and for the record I didn't use, then dump, Josh. He's the one who decided that a woman with only one breast was just a little too freaky for his tastes." She wiped a hand across her cheek and was horrified when it came away damp. Furiously she commanded the tears to dry up. This wasn't the time to show such weakness or, God help her, the person to show it to.

"Those are excuses," Natalie said flatly. "Because you're afraid. You're not making any plans for the future because you're afraid you won't have one. And so is Josh."

She was wrong, Candace comforted herself. Heavens,

only a few months had passed since she'd finished her treatment. There was no law setting a time limit for when she had to start planning her future, to start giving some sense of permanency to her life. She wasn't even forty yet. She could start making it real and permanent anytime.

But Natalie was also right. People had offered their friendship—Martha, Cal and Theresa Martin, for starters, as well as neighbors and other cancer patients back in Atlanta—but she'd kept a polite distance from them all. She'd pretended for months that the only friendship that really mattered was Natalie's—the one she was least likely to get.

*Was* she afraid? Was making friends beyond her capabilities? Or was she afraid she wouldn't live long enough to truly enjoy them?

After unfastening Luther from his leash once more, she took a few halting steps back toward Natalie. "Yeah, I guess you could say Josh is afraid," she agreed, then added, "If by *afraid*, you mean repulsed."

"That's not true and you know it."

"I know he couldn't get out of here fast enough Tuesday morning. I know he stood me up Tuesday evening, and I know that when I ran into him later, he couldn't even look at me." She *hadn't* known that silence could cut so deeply. The way he'd turned away, as if doing so could make her disappear....

"Josh is thirty-three years old," Natalie said, "and he's never been really serious about a woman. He always figured someday he would fall in love, get married and have kids, and they would be together fifty or sixty years, like his grandparents. Then he fell in love with someone who might not have even five years to spend with him, who might not be able to give him kids, or who might give him kids, then die and leave him to raise them alone. You bet he's scared."

"I wish more than anything in the world I could believe you...but I don't. I saw the way he looked at me, the way he turned from me.'' She wiped the tears away again. ''Besides, he never said a word about love. He made it clear from the start that all he wanted was an affair, nothing else.''

With an unsteady sigh she walked to the water's edge, picked up a handful of stones and tossed them one at a time into the lake.

After a moment, footsteps crunched across the ground behind her, then Natalie said, ''You've got a sorry arm. My three-year-old can throw farther than that. Of course, you always were kind of puny, and I doubt having surgery and chemo and radiation helped any.'' Her own stone sailed yards beyond where Candace's had plopped into the water.

''At least I don't have as much weight on my chest to interfere with my windup,'' Candace replied with a sniff.

Natalie gave her own sniff. ''You never had much to start with.''

Too true. Before the cancer she'd dressed to distract from the facts that she was slim, not too curvy or well endowed. Natalie, besides being tall, had been blessed with lush curves that Candace had envied, along with her connection to the great Thaddeus as well as her talent and her position at the paper.

Candace hadn't been able to steal the curves or the talent, but she'd greedily taken both the job and Natalie's place in her father's life.

And she'd lived to regret it. She'd been convinced for a time that she'd also lived to make it right, but today she wasn't so sure.

''What are you going to do?''

''I don't know.'' Feeling Natalie's gaze on her, she glanced her way. ''What…?''

''I can't remember a time when you didn't know exactly what your plans were for the next five years. This has really knocked you for a loop, hasn't it? The cancer, the treatment—'' Natalie grinned broadly as she went on ''—falling in love with my brother-in-law. You've lost control of your life, and you don't know how to get it back again.''

Candace threw her last rock, then dusted her hands. ''Maybe you're right. Maybe I'm not making any plans because I'm afraid I'll die before I can carry them out.''

''Of course I'm right. That's my job now—giving advice and running other people's lives. My title is Mother.'' Natalie made the statement with a large dose of dry humor, then slowly started back toward the quilt. ''Of course, there was a time when my own life was in shambles. I ran all the way home to Montgomery because Tate had broken my heart, and I was preparing to run even farther. I wasn't counting on much of a future, either, not without him and Jordan.''

''But he went after you.''

''Not exactly.'' She sat down once again on the boulder, and Candace dropped down on the quilt. ''Jordan went after me, and Tate went after him and got me, too.''

''That's very nice,'' Candace said huskily, and she meant it. But Josh didn't care enough to drive a few miles from his house. He certainly wouldn't follow her all the way back to Georgia.

''What guarantee did you have before the cancer?'' Natalie asked abruptly.

''I don't know what you mean.''

''About life. How many years were you promised? When were you going to die and how?''

Candace scowled at her. ''Of course I didn't know that.''

''No. And you don't know it now, either. You could live to be a hundred, or you could die next week. The cancer could come back, or you could get hit by a drunk driver, or you could be killed in a robbery gone bad. Candace, there are so many endless possibilities of when and how that you could go crazy thinking about them. So don't.''

*Don't.* Such easy advice—so foolishly and naively obvious. Shaking her head, Candace argued, "It's not that simple."

"It can be." Natalie stood up and took the few steps that brought her to the edge of the quilt. She stared down, her blue eyes stormy, her tone fierce. "You've already started a future here. You have a job, you have friends, you have Josh…and you could have the best, most loving family in the world—*my* family. But not if you run away to Atlanta. Think about it, Candace."

Then she turned on her heel and walked away. She wasn't finished yet, though. At the truck, she looked back. "Is that dog's name really Luther?"

Candace nodded. When Natalie grinned, she asked, "What's so funny about that?"

"That's Josh's father's name. Luther Boyd Chaney. Just my opinion, but your Luther's a vast improvement over the other one." And with that she was gone.

Candace sat on the step and watched the sun set and the clouds drift across the sky, and the dusk creep from east to west, slowly blotting out everything else, even the last pink and purple rays of the sun. Compared to the city, it seemed quiet, but she'd come to identify most of the sounds—the plop of a fish breaking the lake's surface, the owl that nested in a tree behind the motor home, the distant hum of the Conways' central heat, the even more distant chug of a boat motor and the usual assortment of birds, tree frogs and insects. It was peaceful. She would miss it when she left here.

If she left here.

She'd been so naive. When she'd seen Natalie step out of that old truck this afternoon, she'd thought she would say her piece and then she would be free to leave. Instead she was even less sure than ever about what to do.

But that had been Natalie's intent, hadn't it? She'd known Candace wanted—needed—her friendship again, she'd known Candace was in love with Josh, and she'd probably suspected how much Candace wanted a place and people to belong to. And she'd teased her with the promise of all that. All Candace had to do was stay. Quit being afraid. Stop thinking about dying and start living.

All she had to do… Sure, and then she could flap her arms and fly a circuit or two around the lake.

Besides, those promises weren't Natalie's to make. Sure, she could decide whether she wanted Candace in her life, and she could probably, to some extent, make that decision for her husband, too. But not for Josh. If he didn't want her, nothing Natalie could do would change his mind.

And if he didn't want her…

Blinking back the tears, Candace rose from the step, picked up her quilt and crossed to the fire ring near the shore. She spread out her quilt one last time, then knelt next to the ring. The Conways kept a supply of firewood for their campers, protected from the rain by a heavy-duty tarp. She was going to sit by a campfire, roast some hot dogs and marshmallows and look for falling stars, and hopefully by the time she grew tired, she would have some answers.

She crumpled pieces of newspaper and stuffed them under the small branches she'd arranged earlier. She'd gathered a big stack of logs, preferring to put back what she didn't use in the morning over the possibility of running out tonight, and once the burning newsprint had caught the smaller pieces, she added a log or two.

She sat back, the ground cold under her, even with the quilt, and watched as the flames licked all around the logs. Inside the RV, Luther barked periodically, irate that he'd been shut inside when he really wanted to join her. After watching the fire for a few minutes, she returned to the motor home. She put Luther on a leash, then picked up the box she'd prepared earlier. In it was everything she needed for tonight's treat.

A wiener roast for one and a dog. How pathetic.

She'd learned to pay particular attention when coming outside with Luther—he moved in leaps and bounds and as often as not left her stumbling behind. Once her feet were safely on the ground, she closed the RV door, turned toward the fire and stopped short.

Luther had been making so much noise inside that she hadn't heard the pickup pull in, but there it was in its usual spot, and leaning against the front end was Josh. The urge to cry swept over her, but she kept it in check. She wasn't going to become one of those annoying women who cried at the drop of a hat, not even if she had reason to.

He pushed away from the truck and met her in the middle, taking the box from her and falling into step with her. She secured Luther's leash to a stake in the ground, where he could reach the quilt but not the fire, then sat cross-legged on the quilt and leaned forward to add another log to the fire. The added weight sent up a small shower of sparks and embers and put out a rush of heat.

Josh sat down beside her, also cross-legged, his knee only a couple of inches from hers. She was tempted to move so they would bump, but instead she sat motionless, barely breathing. From the corner of her eye she saw that he was staring into the fire, so she did, too, while she tried to think of something to say. When she did, and blurted it out, it was so meaningless that it made her cringe.

"Do you mind that my dog and your father have the same first name?"

The corner of his mouth lifted in what might have been a smile. "Nah. He brings a little respectability to the name that my old man's not capable of."

The silence settled again, heavy and uncomfortable. She wished he could forget that she'd had cancer, and she could forget that he couldn't deal with it—wished they could be the way they were a week ago, or two or even three. She hated this stiffness, this terrible dread.

Finally she reached for the box. "Have you eaten?"

"No."

"We're having hot dogs and roasted marshmallows. Neither Luther nor I have ever had wienie-roasted hot dogs and marshmallows." She handed him a long-handled metal fork, courtesy of the Conways, then opened a package of hot dogs.

"I have. I learned how to roast marshmallows just right out here. But if I'd known you were doing this, I would have brought the good stuff."

"What's that?"

"Graham crackers and chocolate bars—for s'mores."

She gave him a sidelong look. "I make s'mores in the microwave."

After fixing a wiener on the fork, he gave a long-suffering shake of his head. "City girls. I bet you prefer steamed hot dogs, too, and you probably wouldn't even eat one that had been dropped in the dirt."

"Probably not."

He crouched closer to the fire so he could hold the wiener in the heart of the flames. They cast a golden glow over his features, highlighting his stubborn jaw, the sensuous curves of his lips, his almost perfect nose—and the stress lines that edged his mouth and eyes. Presumably, the past few days hadn't been easy for him. She tried to find some satisfaction in that, but she couldn't. They'd been too damn hard for her, as well.

Glancing up, he caught her staring, and he stared back. For a moment there was such pure hunger, such sweet emotion in his expression. Then he blinked, swallowed hard and asked, "Am I doing all the cooking?"

Candace took a cautious breath, afraid her lungs couldn't expand to accept it. "I think so," she said hoarsely. "I chopped all the onions *and* arranged for a perfect night."

He looked up at the sky, then removed the fork from the fire. "You did pretty good."

"Later, stars are going to come out, so I can watch for shooting stars."

"You can usually catch a few here. This one's done. Do you have a bun?"

She held the bun while he slid the wiener onto it, then laid it aside. "That's Luther's. It needs to cool."

"You're spoiling that dog."

She considered it a moment as she removed napkins, mustard, two cans of pop and a dish of chopped onions from the box. "Yes," she finally agreed. "I am. Do you have a problem with that?"

"Nope. Just making an observation." He cooked two more hot dogs, then sat down beside her again. She was about to take a bite of hers when he spoke, his voice thick and unsteady. "You have to promise me one thing."

Hot dog halfway to her mouth, she waited.

"You won't die unless there's just no earthly way around it."

Her hands started trembling so badly that onions showered onto the quilt. She set the hot dog on a napkin and clasped her hands together.

"I always thought falling in love was, like, this nice, kind of harmless thing. I mean, I've loved people before—my mom and Tate and Natalie and my nephews. But this…this is so damn scary anyway, and the cancer…" He gave a shake of his head. "After I left here Tuesday, I kept thinking I couldn't handle it. What if the cancer came back? What if we got married, if you became the most important part of my life, and then you died? I couldn't do it. Better to walk away now than wait until it's too late."

The tightness that had settled in her chest earlier spread to her throat, and tears slid down her cheeks, but that was all right, because there were tears in his eyes, too, as he laid one trembling hand against her cheek.

"But I learned something the last couple days. It's already too late. You're already the most important part of my life, and having had cancer or getting it again can't change that. I love you, Candace, and I want to marry you. However much time you have left to live, however much time I have, I want to live it together.''

She wasn't aware of moving, but suddenly she was in his lap, his arms wrapped tightly around her, her palm cupping his jaw. ''But what if the cancer does reoccur?'' she whispered.

''We'll deal with it together.''

''But…you can't imagine what it was like. I was cranky, I lost weight, I got sick, all my hair fell out and—''

He brushed his mouth across hers to silence her. ''Honey, I'm not in love with your hair, and I'll love you cranky, skinny, sick, whatever. If it happens again…well, you beat it once all by yourself. Just think how much easier it would be with me, Natalie, the family, Cal and Martha and the whole damn town beside you.''

She was contemplating that when he kissed her forehead. ''Besides, what if it doesn't reoccur?'' he asked. ''What if we live the next fifty or sixty years in perfect health? You can't turn your back on that possibility, babe. Whatever happens with your health—or, for that matter, with mine— is going to happen. We can deal with it together or alone…but, honey, trust me on this. *Alone* is an awfully lonely way to live.''

Oh, she knew that from experience. But…

Don't think about the endless number of things that could go wrong, Natalie had advised. And the corollary to that advice: think about the things that could go right. Getting married. Having a family by marriage even if she couldn't have one by blood. Living with Josh, working with him. Lying beside him every night. Loving him.

''I love you, Josh.''

He gazed down at her, searching her face, then slowly smiled. ''And you'll marry me.''

''I'll marry you. And I'll never, ever leave you.''

Closing the distance between them, he kissed her, a sweet, tender kiss that made her feel treasured, cherished and well and truly loved.

Loving Josh and being loved by him. Every day for the rest of their lives.

Could anything be more right than that?

√Make amends with Natalie.
√Sit by a campfire.
√Roast marshmallows.
√Look for shooting stars.
√Accept Josh's marriage proposal.

## *Epilogue*

As the ten-o'clock news came on, Josh yawned, stretched his arms over his head, then got up to head off for bed. He shut off the television and switched off the lamp, then crossed to the switch for the overhead light. For a moment he stood there, simply looking around.

In four years the house hadn't really changed much at all. The sofa still faced the television rather than the fire-place—though a comfortable armchair was angled directly in front of the stone hearth. The wood floors were still a little dusty, and there were still things growing fuzz in the refrigerator from time to time. The bedroom was still painted Terra Cotta Dust, and there still weren't any flow-erbeds out front—but there was a swing and two rockers on the porch. They had been entirely his idea, though.

The biggest change was in the extra rooms they'd added on three years ago—three new bedrooms, a bathroom and a laundry room. That had been his idea, too, as well as a necessity. After all, kids couldn't be asked to bunk down in odd corners of the living room and kitchen forever.

He flipped the porch light on, shut off the overhead light, then turned off the light over the stove in the kitchen. As he made his way down the hall in the dark, he stepped on something small and metal that made him yelp and hop onto the other foot. Grimacing, he hit the next light switch he passed, illuminating the various toys scattered along the hall.

The first room he came to belonged to Sara Elizabeth. She was three years old, a perfect miniature of her mother except with brown hair. She'd been born in the middle of a thunderstorm and still took great delight in blinding lightning and crashing thunder, and she was best buds with her cousin, Will, Tate and Natalie's thirdborn. And she could wrap her daddy around her finger with nothing more than a smile.

Hadn't he said she was just like her mother?

"Good night, angel. I love you." He tucked the sheet around her, smoothed her hair from her forehead, then bent to kiss her. Worn-out from a day's play, she didn't stir.

Down the hall was Alex's room. He was twenty-two months old and was a perfect miniature of his father, including the brown hair. Where Sara was slender, he was sturdy. Where she was, oh, so feminine, he was all boy— and he could wrap Sara around his finger.

Josh crouched next to the bed. Alex had just moved out of the crib a few months earlier, so his bed was low to the floor, like him. He opened his eyes when Josh gently touched his cheek, and he grinned a way-too-familiar grin. That boy was gonna be trouble, Lucinda teased, just like his daddy. A heartbreaker, Candace had agreed, just like his daddy. But Josh had been out of the heartbreaking business for four years, and he was never going back.

"I love you," he whispered.

"I love you," Alex whispered back.

"Sleep tight."

"Sleep tight."

"See you in the morning."

"Okay." Alex's eyes drifted shut and, like that, he was asleep again.

Stepping over Luther, who'd taken up his usual position at the foot of the bed, Josh went back into the hall and across to the last bedroom. A carousel lamp cast soft light over the crib and eight-month-old Hank. Henry, his mother called him, but Josh intended to make sure that didn't last long. Hank was a strong name, a good cowboy name, while Henry was the kind of name that got you a punch in the nose in kindergarten. And while he was sure Hank would get his share of punches growing up—after all, he *was* Josh's son—they wouldn't be over something so prissy as a name.

Hank was good-natured and had slept through the night since his third night on earth. He laughed at his brother and sister and all his cousins, with the exception of Emily, Tate and Natalie's youngest. Of course, Emily did little to laugh at, being only six weeks old.

Resting one arm on the crib side, Josh rubbed Hank's back. "Hey, buddy," he whispered. "Sleep well."

The baby's only response was to suck vigorously, puffing his cheeks, before his mouth stilled again.

Back in the hall, Josh picked up toys as he went, dumping them all into a basket just inside the kitchen, and then he moved down the shorter, original hallway to the bathroom. The door was closed, the light on, and soft splashing sounds came from inside. He didn't hesitate to walk right in—he wasn't shy, and these days, neither was his wife.

Candace lay back in the big old claw-foot tub, mounds of bubbles floating around her. Her hair curled damply at her neck, and one leg was propped provocatively on the side of the tub. "Hey, cowboy."

"Ma'am. You look mighty comfortable there."

"Oh, I am." She subjected him to a long, heated gaze. "You look mighty comfortable yourself. Hmm, I do love a barefoot cowboy in jeans with no shirt."

He sat down on the floor and slid one arm into the water. It was warm and smelled of tangerines and spices. Damn. He got turned on often enough around her. Now the smell of citrus fruit and cinnamon was going to remind him of her naked, and was liable to leave him in the same aroused condition.

Underneath the bubbles his fingers brushed across her belly, then her rib cage, then higher to her breasts, skimming across the silken skin. After Hank was born and she'd gotten her five-year clean bill of health, she'd finally gotten a referral and gone into the hospital for a few days for reconstructive surgery. It was something she'd always planned to do, but after they'd gotten married, she'd kept delaying it. There was always something else to do with the money—having babies, building on to the house, buying a new bull.

But Hank was their last baby, unless God surprised them with another, and for once they'd had the money to spare and no other pressing needs. It was time, she'd decided. And since the tissue for her new breast came from her abdomen...hey, after three babies, she *needed* a tummy tuck, she'd teased.

Josh had fully understood and supported her decision, but truth was, it hadn't mattered either way to him. Her new breast was very nice, as all breasts tended to be, but she'd been beautiful without it. He loved her more than life itself, with or without breasts.

"What are you thinking?" she asked.

"Oh...just wondering what I'd have to do to get you to make love with me."

She made a rude noise. "Oh, gee, let's see...maybe *breathe?*"

"Oh, babe, I'm breathing."

She caught the chain of the old-fashioned stopper between her toes and yanked it out, then slowly stood up. He held out a towel, which she wrapped around herself and anchored between her breasts before stepping out of the tub. Rising onto her toes, she leaned close to his ear and whispered, "Race you to the bedroom," then darted out the door.

Grabbing for her, Josh succeeded in pulling the towel away and was rewarded with an enticing glimpse of fair skin, womanly hips and a flash of leg. He kicked off his jeans and briefs, then followed her to the bedroom, where she lay beautifully naked in the middle of the rust-tan-and-turquoise Southwest-patterned spread.

The sight brought to mind a long-ago memory, when he'd wanted to see her naked on this bed. She would look like an exotic plaything, he'd thought, and he'd wanted to spend the next several years doing nothing but playing with her.

His wish had come true. They'd had four years of playing and loving and making a future and a family and a life, and he was looking forward to forty more. Thank God she'd finally understood one thing about him all those years ago.

He might have been playing...but he was playing for keeps.

√Marry Josh.
√Have kids.
√Live long, be happy and love well.


√Very long, very happy, and *very* well.


\* \* \* \* \*

# SILHOUETTE®
# SPECIAL EDITION™

## AVAILABLE FROM 16TH JANUARY 2004

### MICHAEL'S DISCOVERY  Sherryl Woods

*The Devaneys*

For years, physiotherapist Kelly Andrews had wanted marine
Michael Devaney to notice her.  But could Kelly heal his body—
and his heart—with her touch?

### HER HEALING TOUCH  Lindsay McKenna

*Morgan's Mercenaries*

Sergeant Burke Gifford had come to learn from renowned military
medic Angel Paredes.  But the rugged Special Forces man hadn't
expected the passionate connection they shared.

### TAKING OVER THE TYCOON
### Cathy Gillen Thacker

*The Deveraux Legacy*

Connor Templeton never mixed business and pleasure—until he
met stunning single mum Kristy Neumeyer.  Could this tycoon be
assuming the role of husband and father?

### BABY 101  Marisa Carroll

*Maitland Maternity*

Lana Lord could teach tycoon Dylan Vanguard about caring for his
little son but could she help him overcome his past and embrace a
future with her and tiny Greg by his side?

### THE WEDDING BARGAIN  Lisette Belisle

*Stone's End*

Olivia DeAngelis needed a husband!  According to her father's
will, she had to marry within six months or lose her family's
homestead.  Would a handsome stranger come to her rescue?

### THE MISSING HEIR  Jane Toombs

For Russ Simon, agreeing to find out if beautiful Marigold Crowley
was a gold-digging impostor or truly a missing heiress was hard—as
he'd never expected to fall for his golden-haired quarry.

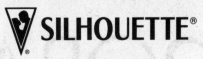

_Ml0311_

# 4 FREE

## books and a surprise gift!

We would like to take this opportunity to thank you for reading this Silhouette® book by offering you the chance to take FOUR more specially selected titles from the Special Edition™ series absolutely FREE! We're also making this offer to introduce you to the benefits of the Reader Service™—

- ★ FREE home delivery
- ★ FREE gifts and competitions
- ★ FREE monthly Newsletter
- ★ Exclusive Reader Service offers
- ★ Books available before they're in the shops

Accepting these FREE books and gift places you under no obligation to buy, you may cancel at any time, even after receiving your free shipment. Simply complete your details below and return the entire page to the address below. *You don't even need a stamp!*

**YES!** Please send me 4 free Special Edition books and a surprise gift. I understand that unless you hear from me, I will receive 6 superb new titles every month for just £2.90 each, postage and packing free. I am under no obligation to purchase any books and may cancel my subscription at any time. The free books and gift will be mine to keep in any case.

E4ZED

Ms/Mrs/Miss/Mr ...............................Initials.................................
BLOCK CAPITALS PLEASE

Surname ......................................................................................

Address ......................................................................................

...................................................................................................

......................................................Postcode..............................

**Send this whole page to:**
**UK: FREEPOST CN81, Croydon, CR9 3WZ**
**EIRE: PO Box 4546, Kilcock, County Kildare (stamp required)**